CW00537007

Roberto Quaglia

Ian Watson

A special signed edition, limited to
150 numbered copies.
This is number:

REVIEW

REVIEW

The Beloved of My Beloved

Für Damar und Anthea (handwritten)

The Beloved
of My Beloved

Ian Watson & Roberto Quaglia

Roberto Quaglia & Ian Watson

April 3rd 2010 (handwritten)

! Bitte schön (handwritten)

NEWCON
PRESS

NewCon Press
England

First edition, published in the UK April 2009
by NewCon Press
41 Wheatsheaf Road, Alconbury Weston, Cambs, PE28 4LF

NCP 013 (signed hardback)
NCP 014 (softback)

10 9 8 7 6 5 4 3 2 1

This collection copyright © 2009 by Ian Watson & Roberto Quaglia

All rights reserved.

No part of this book may be reproduced in any form without the express
permission of the authors and publisher.

ISBN:

978-0-9555791-8-9 (signed hardback)
978-0-9555791-9-6 (softback)

Cover layout and design by Ian Whates
Utilising photographs supplied by Roberto Quaglia

Book layout by Storm Constantine

Printed in the UK by the MPG Books Group

Contents

The Illustrated Tumour of My Beloved – part one

Cancer of the womb had ravaged my beloved Amanda. Not until far too late were she, nor I, aware of the vile malignancy which had taken root inside her. By the time we did realize the truth, the swelling tumour had sowed lethal seeds elsewhere in her bones and even in her brain – so she was doomed.

We'd noticed no symptoms. Slightly surprising but not totally so. A womb exists to be occupied by a sort of intruder growing within it – the embryo which becomes a foetus which becomes a baby. A foreign sperm goes inside a woman and produces a kind of parasite that feeds upon her. The womb is designed to expand to accommodate this. Being occupied by a foreign body doesn't necessarily interfere with the womb's function in quite the same way as a tumour of the kidney or the liver interferes with those organs. It's possible not to notice anything amiss until the fifth month of pregnancy, or rather tumour-acy.

A foreign body! What am I saying? It was as if Amanda was having a baby which was her own self. An undifferentiated baby, true! A cell in her body reproducing itself uncontrollably. No arms nor legs nor head, simply a mass of identical tissue. But identical to her.

Immediately after diagnosis Amanda's wayward womb was promptly removed by a private surgeon, Mr Moravec, who was rather a connoisseur of tumours. However, nothing could be done about the secondary tumours in her brain.

It was Moravec who gave me my idea – while Amanda was "recovering" from the hysterectomy and tumourectomy.

7

Recovering, in a very limited sense – I would lose her within three months.

"If only you could clone my beloved Amanda for me!" I had exclaimed.

Cloning a human being was strictly forbidden worldwide, mainly because of the Americans and their superstitions. Most people in that God-fearing country of tele-evangelists believe that only God creates a human being. Effectively God is present in bed with a married couple (and with an unmarried couple too, I suppose), and He inserts an immaterial finger to bless the union of sperm with egg. Personally I think this is quite pornographic, but Americans thought it was sacred. Consequently, if scientists cloned a person, that would be an insult to God. God might retaliate by means of more rapid global warming or a stock market collapse. American influence is so powerful that breach of the cloning ban in, say, Tadjikistan or Indonesia could well lead to military intervention to bring about regime change, so as to restore respect for the miracle of conception; and nobody would risk that. The Vatican backed this policy. The Chinese didn't, but they had a big enough population anyway, so they wouldn't make an issue of it.

"You can always have her plastinated," Moravec pointed out.

I was perfectly aware that grieving relatives quite often paid for a loved one to be plastinated in a characteristic pose – sitting in a favourite chair reading a newspaper (which could be renewed each day), digging the garden, or watching television.

Over the years, as more loved ones died, a house could become a bit crowded with plastinated dead bodies. Those who deeply cared about their departed relatives might themselves die. Younger family members would wish to dispose of their plastinated elders. So the younger relatives would take the relics of their elders to the various Plastination Recycling Centres which are very like supermarkets except that customers themselves stock the shelves with plastinated bodies, although of course they

8

can also buy bodies. Leave your plastinated grandparent there; in due course he or she would sell to a landscape gardener, or to a senior citizen department store as a mannequin, or to a civic architect who wanted his plaza to look populated. Did Moravec think I was oblivious to all this? I felt revulsion at the idea of myself dying one day with the result that a total stranger acquired plastinated Amanda for any purpose he or she had in mind. But irrespective of this…

"I'm not sure if a plastinated body is flexible enough."

"If you want flexible," said Moravec, "how about a silicone model of her? Fully poseable with a fleshlike feel. Check out *realdoll.com.*"

"But that is not *herself.* I want herself!"

"I can assist her tumour to carry on cloning itself, but herself I cannot clone. I'd be crucified. In a manner of speaking. US Special Forces, who knows?"

Moravec was a portly, dignified chap. I suspected his neat wavy brown hair of being a wig. I'd hate to think of him being crucified, squirming tubbily and maybe losing his wig in his agony. Only slim muscular people ought to be crucified. Though of course Moravec was speaking metaphorically.

A model would need to be formed in a mould. A mould – not the stuff that forms on cheese, but a receptacle the exact size and shape of… *my Beloved.*

I asked, "Can you continue growing the tumour inside a full-size transparent mould of Amanda's body? Could you accelerate its growth so that the tumour fills the mould completely in, say, three months?"

Thus my Beloved would continue without interruption, in a manner of speaking, her DNA in every cell of the tumour.

"Can you? Could you?"

This would be innovative, cutting-edge work, and the idea excited Moravec, who loved tumours – although not literally. Yet, as we talked, the possibility of *literally* loving a tumour which enshrined the DNA of my Beloved – and which even immortalised that unique DNA deathlessly – dawned upon me...

A tumour which copied her shape perfectly because of the mould – her face, her limbs, her belly, her breasts – would superficially be identical with Amanda, apart from the colours of the outer surface and of course the absence of a mind. Or a heart. But this is a post-Cartesian era, is it not? Speaking of superficialities, when do we ever look *within* a human Beloved, at her lungs or intestines? Do we love and desire the lungs and intestines as passionately as we love the breasts? Arguably a Beloved may just as well be solid throughout.

Although equipped with entrances, and exits...

The tumour would need to take in liquid nutrient to feed itself – and it would need not only to excrete waste products but also to extrude *its own self*, for when Tumour-Amanda reached full size she would keep on growing irrespective. Surplus tumour must be expelled from a sort of anus like a string of sausages from a sausage machine, each sausage to be pruned as it emerged under the pressure of growth. Rather like going to the toilet.

One entrance could be designed for love, namely a tumour-vagina.

"Hmm," said Moravec, "once the mould is full I shall use nanotechnology to inject a smart membrane around the shaped tumour."

"A smart membrane?"

"As in smart plastics or fabrics. They resume their original shapes after being twisted or whatnot. Smartness should keep her in shape so long as there's a vent for excess growth."

"Will she be able to stand?"

"I doubt it. You might be able to lean her against a wall. I think she'll sit without slumping, and of course if she's lying in bed..." He shrugged suggestively.

"And her smart sheath can be tinted, so that she looks less

10

like a tumour?"

"But tumours can be beautiful. The mottling effects. Let me show you."

"I'd rather not. Ah, but what about her tattoo?"

My Beloved boasted a magnificent huge tattoo of a bird's wings upon her back, green and gold feathers outspread from her spine. She'd been intending to have both her legs tattooed – with a leopard descending her right leg, a flowery tropical plant ascending her left leg. Amanda loved the paintings of Douanier Rousseau.

"Can the smart skin be tattooed?"

Although Moravec shook his head, a mischievous smile played upon his lips.

"Yes?" I asked eagerly.

"The nano-skin can probably be programmed with patterns."

"Ah! Pre-programmed patterns. I see."

Again came that mischievous smile. "I think that exposing part of the nano-sheath to a magnetic field could cause a pattern to express itself in that area – and to be erased if necessary! One of the problems with tattoos is that they're for life. A person might change her mind about having a leg covered in orchids, but the tattoo is irrevocable…"

"Whereas a sheathed tumour *can* change its mind, supposing it had a mind."

I described my inspiration about tumourisation to Amanda, and she sighed deeply.

"Beloved," she declared – we called each other by the same name since we experienced the same sentiment for one another. "Beloved, oh how much happier it makes me to imagine you making love in the future to the tumour of me than to other women! This is such a consolation – it's so romantic of you, so devoted, so ingenious! I admire you so much. Of course I'll let a mould be made of me. How can you doubt it?"

So I also explained about the patterns, and Amanda clapped her hands with glee.

"Beloved, forget about the bird and the leopard! You know how much I like you to tell me a story after we make love."

Indeed, our love-making resembled the 1001 nights of Scheherazade, except the other way round.

"Why not cartoon stories on my back and my belly and my legs and my arms? Different stories everywhere? Could a speech-recognition program mated with Photoshop design the cartoons while you tell my tumour the stories? You end off by exposing part of my sheathed tumour to the magnetic field?"

"Wow," I said.

True, these were early days yet, but my Beloved was certainly entering into the spirit of the concept. The very idea seemed to be giving her far more comfort than would weeks in a hospice for the terminally ill, attended by banalities.

"I think," she said, "when I am dead in heaven I will dream the stories you tell to my tumour!"

"And I, listening to the silence in which you'll listen to my stories, will hear the echo of all the marvellous things that you have said to me during all the life we shared together."

"I love you."

I love you echoed in my brain and *I love you* in the tones of my Beloved would have echoed within myself for all of my remaining future each time I would watch, caress, kiss and love her tumour in her shape, illustrated by the dreams that my fantasy would transmit to her in the afterlife. Oh if only, beyond the bounty of her appearance, her tumour could also have the gift of words!

I had an idea.

I consulted a friend who's an insider in the mysteries of artificial intelligence, and he didn't disappoint me.

"The problem would be a serious one if the human subject to be simulated was already dead. But since she's alive, we can easily model her linguistic behaviour and fully reproduce the illusion of eloquence later."

We attached to my Beloved a set of excellent microphones which henceforth would record every word of hers, every sentence, every laugh and every moan. All of these sonic inputs would be transmitted to a computer, interpreted by a voice and semantic recognition system, and catalogued.

"The variety of our utterances," my friend explained to me, "is even more of a sophisticated illusion than that of free will. With some rare exceptions, when people talk they all more or less repeat the same things, and the sequence of utterances is basically random, partly influenced by what others around you are saying or expecting to hear from you just then. We're all much more banal and predictable than we like to believe."

"My Beloved *isn't* a banal woman. I wouldn't have married her if she were."

"That merely means we'll need to assign a slightly higher value to the variable of eccentricity in the A.I. algorithm simulating your Beloved."

My Beloved spoke without difficulty for another two months. Throughout this period she strove to say as many things as possible, to express every least thought, to develop arguments sparked by whatever pretext, well knowing that upon this would depend the quality of representation of her that the tumour would exhibit after she was dead. In the third month, words were often replaced by groans. Just like MacDonald's spreading throughout the world, the tumour had installed an embassy in every vital part of my Beloved.

All this while, the clone of the tumour was growing rapidly inside the mould of my Beloved before her very eyes. We'd put the mould in the same room where she was preparing to die, right beside her bed. It was she who had wanted this. The tumour in its transparent mould was providing her with that sense of continuity of one's own DNA which human beings care so much about, and ever have. Even if now it was aberrant DNA, this was a great consolation to my Beloved.

Due to the physical pain she was feeling, the love for her own tumour – with which I would live and couple in future – now and then turned into hatred or jealousy. Yet she never called for the execution of the tumour, or its burning at the stake, as others in her position might have done. Her hatred seemed more spiritual in its symbolism.

For instance she insisted, "Promise me you'll sodomize my tumour."

"If that's your wish, I'll do so, even against my will."

"You have to humiliate it, the way it's humiliating me. I want you to fuck it in the arse."

During our life together, my Beloved and I hadn't dedicated ourselves to anal sex – not due to moralistic taboos, but simply because this activity always seemed to us silly.

"I want you to put it in chains, whip it and ejaculate on its face and piss in its mouth. I want you to do to it all the filthy things you never did to me."

Was this really hatred? Or was it instead that, since she herself couldn't do so any more, she wanted her tumour to complete for her the whole repertoire of fringe sexual variants of which we had never had need? I promised everything she asked of me. But I also told her that I would do all those things with love, with no trace of hatred. Hearing my words, she calmed and fell asleep peacefully, smiling.

The time came when my Beloved was scheduled to die – but she didn't die. Despite enriched growth promoter, that exogenous tumour hadn't filled the mould yet, and Amanda confided to me that she couldn't die without seeing her tumourous alter ego fully formed, ready to replace her beside me in our bed.

"You won't get any window of opportunity to betray me with another woman on the excuse that my tumour isn't sexually mature yet!" Amanda was even able to joke at the time when she ought to have died, instead.

"Good thinking!" I answered. "For the moment, don't die."

Several more weeks passed before the tumour of my Beloved grew to fill the mould completely. Then the mould was opened to finalize and stabilize the body-shape within that smart sheath, and the chip was implanted containing all the digitalized utterances and noises that Amanda had emitted during the months of her disease – together with the A.I. program to assemble those at their best, plus some microspeakers hidden inside the throat which would perfectly reproduce the sound of her voice.

When the moment came, my Beloved gazed into my eyes with a light I will never forget.

"Kiss me," she asked in a tiny voice.

I kissed her.

She whispered sweetly, "Now kiss my tumour."

Turning to where the tumour now lay on the bed behind me attached to its nutrient supply, I did so.

"Hold my hand."

Which I did. As she stared from the pillows towards her tumour, instinctively I also took its hand.

Then there was only silence, and I began to cry, for I realized that in that room of a sudden there was nobody other than me.

That very same evening I made love to the tumour of my Beloved. First I moved the tumour next door for a candlelit dinner, me feeding myself in the usual oral way – a tagliatelle carbonara, which my Beloved used to adore – while the tumour obliviously sucked the regular liquid that kept it alive. Then I transported it back to the bed, and after several months of sexual abstinence I could finally experience once more the intoxication of passion and the heat of a body against my skin. Unlike a banal sexdoll, the tumour of My Beloved was as warm as Amanda had been.

"It's so beautiful to make love with you again after so long," the tumour told me without moving its lips. It sounded sincere, though a little ventriloqual. Rationally I knew that this sweet sentence was only the product of a program of artificial intelligence, but the emotion I was feeling wasn't affected by consciousness of the deception. What's reality, after all?

After the first pleasuring – short, intense, and passionate – the tumour insisted on a repeat, just as my Beloved would typically have done, at least when we were younger. Unfortunately, unlike my Beloved, her tumour couldn't help restore the needful erection with the old but always efficient trick of oral sex, since – even though it was alive – it was inert. So I explained that it needed to be patient a while longer. The tumour of my Beloved proved to be patient, and could wait. Could it be that tumours are the most patient creatures in the universe? When we pleasured again a while later, that was even more beautiful than the first time. In one regard at least this was our first night of marriage, start of a long honeymoon. Time for buggering it, whipping it and humiliating it – as my Beloved required of me – would come later, much later in time.

In the depths of the night I felt that the moment was ripe to complete my spiritual union with my Beloved, who was beholding me from up there in paradise and certainly was proud of me. This was the moment to tell the tumour the first of the stories that would decorate its skin with ephemeral tattoos, a new species of mandala destined to disappear every time a new story generated a new picture. We'd had to discard the idea of accumulating a multiplicity of illustrations. The body of the tumour of my Beloved would retain each picture indefinitely on its skin until I told a new story, which would generate a new picture to replace the first, and so on. This was like life. This was like love. Ultimately, everything in the whole universe is merely one form or other of ephemeral mandala.

For as long as each picture endured on the new and immortal body of her tumour, my Beloved would dream time and again the story that I told – a story which would speak of a Beloved, for from that day on I would only tell stories about Beloveds. And because my own Beloved had just died, my first story would need to be that of the Grave of my Beloved.

So, my heart swelling with love and my eyes overflowing with tears of joy, I began to tell the following tale...

The Grave of My Beloved

I do not wish to say how my beloved Mirabelle died, but when that terrible misfortune first happened I contemplated a veritable mausoleum for her, a place where I could sit of an evening to commune with her. I imagined marble and lilies in vases and an alabaster sarcophagus, for her skin was so white.

Unfortunately I did not have enough money for a mausoleum, consequently Mirabelle must be buried in an ordinary grave.

Yet then I thought to myself: the body below ground will forever be out of my reach. It is beside the gravestone that I would place, and replace, lilies. Thus in a sense the body is displaced into the gravestone. Just as, by being dead, the real Mirabelle was entirely displaced out of her precious body.

And then I realized that thanks to cyberspace a further, more consoling displacement was possible. I had not previously given much attention to this because my Beloved was so real to me. But her grave need not be in the physical world at all. It could be in the virtual world. Indeed, this etherial realm might be a more appropriate location – for was my Beloved not an angel? I would arrange for Mirabelle's body to be cremated. I would scatter the ashes in a lake. And from within my own home I could visit her cyber-grave constantly.

Nothing material survives beyond the grave. In cyberspace nothing is material. Therefore cyberspace must be the real kingdom of spirit on Earth! Surely the whole of mankind would realize this sooner or later. Old-style physical cemeteries will come to seem relics of a primitive era, of concern only to archeologists.

What's more, the inscription on the gravestone could be as outspoken as I wished, since it would be totally private, and I could incorporate a picture of her face without fear that this might be defaced or prised loose and stolen.

I swiftly discovered that several cyber-companies offered this service, and I obtained on-line brochures. Definitely the cream of the companies was Undying Love. Undying Love served film stars and rock stars and such – or rather the estates of dead film and rock stars. Imitators of Undying Love charged less money but apparently none possessed the same cachet.

I couldn't possibly economise in my devotion! Yet I couldn't afford to pay all at once (the interest from that lump sum funding the permanent maintenance of the virtual grave). Apparently most customers of Undying Love recouped the payment by charging fans to visit the virtual grave of the star in question – which fans did in their droves. A hundred thousand hits, and payments, per day was not unusual. Such numbers of devotees could never visit a physical grave in a fixed location, so this made good business sense.

My Beloved did not have a retinue of fans to fund a virtual grave. She had not been the Beloved of millions of people world-wide, but only of me.

Nevertheless it was possible to pay, month by month, a sum which I could afford. This option was discouraged. A lifetime "subscription" (perhaps I should say a deathtime subscription) was equivalent to thirty years' worth of monthly payments. During this period a star's fame might very easily go into eclipse if one was funding the grave site solely from payments made by visiting fans – besides, that tactic seemed mean, failing to honour the star sufficiently. Most stars, in any case, were quite rich and wrote into their wills an insistence upon lump-sum payment all at once.

Still, monthly payment was possible.

Accordingly I made arrangements with Undying Love for my Beloved's burial in cyberspace. I signed an on-line contract for the permanent upkeep of Mirabelle's grave, and for additional realism supplied details about the body to be interred. The grave would be tended virtually. As per my requirements, virtual lilies would be placed in a vase once a week, programmed to wither, it is true, exactly as natural lilies wither, but then each week fresh lilies would appear. The miniature rectangular lawn of the grave would be trimmed regularly. Weeds, programmed to grow, would be removed.

Alas, within two years financial difficulties overtook me so that I could not afford those monthly payments.

I watched the lilies wither one final time and knew that they would not be replaced. The grave still looked serene to my eye, albeit melancholy, as I continued to visit it. Naturally I did so, every day. How could I not? My Beloved was there, nowhere else.

Very soon I received an automated payment reminder from Undying Love, tactfully phrased. The next reminder was still quite tactful, but the third conveyed a note of vague menace.

I did respond to the initial demands with an explanation and a plea for patience, but evidently only a computer was reading (or failing to read) my comments and either failing to understand them or ignoring them. There was nothing I could do except hope for a change in my personal fortune, or lack of it.

Undying Love did not threaten to delete the grave of my Beloved, but presently an obscene item of graffiti appeared on the gravestone. It would disgust me too much to quote the words. The next demand for payment, plus arrears plus interest, threatened that "worse will happen."

I attempted to phone a human being, but only succeeded in speaking unsatisfactorily to synthesized voices.

More vile graffiti appeared until I shuddered to visit the grave. What a torment to see on my screen, only inches away, the defaced gravestone, and nothing I could do to scrub it clean!

Soon the grave bore so many graffiti that they were mutually illegible, which was one small consolation.

By now the virtual grass had grown long and many ugly weeds had arisen.

One evening, as I watched, a mongrel dog wandered on to the overgrown grave – and shat, straining to produce a big white turd. Evidently the dog suffered from distemper. This made the mongrel and its excrement seem doubly unclean.

Who had devised this sadistic and complicated programming for a failure to maintain payments? Perhaps Undying Love itself knew nothing of what the programmer had inserted.

To appeal to the higher management of the company appeared as impossible as an appeal to God. Beside, I was relieved that the grave, however untidy and polluted, continued virtually to exist. This was also what deterred me from contacting journalists to decry this cruel bullying by Undying Love – not to mention what might have passed through those journalists' minds willy-nilly. *Is this what you let become of your Beloved's grave? Can't you move into a cheap slum or sleep rough?* (Then how would I be able to visit my Beloved's grave?) *Why don't you sell a kidney or an eye?*

Although not dead myself, truly I was in Purgatory.

Then the necrophile came. I recognized that he was a necrophile from the way he sidled around my Beloved's grave, stooping and sniffing, and from the bulge in his trousers. He began to uproot weeds and to tear grass loose and to rake his fingers tentatively through the soil thus loosened.

Touching his now dirty fingers to his lips, he licked them. Then he went away, as if reluctantly. Unless I paid a by now impossible sum to Undying Love I was sure the necrophile would return.

Suddenly I was granted a reprieve – of a sort!

When, dreading the worst, I visited the grave once again I beheld not the Necrophile commencing an attempt to disinter my

Beloved, but an advertisement upon the gravestone – a banner ad for a porn site. The naked girl flaunting herself beckoned me to enter – as if the route to vicarious pleasure was directly through the gravestone of my Beloved. Worse yet, as I realized very quickly in shock, that posturing naked girl bore the angelic countenance of my Beloved. She whose beloved face graced the headstone had become a whore.

How many more twists of the screw could I endure?

Advertising upon this gravestone couldn't possibly attract revenue. Who would visit this grave except myself? Connoisseurs of Gothic dereliction, of weeds, of dog stools?

Perhaps the ad for the porn site was designed to trick me. If I did enter the site, madly determined to be reunited erotically with some semblance of Mirabelle, this would demonstrate that I was perfectly capable of paying for *some* intimate services in cyberspace.

Whatever face that girl bore, in body she wasn't much like Mirabelle, whose breasts were small. I mean, *had been* small. By now Mirabelle's body would no longer conform to my memory of it. Oh what was I thinking? Her body had ceased to exist. Underneath the virtual soil did a virtual coffin really contain a virtual body? What else could the necrophile be hoping to find?

I wondered how long the porn site would beckon and hold the necrophile at bay, as a cross and garlic banish vampires. A site advertising a body of living flesh could scarcely appeal to a necrophile.

Because I took no action, within a few days the porn site disappeared – and the necrophile returned. First he tore off all the sods of grass and threw those out of sight, then he set to, digging with his hands. Whenever I looked, he removed more soil. Rather like a dance of the seven veils, although in this case it was the seven or seventeen soil layers.

What use would it be to shout at the screen, "Go away!

23

Leave my Beloved alone!'"?

I was forced to contemplate the possibility that my Beloved might presently be revealed in whatever condition the programmer chose her to be in. Rotting flesh and maggots. Bare bones which the necrophile would embrace, breaking them apart in his lust.

Ah, but Mirabelle must be inside a coffin – let the necrophile possess no screwdriver! Let him be frustrated at the final stage! You perceive how I clung to a thread of hope throughout this whole purgatorial episode.

Because the necrophile's activities seemed to correspond with whenever I viewed the grave (otherwise it would have accomplished more) for two whole weeks I only visited the grave very briefly, logging off almost immediately in the hope of delaying excavation for as long as I could. Since the whole point of the virtual grave was to be able to spend time contemplating it, this too was a torment. Anxiety possessed me that in my absence events might unfold willy-nilly if the programme diagnosed that I was employing delaying tactics.

Sure enough, the next time I looked in on Mirabelle's ravaged grave, the necrophile had made much more progress. He had uncovered the lid of a coffin, and was in the process of wiping it clean. In his case, I couldn't help feeling that he was wiping it *dirty*. The wood was a dark brown hue bearing long, thin, blackish streaks as though a cat had dragged its crappy bum across several times.

A quick googling revealed that the wood was Yew, *Taxus baccata*, of the Irish variety often planted in churchyards perhaps because it can live for 2,000 years and thus represents a sort of eternity – although not for cattle which might nibble its needles, nor for any child foolish enough to snack on its pinkish, cup-shaped fruits which are not true berries but *arils*, so called because the seed lies at the base of the cup rather than being enclosed by flesh. Too much googling can fill one with useless knowledge. I noted that the Yew tree was of pagan religious significance before it was christianised in churchyards. Rather than choosing any old lumber for the coffin, at which the necrophile now pawed, the programmer had selected a wood that was eminently symbolic, although not used for many actual coffins, paradoxically because of an association with death.

By now I was beginning to wonder whether the programmer was human at all or might instead be some kind of artificial intelligence. Seized with inspiration, I decided to resort to prayer that my Beloved should be respected.

I would not have dreamed of praying to a god called God, but I felt it was acceptable to pray to a god which made no pretence of divinity, yet which nonetheless presided over – and created on an on-going basis – a world, the virtual world of my Beloved's grave, the lilies (long departed), the weeds, the mongrel, the necrophile.

The programme obviously took some heed of my actions, or inactions. So what I did was place my fingers on the keyboard and type: I PRAY YOU, RESPECT MY BELOVED – followed by many variations upon this. No words appeared on the screen, which was occupied by the grave, but this seemed of little consequence when security services are able to spy on what a person is keyboarding by snooping from a distance on the tiniest electrical impulses produced by touching different keys.

I did this for a long time – until, I was about to say, sweat broke out upon my brow; except that touching a keyboard isn't a very strenuous activity. And yet I did perspire, as if attempting to wrestle with the necrophile, apparently to no avail.

I recalled that faith was important in prayer, not simply the demand of favours.

Time wore on, and I persevered.

Having cleaned the coffin thoroughly, the necrophile proceeded to use its virtual fingernails to unscrew the lid. Somehow I felt that this was cheating.

Finally the necrophile heaved the lid aside. From my viewpoint I could not see what was inside.

He reached down with one vile, grasping hand. *And he raised my Beloved.*

Yes, Mirabelle arose, radiant in her white shroud, unblemished by corruption!

I was beholding my Beloved's actual (I mean virtual) countenance and hair – and her very own figure within that shroud which had become a lovely white dress embroidered with daisies. It was she. It was her. Grammar fails me. In no way did she resemble the body of that girl on the sex site.

Conducted upward almost chivalrously by her excavator, Mirabelle stepped upon the coffin lid, and thence up on to the side of the grave.

"Mirabelle!" I bellowed. "Beloved!" Of course she could not hear me.

On the gravestone of a sudden appeared the words, FIAT VITA, Let There Be Life. Rather than the traditional FIAT LUX, Let There Be Light.

The necrophile was speaking to my Beloved, and she to it, but I am not a lip-reader. Tendrils were arising from the virtual earth all around, and flowering. Trees bent leafy boughs. A virtual bird flew by. I imagined a whole new world of paradise exfoliating from that place.

I began to understand. Due to my prolonged failure to pay, the programme had proliferated and evolved. Now it had performed a virtual resurrection. And by a corollary, perhaps the programme itself was now alive and fully sentient. I was perceiving a cyber-miracle – the dawn of true life within virtuality.

My sins of omission were forgiven. Or were they?

"Mirabelle!" I shouted, in vain.

Did she have any idea that I existed, and adored her? How could she, when her *mind* had not been buried in that grave, nor even strictly speaking her actual body?

Not once did Mirabelle look in my direction, at me who had prayed for this.

No, I had not prayed for *this* – I had simply prayed that her virtual corpse not be sullied and dishonoured. Unless the necrophile told Mirabelle, she could have no idea that I had paid (then failed to pay) for a virtual grave. She could have no idea whatever of me, for this resurrection could scarcely have restored her memories of life. Whatever was in her mind must be the creation of the artificial intelligence.

Although tormented anew by her indifference to me, I had an idea. Many scientists and religious people would *now* pay to visit this grave because of what was happening...

What a mercenary idea! How could I think something like that?

While I was wrestling with scruples, a development was occurring. The necrophile had taken my Beloved by the hand once more. He was gazing sweetly into her eyes – and his look was being reciprocated by Mirabelle! In her countenance I saw a gleam that I remembered so well. Yet now – what agony for me! – that look was directed at the necrophile.

All the joy I had been feeling at her miraculous resurrection was thrown into utter turmoil. Horror gripped me – and rage. I felt vilely cuckolded. Pangs of impotent jealousy pierced me. What a ghastly cocktail of emotions I experienced. I almost screamed as the necrophile led my Mirabelle – herself visibly consenting – towards the edge of the screen... and away out of sight.

In that moment of her disappearance my world fell in upon me. All that remained of love and devotion – and, latterly, of hope and exaltation – was the profaned grave now empty and abandoned. I tell you that I wept.

A sudden slinking movement: what was happening?

Hastily I wiped my eyes – only to behold that dog, that very same dirty sickly mongrel!

The animal positioned itself on the edge of the ravished grave – and it shat. Yes, the cur emptied its diseased bowels into the very space where my Beloved had rested in peace not long before. Were she still lying there, exposed, its turds would have fallen upon her face.

My sins of omission, in not paying Undying Love, had not been forgiven after all.

I was to be tormented to the utmost, like some prisoner of the Inquisition. My prayers had been understood as the pathetic cries of a heretic, who had failed to keep faith with Undying Love and consequently deserved even more agony upon the rack. Mirabelle, *my* Mirabelle, had been resurrected for the sole purpose of being kidnapped and taken far away from my love and devotion.

No longer could I bear such misery alone. I desperately needed help. Mirabelle must be able to rest in peace. And me too, me too.

Consequently I logged on to Cyberpol. Nowadays so many crimes occur in the virtual world that virtual police must handle these cases. No human officer can keep pace since response time needs to be fast in the cyber-realm.

I was positive that, at last, Undying Love had committed an actual crime. A virtual crime? A crime, nonetheless. Abduction. Cyber-abduction.

Quickly a menu of crimes appeared. Arson, which is to do with firewalls, Copyright Breach, Data-Theft, Embezzlement, Impersonation, Poisoning by Viruses, many, many cyber-crimes.

In vain did I search the menu for Profanation of Cybertomb, Kidnapping of Virtual Corpse, or Abusive Resurrection. At least there existed a category for crimes which didn't fall into a category. Consequently I clicked on `Other Crimes.' On my screen a cartoon of a sleuth-wizard promptly popped up, long wise beard, policeman's cap on his head.

From my speakers issued a synthesised voice:

"Please voice or keyboard your problem."

Since my speakers were not microphones, I was obliged to keyboard my explanation.

"Please clarify your relationship with the disappeared corpse," said the digi-detective moments later.

She was my Beloved, I typed. I think I might have felt ridiculous uttering these sentiments aloud to a cartoon character.

"But did the corpse belong to you?"

What sort of question was that?

Of course it didn't belong to me! I am not the dead person.

"Sir, you need to demonstrate ownership before the removal of the corpse can be treated as a crime." The digi-detective knew that I was a sir because my computer had conveyed my identity. "Did the corpse make a will with regard to her corpse before becoming a corpse?"

She didn't make a will. Anyway, I told you that her corpse was resurrected. So it must belong to herself! I want her remains – even though virtual – to be respected. I adored her.

"Love is a wonderful thing," the sleuth said sympathetically. "But I believe that the corpse in question did not belong to you any more than to herself. I must ask formally: are you the registered owner or did you own copyright in the corpse?"

I wracked my brains. Undying Love had created the corpse, although to my specifications. Did that give *them* copyright? If so, they would hardly denounce themselves!

It was almost with relief that I heard the next comment from the digi-detective:

"If a corpse dies intestate, all property defaults temporarily to the state to disburse to blood relatives according to the correct procedures."

Mirabelle had no property apart from herself, and she had no blood relatives. Anyway we aren't talking about her physical corpse. (I was beginning to fear that I might be accused of irregularities in the matter of her funeral.) *We're talking about her virtual corpse.*

"As regards this legal principle the virtuality of the corpse is irrelevant. Consequently only the state can protest at a theft. Are you requesting the state to proceed in this matter?"

Hope leapt in my bosom.

Yes, yes! Can you help find my Beloved?

"In theory, yes. In practise, no. Currently the corpse belongs to the state, it is true, but since a virtual corpse merely consists of some magnetism on a disk somewhere or other the state is most unlikely to invest resources. If the corpse belonged to you things would be different. If that was so, Cyberpol would be obliged to pursue your complaint."

I was at my wits' end.

Is there no way the corpse can belong to me legally? I lived with her, I loved her!

I typed no more, in case I seemed like a necrophile myself.

"Do not despair yet, Sir." The digi-detective grinned at me somewhat smuggly, suggestive of superior knowledge. "You can *adopt* a corpse – provided that it isn't adopted already – by payment of a fee to the state. Thus you can become the guardian and de facto owner of the corpse."

Are you sure? I can understand adopting a person on their deathbed when they're virtually dead.. But a corpse – or a virtual dead person?

"For hygenic reasons the law does not permit the adoption of physical corpses. But virtual corpses are another matter. The essential reasoning was that the dead cannot continue to pay taxes – except indirectly, by such a means. But the law makes no distinction between virtual actual corpses and invented virtual corpses which may of course be composites of digitised actual corpses."

Sometimes I thought that the world was becoming too alien and complicated for me.

What exactly do I have to do in order to adopt the corpse of my Beloved?

"First of all, you must have it. Habeas corpus."

But she has been kidnapped!

"Stolen," the digi-detective corrected me. "You can only kidnap someone who is alive."

BUT SHE IS RESURRECTED, I shouted by typing in capitals.

The digi-detective seemed to be consulting deep data-banks, for it was several moments before he replied:

"Virtual resurrections belong in the realm of metaphysics. In law they have no substance. Therefore she was stolen."

SO HOW DO I FIND HER? I shouted again.

The digi-detective winked.

"Why not try a search engine?"

This was mere mockery. How dare the digi-detectives of Cyberpol be programmed to mock citizens in time of need! I shut the link in a fury.

Yet then I began to think.

Seemingly an artificial intelligence had awoken within Undying Love. Could it be that the same was happening within Cyberpol? An artificial intelligence with a sense of humour, and even compassion? Obviously compassion was important in dealing with victims of crime, even electronic crime. Could the suggestion have been intended helpfully?

Feeling quite ridiculous, I visited a search engine site and typed the entire name of my Beloved.

As I should have foreseen, I found nothing.

Nevertheless I tried again, on the next day then the next, several times a day in fact – more out of desperation than any real hope.

On the fourth day, to my astonishment, I found Mirabelle.

This wasn't what you would call a pleasure. The search engine took me to a necrophilia porn site.

Cyberzombies were the performers, if that's the appropriate word. Exclusively cyberzombies. The FAQ of the site boasted of *real* dead people, whose spirits had awoken to apparent life in

31

cyberspace – as opposed to mere simulated animated corpses in various states of pristineness or putrefaction. I would have never thought that something like that could ever exist. What kind of human being could ever have conceived of such a perversion? Now my Mirabelle was one of those virtual zombies whose virtue was constantly being assailed. As if in a brothel!

What's more, devastatingly more, her beautiful face was outside the brothel on the splash page of the site, together with other victims who had been stolen away from their eternal peace to be exploited sexually.

Stolen? Ach, Undying Love must have sold her to the pornographs – or maybe the cyberzombie site even belonged to the same corporation that owned Undying Love.

I started to cry.

When I had recovered enough composure, I linked to Cyberpol again and very soon was confronting the same sleuth-wizard. At least he looked the same. Maybe there were hundreds of him. This one at least was immediately conversant with my case.

They are abusing my Beloved in the most monstrous way! I typed on the keyboard, now wet from my tears, then I summarised the whole situation.

The digi-detective spent a few moments in cyber-reverie before announcing:

"Unfortunately there is nothing illegal in that, Sir. The virtual corpse of the lady has been adopted by the company who owns that site."

But she is MY Beloved!! MINE MINE MINE MINE. Not theirs!

"Possession is nine parts of the law, Sir. Obsession is no part."

My heart sank even further, if that were possible. It seemed to me that this was a different digi-detective, although identical to the previous digi-detective. This one neither winked nor grinned nor offered any hints or assistance. I thought furiously.

What if there existed a little-known Convention of Rights for the Deceased?

Surely even a corpse has basic human rights, of dignity and decency!

"Undoubtedly, Sir, but a virtual corpse has virtually none."

Was that a *joke?* A hint of humanity on the part of this smart programme? Or of inhumanity? The situation was grotesque. Scientific progress had transformed my human tragedy into farcical grotesquery. Maybe this is the ultimate outcome of science – to diminish us all into ridiculous clowns before the artificial intelligences take over to muse sublimely and serenely.

I went through a period of utter prostration. At times I tried to pretend to myself that nothing terrible had really happened. Mirabelle was dead. She wouldn't ever come back. Her memories and her personality were *not* in the virtual mind of the cyberzombie in which she was resurrected. I was stupid to agonise.

However, all that still existed of Mirabelle in this world was there in cyberspace. There, it had to find rest and respect. How else could I love her? How else could I commemorate her devotedly?

Eventually I went to a living lawyer, to assess the possibility of taking some kind of legal action. The ways of law are mysterious.

Maybe technically I did own some copyright in Mirabella because I had supplied her semblance to Undying Love. Maybe I could demand a royalty, a percentage of her time in cyberspace, say twenty per cent, to be spent peacefully in her grave, the other eighty per cent in the zombie bordello. Vile though this compromise might be, at least it would grant Mirabelle some peace. Consequently her work in the bordello might more resemble employment than slavery. She would be able to sleep for 4.8 hours per day – or per night – to refresh herself for the remaining 19.2 hours.

No, not to *refresh* herself – what was I thinking? That her refreshed corpse might provide better service? Maybe the owners of the site might be persuaded to see things in this light, and believe it was to their advantage to exploit a refreshed cyberzombie.

And I would be able to spend 4.8 hours daily or nightly communing by her graveside, which would be open – as would the bed, her coffin, be – before the loathed necrophile led her away once more. In a sense this procedure might even become beautiful, or at least tolerable, or at least mythic – akin to the myth of Eurydice and Orpheus. No, I was confusing Eurydice with Persephone, compelled to live in Hades, or with Hades, for 33 per cent of the year. Just suppose, though, that Eurydice was Persephone. Myths often mingle. The discrepancy in percentages I would have to live with.

Alas, the lawyer poured cold water on my notions. Forget about her, he said.

I couldn't.

Now and then, guiltily but inexorably, I found myself in front of the monitor screen observing her candid face with that immaculate expression exposed like a trophy at the entrance to the most ignoble of sites I had ever seen. I sought to focus all my attention upon her countenance, seeing nothing of what surrounded her.

Consequently it was a long time before I noticed by accident a small notice on the web site:

Adopt a cyberzombie today for free!

I cursed myself. How long had this notice been on the site? Or had my peripheral awareness only just now spotted this as something new?

Although I had sworn never to enter any further into this abominable site, immediately I clicked on the notice.

34

And this was the offer…

For each new client I introduced to the site, I would receive an electronic corpse-token by way of commission. If I accumulated one hundred tokens, I could convert these into the adoption of any cyberzombie from their catalogue.

The chosen cyberzombie would be mine! Mine, to move to wherever I wished!

What a diabolical dilemma. Either I must become an accomplice of this vile site, recruiting customers for it in the hope of eventually giving my Beloved eternal peace – or else I must abandon the soul of my Beloved and let it rot inside that virtual brothel of cyberzombies, eternally prostituted by her virtual necrophile pimp.

For many nights I tossed sleeplessly, tussling with the dilemma – until one morning I switched on my computer almost unthinkingly, as if I myself was a zombie, and affiliated myself to the dirtiest evil.

I shan't go into details of what I had to do in the months that followed. I shan't admit to the things I had to learn to be able to find clients for that site. Suffice it to say that it cost me two years, every hour of my free time, and the loss of all remaining innocence. An enormous sacrifice, probably excessive. And yet my Mirabelle had meant everything to me. I couldn't have lived with myself if I'd washed my hands of the destiny of her virtual remains.

During that terrible period I consoled myself by imagining that my Beloved was inhabiting not Hell but some sort of purgatory, where she was expiating sins which were not hers at all, and that in the end paradise would be her reward.

All the while, terror tormented me that some other recruiter might rack up hundred electro-corpse tokens before I did – and that the swine might choose to adopt my Beloved.

Finally the day arrived when I earned my hundredth token. Mirabelle was still in the catalogue. The site did not default nor try to cheat me. Indeed the site sought to employ such an enthusiastic recruiter as me on a more permanent basis. I declined with a staccato S*N*A*R*L. She was transferred into my keeping.

Where should I dispose of my Beloved?

No way would I ever go near Undying Love again. Anyway, I couldn't afford their services, which was the root source of all my travails in the first place.

Very carefully I calculated my incomings and outgoings, then I researched all the copycat sites until I found one that seemed adequate and affordable – namely, Eternal Peace.

The monthly fee for Eternal Peace was quite low. True, the flowers in the vase would be virtual artificial ones – but I could choose which ones, and already I knew that I would choose camellias; I had bad associations with lilies. Candles on either side of the headstone would likewise be virtual artificial candles rather than virtual real ones. An enormous plus was an excellent Korean filter against intrusion by perverts, profaners, or incontinent dogs. Apparently the number of virtual strays was on the increase due to the irresponsibility of ex-owners who couldn't be bothered to keep up the virtual feeding and walking.

After her enforced imprisonment in the purgatory of the cyberzombies she was unchanged, my Mirabelle. The candour and innocence of her eyes survived intact. Her countenance was still so lovely. My own face had degraded due to my own hideous experiences. There were lines and wrinkles, there were bags, and my skin looked grey and depraved. I thought of the picture of Dorian Gray.

To bury Mirabelle again was almost like making her die a second time. Rationally I knew that she had been dead for a while now, but what my eyes beheld on the screen was an illusion which it was difficult to counteract.

I did what needed to be done, then I let out a long sigh. My humid eyes blurred the image of the new grave so that this creation of Eternal Peace seemed as luxurious as that of Undying Love. I admired how a willow tree bent over the grave, its fronds like the calligraphy of a Chinese painting.

REQUIESCAT IN PACE, I typed. Only the solemnity of Latin seemed to suffice for this moment.

At first I thought that it was on account of the moisture in my eyes, yet surely the fronds of the willow were moving fitfully? A breeze was blowing up. How could this be?

Of a sudden, a small pop-up appeared on screen:

Peace Reservoir low
Click here to buy more peace

Beloved Vampire
of the Blood Comet

Nowadays aristocratic vampires hang out far away from Transylvania, which is only for tourists. Aristo-vamps live in posh places such as Antibes and Baden-Baden or Venice, and they bank in Switzerland.

Incidentally, they only bank money and gold and jewels, never blood. Plenty of blood-banks exist, but after a few months bottled blood isn't at its best – and supposing interest was paid on a blood deposit, would this come from the veins of shareholders? Blood must continue circulating, otherwise it loses value.

A few hundred years ago Transylvania was *the* cutting-edge place to be, as my beloved vampire explained to me.

His name was Silviu Romanescu. He was tall and slim, with shoulder-length white hair, and he looked about forty years old, though probably he was at least 200. Silviu's charm was extraordinary. By now I had been captivated for a year.

"Well now, my little dove," he narrated to me, "the first expedition into outer space was actually an expedition of vampires led by Vlad Tsepesh (speaking phonetically, as one usually speaks), aka Dracula. History tells a lot of nonsense about Vlad. That business about him impaling his enemies on account of sadism and to inspire horror, for example! Horror wasn't the reason at all. Vlad needed a method of propulsion to lift a heavy body into outer space."

"There were no rocket fuels at the time…"

"Exactly. So he needed to use a paranormal method."

"He needed to find people who could levitate something by the power of mind?"

"What better motive to levitate a heavy weight than if that weight is yourself impaled on a semi-sharpened stake! So he, shall I say, *auditioned*, tens of thousands of, shall I say, *candidates*. Those who succeeded, he used as strap-on boosters and as on-board propulsion – the Impalement Drive – for the Transylvanian spaceship."

"It sounds cruel. This is supposed to be my bedtime story, Silviu!"

Silviu and I were lying on a bed of compost in an open twin-size coffin, and Silviu liked to have worms in the compost, which would tickle me, sometimes very intimately like boneless fingers. *The worms keep the soil fresh*, was his reason. I was accustomed to unusual bedtime stories, told at dawn of course since dawn was bedtime in his heavily curtained palazzo in Venice. However, this story was making me shivery, and to cling to him was of little help since his body wasn't at blood-heat but many degrees lower. That's why I usually had a rug over me except in the hot smelly Venetian summer, when the touch of Silviu's cool limbs was enchanting.

By the way, vampires never empty a victim's veins – would *you* want to drink five litres of soup for supper? – but often on a Friday or Saturday night vampires are thirstier than usual and their victim's blood pressure drops too low to sustain life. Thus not too many vampires tend to live in the same city, otherwise the number of semi-exsanguinated corpses might arouse suspicion.

Silviu had mesmeric powers, and influential local contacts. Consequently stories appeared in *Il Gazzettino di Venezia*, blaming MacDonald's for the semi-exsanguinated corpses which the Carabinieri fished out of the canals or found in alleyways. Anti-Americanism was popular, and it's well known that capitalists are blood-suckers, so many people believed that the seats in

40

MacDonald's contained anaesthetising needles which sucked blood from customers, to be replaced with cholesterol. Thus Venetians ate their hamburgers standing up, whereas Americans always need to sit down. Where possible at the weekend, Silviu hunted fat tourists.

"Vlad's spaceship was made of armour in Gothic style held together by interior leather straps riveted to the plates – and reinforced with internal braces so it wouldn't be too flexible, unlike armour which needs to be flexible."

"How do you know all this?"

"I was on that expedition." Quickly I revised my estimate of Silviu's age.

I didn't much wish to ask the next question, but the point had been niggling.

"Um, why were those candidates' stakes only *semi-sharpened?*"

"Because otherwise they might die too suddenly from shock. However, after leaving Earth's gravity behind, the stakes used for the Impalement Drive were fully sharpened because in outer space there's no weight to impale you."

"Um, what happened to the strap-on boosters?"

"Once we achieved escape velocity, those were unstrapped from within the ship. By then the bodies were frozen solid. Ice-corpses rained on what are now Romania and Hungary."

"Were you all wearing space-armour inside the ship?"

"No, my little dove. Vlad needed to limit the weight. As you know, cold means little to a vampire and we don't need to breathe, although sometimes we pretend to, as when I make love to you. Vampires are the best astronauts."

"But what about those Impalement Drivers? Didn't *they* need air?"

"You mean the successful candidates who pushed the ship along paranormally, strapped to the inside?"

"Yes, them."

"Little dove, are you by any chance trying to poke holes in your bedtime story?"

"I'm just fascinated by the details."

"Well, we had alchemical apparatus that stored solid air created earlier. You'd be amazed at how much air you can solidify into something as small as a brick. The Impalement Drivers, as you call them, wore bladders over their heads joined by tubes to the alchemical apparatus. Also, we used the drivers now and then as food-animals, akin to the way the Martians behave in *The War of the Worlds* by H.G. Wells. Do you realize that Orson Welles named his radio company the Mercury Theatre, and that Hg is the chemical symbol for mercury?"

Seemingly I couldn't fault Silviu on any detail!

"But what was the reason for this expedition?"

"To discover if our kind dwell on the Moon!"

Once again, how I envied and admired Silviu. He was undoubtedly a superior being. Admittedly he was also dead – all vampires are dead – but Silviu only smelled slightly sweet in a nice way, like Parma Violets. Didn't Nietzsche say God is dead? Being dead may be why God is a superior being. The crucifixion was a cunning plan.

"Will you ever make me into a vampire?" I asked wistfully.

"That would spoil our relationship, my pigeon. I like it as it is."

You could call me a vampire-virgin. That's because Silviu's teeth never once pricked me. I was like a pussy cat to him, to be stroked, or maybe more like a musical instrument, for when his skillful fingers played with me I moaned melodiously; which he enjoyed. Better than Albinoni, he commented. Very soothing, and melancholy in a delicious way. Mature vampires experience aesthetic and metaphysical desires rather than physical ones. In the case of male vampires, I was led to believe, their penises never stiffen with blood flow.

I first met Silviu while I was returning to my hotel on the Riva degli Sciavoni late at night. I had stared in wonder at his beautiful white hair and the long black velvet cloak he wore over a harlequin costume. I, Colombe Duval, had come to Venice from Paris with my camera for carnival time. I was in advertising and was preparing a campaign for an expensive new mascara containing depleted uranium dust, called Maskara, to give eyelids that heavy, sultry, radioactive look.

Silviu was wearing a minimal black mask, emphasizing his mesmeric gaze. I gazed, mesmerized. He also gazed in admiration at my long red hair – and then in a trice he had *collected* me, in his very strong arms, and he ran swiftly and effortlessly along the waterside promenade while I offered no resistance.

Did a maiden struggle when abducted by a Greek god? I think traditionally she did, fearing rough sex followed by a dose of homeric herpes Zeustor. I didn't struggle.

Soon my adoration for Silviu grew and grew. Forget about depleted uranium mascara! Forget about Paris! Forget photography, since flash offended Silviu's eyes and in any case nothing of him appeared on any photos despite the longest exposure in the dim palazzo. After I'd been awake only nocturnally for a few months, my flesh grew white as alabaster, which Silviu liked.

And he told such wonderful bed-time stories. Never before did I know that Marie Antoinette was a vampire. "Qu'ils mangent *du sangfroid*," is what she really said about the bread riots in Paris, not *de la brioche*. `Sangfroids' were a favourite speciality made to a recipe of Grimod de La Reynière – little cold blood-puddings that looked like buns. So she was making an elegant pun. Due to my comparative inactivity, aside from wonderful orgasms at dawn and dusk, I had to be careful not to put on weight. Consequently delicacies were essential, being delicate. Silviu himself only ever ate sparsely, to restore trace elements which his body lost.

"Where were we, my little dove? Ah yes, in outer space, heading for the Moon in a spaceship of best-quality armour powered and steered by the paranormal avoidance of impalement."

"Would the armour be from Milan? Would it be called 'Avant' armour?"

I knew a bit about armour because I'd taken a lot of photos of armour for an ad campaign: Tough Guys Wear Condoms Too. The erect penis of the male model wearing a condom had stuck out through a special hole in the miniskirt of chainmail. We had to show him a turkey porn movie before he erected. There was just no other way to get through to him. And then, the first time, he jammed – but at least the condom didn't tear, which pleased the manufacturers. By turkey I don't mean it was a bad movie. It was about sex with a turkey, digi-animated. By then it was too late to hire a different male model whose childhood au pair hadn't played with him during Disney cartoons.

"My pigeon, I told you it was *Gothic* armour – so that means made in Germany. Well, after three days we landed near the South Pole on the backside of the Moon during the lunar night that lasts a fortnight, and we discovered the frozen lake produced by the blood comet."

"Wait a minute, Silviu. I understand how you took off, but how did you land? Did you threaten the drivers with being unimpaled or anti-impaled or whatever the word is?"

"No no, we steered the ship by turning the main driver around until we were over the place we wanted, and upright. Then Vlad buggered the driver. This was such a relief after the sensation of the stake that the driver felt more relaxed. So the paranormal levitation became less than the Moon's gravity. We sank down gently, controlled by Vlad's thrusts and withdrawals."

"Quite a man, Vlad."

"Much misunderstood. The first space commander."

"How come Vlad's dead penis stiffened for buggery, whereas yours doesn't?"

"That, my dove, is the measure of what sort of dead man Vlad was! He alone fulfills the prophecy, *The Dead Shall Rise*. He was out of this world."

"*Was?* Did he die on the Moon? I mean, did he expire?"

"Since I was part of that expedition, obviously we returned to Transylvania and touched down successfully. However, Vlad then had an even greater inspiration – no less than travel to the stars by an FTL drive, *Faster Than Levitation*. Ordinary Impalement Drivers, inspired to levitate by wooden stakes, wouldn't be adequate to reach the stars – but Impalement Drivers converted into powerful vampires and then inspired by *silver-tipped* stakes: those could provide the levitation power for starflight! So I suppose Vlad is still out there somewhere, unless the light of an alien sun has burned him to dust."

A dramatic pause. We broke off so I could have some orgasms, first from Silviu's fingers, then from his cool tongue. Just then I was having my period, Silviu's favourite time for cunnilingus.

Afterwards I asked, "What about the lake of frozen blood? And did you meet lunar vampires?"

"Oh yes, we met the lunar vampires. They colonised the Moon tens of thousands of years ago by using impalement technology, which Vlad had re-invented. Von Däniken was right about prehistoric technology, though wrong about details. Initially, the lunar vampires fed entirely on the blood of the crews of flying saucers. Flying saucers usually stop at the Moon on their way to interfere with the Earth. The Moon's a convenient rest-stop if you forget about the vampires – the UFO crews always forget because of vampiric mesmerism. So the UFO crews get sucked quite a lot. That's why they're the Greys. When they first leave home, they're the Pinks. This explains why the Greys behave so confusingly when their UFOs reach Earth."

"So the lunar vampires are like antibodies in the immune system? Protecting the body of the Earth from invasion?

Weakening the invaders?"

"But uninentionally. Ever since that blood comet crashed into the Moon and formed a frozen lake, the lunar vampires have had an alternative source of blood. However, they still like to suck Pinks into Greys for old times sake. Nowadays UFO crews are like dessert. Or maybe like blood sorbet, a palate cleanser."

"You mentioned a blood comet. How can something like that come into existence?"

"The universe is never stingy of mysteries, my dear. How do ordinary comets, made from dirty water, come into existence? Nobody really knows. The same with blood comets. Of course the blood is frozen, but originally it must have been liquid, just as the water of the comets must have been. The mystery of the origin of blood comets will one day be solved, but not by human scientists. It will be one of us, a vampire, who finds out the truth. Maybe our forever beloved Vlad Dracul will, if he is still out there."

"But if blood comets actually exist, wouldn't vampires like to take a ride on them?"

"You're really starting to think like a vampire, Colombe," Silviu told me with an appreciative smile. "Maybe I should give you a bite one day, you'd deserve it."

"But you won't. Or will you?"

"Not in the near future."

"So tell me: would vampires ride blood comets?"

"That's entirely possible. It's beautiful to think of the vastness of the sidereal spaces ploughed by thousands of blood comets like spatial vessels. Outer space is the natural environment for a vampire, us being dead and not needing air or tourist comfort, and cosmic darkness protects us from the deadly rays of suns. Imagine an ancient primitive vampire form of life! Maybe proto-vampires originally came to Earth on a blood comet millions or even billions of years ago, and the panspermia theory of the propagation of life though the universe is true – for vampire beings, which have moved through the universe inside blood comets since forever. Life on every populated planet could derive from this proto-vampire form of life, and successive mutations would create the first and little known bifurcation of evolution: superior vampire life in one direction and inferior non-vampire life in the other. The creation of the banal mortal form of life of non-vampires is needed by nature for its trivial tragedies, and even more for producing all the necessary blood which vampires need. Vampires cannot drink the blood of other dead and immortal beings. A vampire's food source must be alive and mortal."

"Why is that?" I asked.

"Nature *loves* complications, my dear. Look at the tail of a peacock."

It was time for more orgasms, since my menstruation was at its peak and Silviu wouldn't miss a drop, which typically results in more and more pleasure for me – and who was I to refuse that? If only I could have permanent menstruation – I'd often thought – I'd be the happiest of the women, since I would be licked almost incessantly by a competent male like Silviu, with hundreds of years of haematocunnilingual experience!

Because Silviu had waited a whole year (which was nothing to a vampire) before revealing something as momentous as his journey to the Moon, reluctantly I decided that his account must be no more than a wonderful invention to enchant me. But then, three months later –

In the vast bedroom of the palazzo we had a plasma-screen TV because Silviu liked to watch operas, particularly ones by Mozart. Early one night, a news flash interrupted *The Marriage of Figaro* performed at Venice's own La Fenice. On the other side of the Atlantic, where it was afternoon, an unidentified spacecraft was heading for Florida – just as American astronauts were preparing to board the re-repaired space shuttle, watched by

President Bush himself. Space experts and Homeland Security thought the intruder was an alien spacecraft. The launch was put on hold. George Bush decided not to leave hastily in Air Force One because this might be `a moment of destiny.'

We watched the `alien' spaceship descend slowly, as if by antigravity, while American fighter jets circled. Cameras zoomed – and we saw a ship made of medieval armour, pitted by micrometeorites.

"It's the return of Dracula," said Silviu, almost in awe.

I spoke without thinking: "No, my love, *The Return of Dracula*'s on Channel Three." Blushing, I asked more sensibly, "How could he be away for so long?"

"For him, my pigeon, much less time will have passed because of time dilation due to Faster Than Levitation travel."

The ship of Gothic armour touched the ground quite close to the shuttle launch pad, near where the seven brave spacesuited astronauts still sat holding their helmets, each in his or her own stretch-golf-buggy. Gantry and shuttle with booster rockets towered high overhead, dwarfing the armour-ship which slumped slightly as if relaxing. Towards the bottom of the Gothic spaceship, a big plate hinged open.

Already the presidential limo was speeding towards the landing site, secret service agents clinging to the sides, police motorbikes accompanying. TV crews raced after the limo.

Down from that doorway in the armour jumped a person dressed in a bear skin with a few big buttons. He had long ringlets of brown hair and a long nose curving over big moustaches. The person staggered because of gravity then drew himself upright.

Zoom-mikes picked up Vlad Tsepesh's voice – which Silviu translated for me, him being fluent in medieval Romanian and many other languages – as he bellowed triumphantly at the seated NASA astronauts:

"I bring news that the Milky Way is not a milky way... but

48

the Bloody Way… I bring news of many blood comets… Hmm, he says many planets are made of flesh… The more you approach the centre of the galaxy, the more often the planets are made of flesh… Old-fashioned non-flesh planets are still a majority only in the periphery of the galaxy, where things happen more slowly and evolution is retarded… Planets are converted to living flesh because of nano-viruses… in a cosmic war between Flesh and Machines… The pressure of shit accumulating inside a living planet often explodes it… Asteroids are haemorrhoids… Vampire life is generally far more common in the universe than the human sort of life… My dove, these are remarkable discoveries. This fully explains the frozen blood lake on the Moon!"

The limo arrived before Vlad could declare more remarkable facts about the cosmos. The car doors opened. The eyes of the world were upon George Bush. He couldn't go on holiday this time. No more New Orleans. Followed by several advisers, he had little choice but to advance, holding out his hand to Vlad Tsepesh, though he could have little idea who Vlad was, even if Vlad bore a certain resemblance to Johnny Depp in *Pirates of the Caribbean*. Vlad also looked a bit like Osama bin Laden (though not so soulful and dewy-eyed), but George Bush had seen too many fake videos of Osama bin Laden produced by the CIA to recognize the leader of Al Qaida, if Al Qaida actually existed.

Vlad glanced up at the towering space shuttle pointing at the sky.

"You impale *big*," Silviu translated for me. "But I impale more."

There was a swaggering braggadocio about the vampire commander.

Bravely, or stupidly, George Bush decided to embrace Vlad in the French fashion since evidently he was a foreigner.

Vlad promptly sank his vampire teeth into the President's neck, sucked for a while, then exclaimed in medieval Romanian (as translated by Silviu), "God, I was thirsty."

Whereupon he spun George Bush around and pulled down his trousers and polka-dot underpants. Obviously Vlad wished to assert himself. The thrust of his penis poking through the bear skin lifted George Bush a little into the air, and not by levitation.

Microphones picked up the President's shaky words:

"Oh my God! ARE YOU GOD, COME TO GUIDE ME?"

For many years to come, the most devout Americans would chant in their churches these inspired and anguished words of their president, and would undergo a sacrament of impalement in the form of a quick colonoscopy performed by zealous preachers…

In the days following the historic meeting between Dracula and President Bush, all TV channels broadcast again and again the already immortal images of the event, just as happened previously with the Twin Towers attack. Publicity spots sold very well. To the surprise of TV viewers, the secret service had done nothing to stop Dracula from taking advantage of Bush. Those men can't be stupid because they work for the Bureau of the Treasury, not the CIA, so they knew perfectly well that vampires are immortal and can't be killed, and that frustrating them makes them really mad. The fairy tale of those wooden stakes which are supposed to destroy vampires is only a cinematographic invention. The only things that can terminate a vampire are an eternally unsatisfied thirst or falling into a black hole (which some vampire-philosophers consider to be equivalent). Oh, and of course blazing sunshine too, but Florida was cloudy that day and none of the secret service agents had a portable sun with them. Plus, the security guys probably didn't themselves much want to be bitten by Vlad Tsepesh, and be vampirized. This may have been ill-advised, since later it would become a status symbol to be a vampire. Another explanation is that they didn't react because

Vlad mesmerised them, with the typical psychic emanation which makes vampires such erotic creatures. But these are all hypotheses.

George Bush became a vampire, and presently he was impeached, not for being a vampire – this actually would be a point in his favour – but on Homeland Security grounds for letting himself be buggered in public on TV by an illegal Romanian immigrant without a visa. The American people love impaling presidents, but not impaled ones. Imagine if Monica Lewinski had used a dildo instead of her mouth. Many millions of Americans who viewed the Bush-Tsepesh encounter (a Bottom, rather than a Summit) got psychosomatic irritations of their anuses, and male homosexuality in the United States rose significantly, though this was outstripped by vampirosexuality.

A new President of the United States was needed. The American Constitution had already been modified so that Schwarzenegger, not born in America, could be elected – but because of this Vlad Tsepesh could become a candidate too, and finally Vlad the Genuine Impaler of History beat Arnie the Fake Terminator of Fiction. The fact that when Vlad was speaking medieval Romanian nobody in America could understand him turned out to be an advantage for his campaign. It wouldn't be so easy as before to disagree with the statements of the President of the United States. What's more, the vampire who came back from the stars had revealed to the world by his pioneering voyage mysteries of the universe that were previously unknown. Mankind could dream about new horizons. The American dream became a Romanian dream. As a result, the White House was completely remodelled in the style of the monumental People's Palace of Ceausescu.

Henceforth American foreign policy found it much easier to prevail. The impalement of terrorist suspects, which became the speciality of the Federal Emergency Management Agency, FEMA, established a new standard of potent folklore worldwide.

51

I thought this was quite bizarre, since Silviu had told me that Vlad mainly impaled people for propulsive purposes. Vlad thus became a victim of his popular persona. At the next G8 meeting, he bit the leaders of the world's eight most industrialised countries, transforming them into immortal vampires. Were they lucky! Polls reveal that the majority of mankind would happily be vampirized – however, the world vampire élite reserve their magic bites for an increasingly restricted circle of privileged people. I'm really afraid that Silviu will never bite me.

However – and this is the scary bit – I still don't really know if Silviu has told me the whole truth. Could the bizarre encounter between Bush and Dracula have been a complete coincidence? Is there really a vampiric shield on the Moon that protects us from the full effects of UFOs? Are most planets in our galaxy made of flesh? And do my menstruations really have a subtle flavour of ginger?

The most ominous doubt emerges occasionally in the dreamy mists of early dawn, as my eyes open from the sleep that each night makes them innocent again. It's then, while I'm neither fully awake nor asleep, that I sometimes wonder this:

Now that the world is ruled by vampires, and people believe in them and piously pray during ceremonial colonoscopies, *do vampires actually exist*, or are they state-of-the-art from the élite's myth factory? Is Silviu Romanescu, now a top figure of the Vlad Tsepesh administration, really the vampire that he purports to be?

An invasion by aliens mightn't be noticed if the aliens imitated, not the widescreen technicolor special effects of *Independence Day* or *The War of the Worlds*, which would shout *invasion* – but instead the black-and-white erotic-noir of B movies of beloved memory set in Transylvania, with which we all feel at home. Imagery is everything nowadays.

The Penis of My Beloved

During my Beloved's lifetime his penis was of great importance to me – how could it be otherwise? Of course there was much more to my Beloved than his penis. For instance there was his tongue. I don't merely refer to his skill at licking, but also to all the words he said to me (except obviously whilst licking). Words are so important to a woman during love, just as they are in the everyday aspects of life. Also, there were his dark eyes, which spoke volumes of silent poetry. Also, there were his arms which held me. I need not enumerate more – there was all of Oliver.

When my Beloved suddenly died of a heart attack, how desperately I craved to have him back again, alive.

This was possible due to advances in rapid cloning. However, a whole body cost a small fortune. Oliver and I had never given much thought to the morrow. Even by availing myself of a special offer from the Bodies'r'Us Clinic, and by paying on the instalment plan, the most I could afford was the cloning of a small part of Oliver.

Which part should it be? His right hand, sustained by an artificial blood supply and activated to a limited extent by a nerve impulse box with control buttons? Even a whole hand was out of my financial reach!

Should it be his tongue, likewise sustained by a costly blood supply?

Minus mouth and throat and vocal chords, a tongue could never say anything even if it wanted to, although it ought to be able to lick, for such is the nature of tongues. Body-parts are aware of the role they play in the entirety of the body, consequently this memory lingers on even when they're amputated or dissected, or in this case cloned. Oh yes, his tongue ought to be able to lick, although the sensation might seem to me more like a warm slug than his robust tongue of yore.

How about one of his eyes, which spoke volumes? The eye could rest upon an egg-cup and form an image of me. Before going to bed I could perform a strip-tease for his eye. Yet to be perfectly frank, what could his eye *do* for me? Also, although I had no intention of ever being unfaithful to my Beloved, a naked eye-ball might seem like a spy camera keeping watch. This wasn't the kind of continuing intimacy I craved.

Really, my choice could only be the penis, especially as the cost was based upon the 'normal' size when flaccid rather than erect. In this instance the money I would be paying in any event for the blood supply, so as to keep the part alive, would provide a special bonus benefit, namely erection when the penis was caressed. You couldn't say about any other cloned body-part that your investment could grow ten-fold, as it were!

"You mightn't realise," the cloning salesman said to me, "that a penis becomes stiff not because of blood pumped actively into it by an excited body, but because certain penile muscles *relax*, which allows the blood to flow in and fill it. Normally the muscles are tense and inhibit the volume of blood – otherwise men would have permanent erections."

"So if you feel nervous and tense, you never get an erection?"

The salesman flushed, as though I had touched on a sore point. He was a young man with ginger hair and many freckles. The wallpaper of the consultation room was Klimt, so we were surrounded by hybrids of slender women and flowers.

"Madam, it's simply that you might be expecting too much. We can't absolutely guarantee erection, for that would be to alter the biology of the penis. In effect we would be providing you with a bio-dildo rather than with a genuine cloned organ – and we don't supply such things. Prostho-porn isn't our profession."

This was spoken a shade tartly. The salesman may have been upset by my previous remark, supposing that it reflected upon his own virility.

I was sure that my Beloved's cloned penis would remember my own particular touch and wouldn't feel inhibited.

I made like a wide-eyed innocent. "Is 'prostho-porn' *anyone's* profession?"

"I've heard that in China…" The salesman lowered his voice. "Multiple cloned cunts of pop-stars in pleasure parlours…" Now he seemed mollified and was all smiles again. "This won't be the case here! Your commission will be unique to you."

"I should hope so!"

It goes without saying that I'd arranged for sample cells from all of Oliver's important organs and limbs to be frozen in liquid nitrogen – which wasn't too expensive – before the majority of his dear chilled body finally entered the furnace at the crematorium. I'd read that in another few years it might be possible to coax a finger or a penis, say, to diversify and regenerate from itself an entire body, but apparently this was a speculative line of research pursued by only a handful of maverick scientists. Small wonder: it's much more common for a body to lose a penis than for a penis to lose a body! So I was sceptical of this possibility. In the meantime my dream of recreating the entirety of Oliver, to rejoin his penis, would remain a dream because of the cost.

"So that's the famous penis!" exclaimed my neighbour Andorra, who was short and who spoke her mind. Andorra and I were best friends even before the sudden death of my Beloved, about which she was very consoling. Currently Andorra was working for the Blood Donor service.

Her parents chose the name Andorra to suggest that she would be adorable. Naming her after the tiniest independent state in Europe did prove prophetic as regards her stature and personality – she was short and assertive. Yet as regards adorability in the eyes of the opposite sex, the ploy failed. Andorra had only had one boyfriend, and he was a disaster. No one else tried to get into bed with her, or courted her. I think Andorra trained as a nurse due to reading too many doctor-nurse romance novels, many of which still littered her apartment next door to mine.

Next door to *our* apartment, I should say. Oliver's and mine; mine and that of his penis.

Andorra's dog Coochie sometimes chewed her romance novels or carried them around her apartment while awaiting her return from work, and a walk, and an emptying. Coochie was a yellowish Labrador.

"Famous?" I replied. "There's nothing famous about it except in my own eyes." And in my hand, of course.

"It's a bit small…" but then she quickly added, "at the moment." She eyed the apparatus to which the penis was attached by two long connecting tubes. "Will you pump some more blood into it?"

So that she could behold an actual erect penis in the flesh at last?

"That isn't why a penis stiffens. Don't you know anatomy? What's important is the receptive mood of the penis."

"Well, it would be more impressive…" She tailed off.

Did she hope that I would stimulate the penis of my Beloved for her benefit? I almost succumbed to her implied entreaty, if only to demonstrate Oliver's penis in full gory, I mean glory, but this was an intimate matter.

"I'm perfectly satisfied," I told her. Only as I spoke did I realize how this might imply smugly that Andorra herself remained unsatisfied. She had mentioned dissatisfaction with dildos. I might seem to be cock-crowing, lording it over my friend.

Andorra looked thoughtful.

Due to the length of the blood-tubes it was easy to take the penis
to bed with me so as to stroke it in just the way my Beloved had
liked, then pleasure myself after it stiffened. It remembered me.
Because only Oliver's penis was cloned, not his prostate and
other attachments, inevitably there was no ejaculation, yet this
was no disadvantage – on the contrary! I would hold the rubber
grip-mount, shaped like a small plantpot, in which his penis (as it
were) grew, and much prolonged joy was mine. I was blissful.
Sometimes after an orgasm I would take the penis out of me and
talk to it, or use my mouth for a different purpose. I felt like a
little girl: the penis of my Beloved, my lollipop.

But then came a problem with the blood supply – I don't mean
the tubes and pump, but rather my finances. Bodies'r'Us strongly
recommended renewing the blood each month to prevent
degeneration of the penis. As part of the initial cost, I'd received
five vouchers for replacement blood. Now I'd used those
vouchers, and I discovered that in the meantime the cost of
blood had risen by twenty-five per cent.

BodiesRUs was a significant user and retailer of blood,
needing to buy blood, good blood, too, from healthy sellers.
Nobody would donate blood charitably so that some rich woman
could maintain a clone of her dead poodle, or me a cloned penis.
Andorra had complained to me that the Donor Service, which
supplied hospitals, was suffering a bit of a blood drain because
former donors were choosing to sell rather than donate, but
luckily altruism and generosity still prevailed in society, not to
mention donations by way of the vampire churches as part of
their safe sex campaign.

At this point I consulted Andorra and she made me an
offer…

…to smuggle blood from the Donor Service – providing that

I let her use the penis of my Beloved privately one evening each week, say every Friday.

I was astonished and disconcerted.

"I'm your best friend," she pointed out.

"It won't respond to you," I said.

She pouted at me, full-lipped. "I'll find a way."

I should have refused. Yet if I refused, I might embitter Andorra. It must have cost her dear to make this request, this admission of craving for the real thing – or at least for the cloned and partial thing. Refusal might seem like a slap in the face. But also, of a sudden, I was curious as to whether my Beloved *would* respond to the touch of a stranger!

According to Andorra, the penis did react to her, and very satisfyingly too. She might be fibbing so as to salve her pride, and I could hardly ask to be present while Andorra writhed on her bed. Besides, I wouldn't have wished to behold this personally. Consequently every Friday evening Andorra would carefully carry the pump and the penis along to her apartment and bring them back to me a couple of hours later. During this interval I would watch TV and try not to think about what might be happening. Once the penis was mine again, I would wash it, irrespective of whether Andorra had already done so. Washing excited the penis as much as caresses, since the actions were very similar. The penis seemed to be wishing to make up to me for what had occurred, even though it was I who owed the penis an apology.

I would kiss it. "Forgive me, my Beloved. You earned your blood, that's the main thing."

After some weeks I made a terrible discovery. When Andorra brought the penis back, Coochie was with her, pawing at her thigh and sniffing.

"Stay!" ordered Andorra, but Coochie pushed his way into my apartment. The dog's gaze was fixed on the now-floppy penis. He seemed to want it – not for a snack, which was my first fear, soon dispelled by a much worse realisation: Coochie wanted the penis as a *penis*.

When I stared accusingly at Andorra, she broke down in tears of remorse.

"He's become addicted," she confessed.

"Do you mean… do you mean… you've been giving your dog *bestiality* treats with the penis of my Beloved?"

"He's an unusual dog! I love Coochie, and Coochie loves me, but I knew he was gay!"

"Gay? How did you know that?"

Andorra remained silent.

"Did Coochie bugger some other male dog while out walkies with you?"

More silence. My best friend couldn't tell me an outright lie. Suddenly I realised that if Andorra's discovery had *not* occurred during walkies then only one possibility remained…

"You used to try to get Coochie to fuck you! But no matter how you went about it, Coochie couldn't get it up because – "

"– because Coochie's gay. It's the only explanation."

I felt sorry for Andorra. Yet I also had a persistent image in my mind… of Coochie, who was gallumphing around, his anus frequently visible. How degrading for the penis of my Beloved!

While performing that canine service, Oliver's penis must have been stiff! Was the penis utterly undiscriminating?

"Look," I told Andorra, "you must promise me, don't do it with Coochie again. That's unhygienic."

"I always did me *after* I did Coochie."

That would have cleaned the penis?

Resulting in Andorra's vagina smelling of male dog? In due course Coochie might learn to associate… Andorra had not given up hope.

"I'd be well within my rights to refuse you the penis ever again."

"And I to refuse you blood," she murmured.

She had a point. Consequently we didn't quarrel.

With some difficulty she hauled Coochie away. Alone once again, I eyed the wilted penis.

"Beloved, how could you do it with a dog?"

I tried to come to terms with what had happened by being objective and logical. The episode with Coochie was not my Beloved's fault.

The next week Andorra remarked, "Maybe the penis has erections in a pavlovian way regardless of with whom or with what. Poor Oliver loves you, but he can't resist. You really ought to have more of him cloned."

How would I pay for that?

Oh but she had the answer!

At the hospital where Andorra worked previously, she knew a junior anaesthetist who moonlighted as a stud in porn movies. Mark's rugged good looks and intelligence made him a desirable actor. As for his prowess, before each performance Mark would sniff a stimulant gas to keep himself stiff irrespective of ejaculation. Unfortunately Mark had recently been sacked for stealing gas from the hospital. Now he needed to rely full-time on porn to earn his living just at the time when he'd lost access to what boosted him.

What – suggested Andorra – if I were to offer the penis of my Beloved as a stand-in for Mark's penis while limp? With clever editing, viewers mightn't notice the temporary substitution, the tubes, the little plantpot clutched by Mark, or by whichever woman.

My Beloved's penis would be earning some money with which to recover more of himself for me.

"How is Coochie coping?" I asked.

"I lock him in the bathroom with a lot of cold turkey. He loves that. It takes his mind off the penis."

Andorra made arrangements. A couple of weeks later I watched a copy of the video in order to see with what sort of woman the penis was unfaithful.

The poor editing hid little. It was obvious that part of the time a detached, hand-held penis was in use. Not a dildo, oh no, but a living penis which happened to lack a man attached to it.

What a dream for a woman, you may well say! And you would be right. Thanks to chat on the internet, word spread rapidly. The video became a wow among women. Few men bought it, maybe because of castration fears, but the producer was jubilant. Here at last was a porn video uniquely suited to females. Therefore we must make another video quickly – starring the detached living penis itself. Mark would play the role of a sex counsellor administering the penis as therapy to a patient.

Not long after this second video was released, requests began arriving from dozens of sophisticated high society women requesting 'private performances,' and offering to pay well.

Thus it was that at a private orgy, held in a woodland clearing on the outskirts of the city, the penis of my Beloved was mounted on the bonnet of a Jaguar car in place of the usual little model of a leaping jaguar. Several naked women wearing Venetian carnival masks took turns ascending the front of the car while friends cheered. This gave a new meaning to auto-eroticism.

Because of those private performances I was accumulating money fast. A down-payment on cloning all the rest of my Beloved looked possible, not least because the wife of one of the directors of Bodies'r'Us was one of those who had privately enjoyed the penis of my Beloved. She regarded my quest for the entirety of my Beloved as so romantic.

This woman, Natalie, made short art-films as a hobby. She was convinced that a film made by her about my eventual reunion with my Beloved might win her a prestigious award given for short art movies featuring sexual themes, the Shiny Palm.

This trophy took the form of a polished feminine metal hand grasping an erect penis made of purple glass.

On account of the porn movie about the autonomous penis, Bodies'r'Us had gained new customers. Wives who had seen that movie, and whose husbands failed to satisfy them sufficiently, urged their spouses to have their penises cloned so as to support the men's performance in bed. An identical understudy, or penis-double, would increase the women's pleasure and offer extra possibilities.

Excellent publicity for Bodies'r'Us! In Natalie's opinion an artistic movie would add true chic to the cloning of small body-parts.

Not necessarily always penises, either! A lovely nose might be cloned and mounted on a plaque, like a small hunting trophy, the blood supply out of sight in a hidden compartment. A hand might be cloned. Or a finger. Due to lack of auxiliary muscles, one couldn't expect the hand to flex its fingers dramatically, or the finger to bend much. A finger is not a penis. Probably penises would be most popular.

"Rivalry might even arise among men who have cloned penises," Natalie declared to me on the phone one day. "Those can be displayed on the wall as a talking point at a dinner party. You know how men boast – but it would be most unsuitable for a man actually to pull his own trousers down during a fashionable dinner party! Besides, he mightn't rise to the occasion on account of too much alcohol or shyness. A cloned penis, which wouldn't imbibe, can represent him at his best. Wives will take pride in demonstrating the penis to their guests."

She speculated further:

"Failure to mount your cloned penis on the wall might even give rise to suspicions as to the quality of the original penis. Too small? Too thin? Whatever! Maybe deficient men will buy more magnificent penises not cloned from themselves – provided by third-world companies without the scruples of Bodies'r'Us. On the other hand, the display of a less than splendid penis on the dining room wall might be a form of inverted boastfulness: `It may not look much, but if only you knew what I can do with it, and for how long!' You do want your Beloved back, don't you, dear? If you let me make a film about your quest, I'm sure Bodies'r'Us will be very easy on the terms for a full Beloved. My film wouldn't be intrusive, just a few remote-control mini-cameras concealed in your apartment."

I was so excited I would have agreed to almost anything.

Bodies'r'Us must have exploited some of that research by those maverick scientists I mentioned. Instead of cloning a hundred per cent new body complete with brand new penis, they *integrated* – as they put it – the already cloned penis into the ensemble of all the rest of Oliver's cloned anatomy. The cloned penis which I already knew was precious to me – it stood for continuity. I could hardly discard it, but it would be downright silly to maintain that autonomous penis unused, expensively keeping a blood pump working at the same time as the full Oliver maintained a blood supply to another cloned penis by natural means. It was only sensible that the original cloned penis should be coupled to the rest of the clone.

And so my Beloved came back to me.

Along with some cameras and microphones for my apartment.

In years gone by, scientists predicted that a duplicated brain shouldn't retain any of the memories of the brain that it was cloned from. According to past scientific wisdom, the new brain should only exhibit the same capacities and personality traits and tendencies as the original brain – for instance the tendency to fall in love with somebody looking much like me, or the ability to learn languages easily.

Now we know that a cloned brain actually inherits many of

63

the typical *dreams* of its source brain. This is because dreams are deeply archetypal. The original brain and the cloned brain are genetically identical, so by morphic resonance the cloned brain acquires much of the dream experience of the original from out of the collective storehouse from which dreams emerge, and into which they return.

Thus my cloned Beloved couldn't remember any actual incidents of our waking life together, but he knew who I was in a dreamy way. And because dreams contain speech, he could speak, although in rather a dreamlike manner.

"You are an almond tree," he told me, shortly after Bodies'r'Us delivered him to the apartment. Was that because of the colour of my eyes? If so, this must be an endearment.

Yet to my horror I very quickly found that my Beloved was impotent with me! No matter what I did, or how I displayed myself, his penis remained limp – that very penis which had previously responded so enthusiastically! This shocked and chagrined me – and I regretted the cameras and microphones Natalie had installed.

We have all heard how the arm of the executed German mass-murderer, Sigmund Hammerfest, was grafted on to an amputee, Rolf Heinz, who'd lost his arm in a car crash – and how the murderer's arm subsequently made Herr Heinz homicidal. While Herr Heinz was making love to his wife one night, the arm broke Frau Heinz's neck. The organs and limbs of the body possess a kind of memory, as I've said.

Could it be that, rejoined to its body, the penis conveyed memories of its multiple infidelities to my Beloved's body? And the body, now powering the penis, developed *guilt*, which disabled the penis? Thus the memory of the penis was contaminating the true wishes of its owner.

Yet what really *were* the true wishes of my Beloved? Could it be that the penis had truly loved me, but that Oliver himself as a complete person hadn't been quite so devoted? Could it be that formerly the penis had been ordering my Beloved to love me and nobody else? That it was the desire of the penis, rather than true love, which had made Oliver want to fuck me? Yet I had permitted the penis to respond to anybody; in a sense I had trained it to do so. Consequently now I was no longer a unique focus of desire. My Beloved might call me an almond tree like some medieval Arabian poet, but those were just pretty words! This was very confusing.

Why, oh why, had I cloned all of Oliver at such cost when the penis had been my real lover all along! I had prostituted the penis, the only part of him that truly loved me. Now Oliver was inhibiting the penis from performing, and I might be discovering all too late that my Beloved's flowery sentiments were hypocritical!

I accused my Beloved.

His replies were hard to understand – unlike the formerly clear, if non-verbal, responses of the stiff penis to me.

"You didn't truly love me," I cried.

"Balloons bring roses," said Oliver. "Scent escapes from bursting balloons." Did this mean that love dies?

"It was your penis that loved me, not you!"

"The rubies of your nipples are so hard they could cut glass." Was he complaining about my nipples? In the old days of our passion, had they hurt his chest?

I was shouting at him in angry disappointment when a knock came at the door.

Andorra stood outside, Coochie on a leash.

The blood froze in my veins. Here was the moment I had been fearing.

"May we come in?" Andorra asked with a big, insincere smile. The dog wagged his tail, excited, probably foreseeing who knows which kind of filthy development.

No, no, no! I thought with all the power of my mind.

However, I heard my voice answer politely:

"Yes, of course, feel at home." Oh the hypocrisy of etiquette. I could have bitten off my tongue. But there was no escaping from destiny.

Oliver remained expressionless as he met the gaze of Andorra, then of the dog. Andorra was observing Oliver inquisitively, as if to perceive a penis improbably hidden between his eyes. The gay dog was salivating, detecting the smell of a friendly penis that it knew... in the biblical sense. Coochie pushed close to Oliver and insolently sniffed his genitals through the trousers. Was the trace of an erection swelling in there? Oliver's forehead was knit. Did Coochie awake in him those dreams that I feared? Under no circumstances should I leave Oliver, and above all *my* penis, alone together with these two sexual jackals. As yet we were only in my hallway, which was quite large.

The door-bell rang again and I turned to open the door once more. Etiquette!

Outside, stood two mature women.

"We're from the Church for the Protection of Genital Organs," announced one of the ladies. "We'd like to interview you for our religious magazine."

This church had sprung up recently. Advances in plastic surgery were making it possible to have one's genitals exotically customised. Surely this insulted the sexual organs God designed for Adam and Eve and for all of us! Biblical believers had long since abandoned defending the sanctity of marriage, as a lost cause, consequently they poured their piety into defending the sanctity of copulation as God intended, using the exact organs He provided, not pudenda reshaped into orchids or trumpets, or giant clitorises or bifurcated dicks.

As I later discovered, Bodies'r'Us – who approved of exact copies, not baroque variations – had given some money to the Church of PGO and encouraged them to interview me to make an interesting scene in the movie. Drawing the attention of the

Church of PGO was a big mistake, as subsequent events proved. But meanwhile I got rid of the two women as quickly as possible, although not fast enough. When I turned back to my guests, they were not there any more. Andorra and Coochie had vanished along with my Beloved and his/my penis!

Obviously they had gone into the lounge, but why then had they closed the door? Worry clutched at me. I gripped the door handle to follow them only to discover that the door was locked! With a shiver I imagined the spectators of the movie seeing my face turn pale at this point as the most horrible of scenes formed in my mind, of my beloved Oliver buggering the Labrador, who in turn was buggering Andorra who, between moans, was sipping champagne from one of the crystal glasses my grandmother had left me in her will.

Was the artistic, romantic movie of reunion with the Oliver of my penis destined to turn into the usual bestiality porn reality show, the commonplace of television? I banged loudly on the door, but the only response was what sounded like a suffocated whine. Nobody came to let me in to my own lounge.

"Oliver!" I shouted. "Andorra!" For answer, just another whine.

This was too much. I fainted.

When I recovered, I was lying on the couch in the lounge. Andorra and Oliver were watching me with worried expressions. Coochie was sitting looking sleepy.

"How long have I been unconscious?"

"A few minutes," replied Andorra, whether this was true or not. "We heard a thump and found you behind the door. You ought to have the handle seen to. I don't think it works properly."

Was she sincere?

"Why did you close the door at all?"

"To be discreet. You had visitors." Oh, etiquette again. If I believed her.

I turned to Oliver. "What happened in here before you found me passed out?"

"What is passed or past is the turd of the Fall, come Springtime."

In other words, *No use crying over spilt milk?* By which he might mean spilled semen. Did *turd* allude to a dog's anus? To my mind those two items are always closely linked. Oliver was no help at all. I'd been getting along better with his, or rather *my* penis.

Ignoring the gaze of my Beloved, I looked lower, so as to distinguish within his pants my more beloved penis, probably the only part of Oliver which ever really loved me. That wasn't difficult – an evident protuberance seemed likely to perforate his pants at any moment. Obviously Oliver's penis was completely erect, the way I remembered it, the way I had long loved it. Hidden as it was by trousers I couldn't actually see it, and this seemed unjust. Forgetting about the presence of Andorra and the hidden cameras, instinctively I reached out a hand sweetly to caress my beloved penis, which I hadn't seen – nor felt – in its full, majestic, generous erection for far too long. In the very moment when my hand grazed it, the penis imploded like a Hindenburg airship, deflating at once and evading my contact. Suddenly everything became atrociously clear beyond any doubt!

The penis itself could not know so quickly that it was me who touched it, because the trousers were a barrier to its sensitive nerve endings. Therefore the order to deflate must have come directly from the brain of Oliver. I became furious and shouted:

"You treacherous fuckface prickhead, get out of my home! Get out, but leave my penis here!"

Seizing Oliver, I propelled him with all my strength out of the lounge, through the hall, to the front door. He didn't resist but let himself be thrown out, although of course he took my/his penis with him. Those two damn churchwomen were still loitering outside, index fingers scribbling on smartscreens nestling in their palms. Were they inventing a non-existent interview?

Aurora and Coochie hurried past me without a word or a woof, and I slammed the door behind them. Then I allowed myself the wisest feminine recourse in emergency circumstances: I began to cry.

Oliver took up residence in Andorra's flat. Some days later a man with the face of a mummified pig presented himself at my door.
     "I'm the lawyer of the penis," he introduced himself.
     I discovered that the Church for the Protection of Genital Organs had arrogated to itself the right to represent the interests of Oliver's penis. From Pigface I heard talk about the rights of genital organs to self-determination and about some Treaty of Independence from the Bearer of the Organ. Oh the mysteries of jurisprudence! The ways that lawyers get rich!
     Pigface explained to me that Oliver's penis had gained the status of an individual by virtue of having lived independently for a sufficient time before finding itself again attached to a human bearer. The Church for the Protection of Genital Organs was entitled to represent the penis because it was the first to claim that right, without the penis raising any objection.
     "But the penis wouldn't be able to understand any of this!"
     "Exactly. So it needed legal representation."

Later I learned how the judge at the court in question had become obsessed with making controversial landmark judgements in the hope of being retired soon with a knighthood or some other honour. The Church of PGO had been well aware of this.

In Andorra's flat there were no hidden cameras. Andorra had refused the TV company permission to install any cameras in her home – probably so as not to expose to the world her affair with the dog. For the TV company and for Bodies'r'Us this was unacceptable. On the other hand, the impotence Oliver's penis displayed towards me when it was attached to Oliver hardly made his return to my own home a very exciting prospect for Natalie and the other people involved in the production of the movie. The public doesn't much care for erotic dramas with impotent characters. Therefore the lawyers for Natalie and Bodies'r'Us were petitioning to have Oliver and his penis separated again, so that the penis could go back to performing in the role that had made it so famous, the penis without a man.

The penis without its Oliver had already become a star. A poll revealed that as an anonymous part of a normal person it wouldn't be so interesting to people.

The Church for the Protection of Genital Organs likewise wanted the penis to be separated from Oliver, yet not so that it could perform in porn movies or couple with me again, which they viewed as unnatural. Instead, they wanted it to retire to a zen monastery. Oh the moral obsessions of churches!

Thus there was conflict between the movie producers, with whom I had signed an agreement on behalf of the cloned Oliver, and the lawyers for the penis and the Church of PGO.

"We won't allow you to go on sexually exploiting that poor penis," Pigface told me at a deposition hearing.

"It's a sexual organ. It was born to be sexually exploited," I retorted.

"He's an individual with full rights, included the right of freely choosing the modality of his sexuality."

"It's a penis. If it becomes hard that means it wants to fuck."

"Not at all! Diseases exist, such as priapism. Erection can be the symptom of a pathology."

I decided to change my strategy.

"It's a piece of meat without a brain. It's not compos mentis."

"Another reason to protect his dignity. We will never allow that poor penis to be forced into any more intercourses for which he didn't give written consent."

"How can a penis write anything?"

"If held properly, it can produce a DNA signature."

"Without a prostate it can't ejaculate, so where's the ink?"

"We can prepare all necessary documents *before* the separation."

Suits and countersuits were heard, and the lawyers were all very happy until at last no legal problems prohibited the penis being separated from Oliver. Final judgement was that since the penis was cloned *before* the body, *it* was the one who owned the other, and not the contrary. The penis owned the man, namely the cloned Oliver; Oliver did not own the penis. If it's legitimate for a man to cut off his own penis, provided that he isn't attempting suicide, logically the penis could decide to cut off its own man. The lawyer for the penis, as his legal representative, had full power to act in this regard – and to *steal* the penis of my Beloved, I was thinking in anger and frustration.

The judge duly retired and became a Lord.

However, we live in a strange and unpredictable world.

Under its various Patriot Acts, the USA had permitted itself to intervene in any part of the world in defence of its homeland security and its supplies of oil and cheap obesity fast food full of oil and sugar and additives. To signal to the world its rise as a rival superpower, China enacted the Salvation of Culture Law, by which the Chinese gave themselves the right to intervene anywhere to protect the interests of art. This was something that the American government found hard to understand, so they did not threaten the Chinese with thermonuclear war.

If the USA was the Global Cop, China would be the Global Curator. A popular US slogan was *Kick Ass America!* So Beijing declared *Save Art China!* – and why not, China being the oldest civilisation on Earth? When Venice began to sink rapidly, swift intervention by Chinese technology had rescued the Italian city,

71

preserving it in a dome to the applause of most nations. From then on, China could take great liberties in the defence of art.

Art included Performance Art, and one of the many ways of preserving art was Gor-Gon, a polymerizing nanotechnology inspired by Gunther Von Hagen's corpse plastination factory in the northeastern Chinese port city of Dalian. In just a few seconds, a jab of Gor-Gon administered by injection or by a dart fired from a gun could transform any living being into plastinated artwork, petrifying forever (though by no means as stiffly as stone) the target animal or person at that moment.

The penis had been quite a performer; and the legal case was by now notorious world-wide, as was the prospect of cloned penis and cloned person parting company. So Chinese art-agents targeted Oliver. Already Chinese art-agents had over-enthusiastically targeted several famous opera singers and actors for a Hall of Fame. Since the salvation of Venice the Chinese could do pretty much as they pleased, but plastinating artists suddenly while they were on stage caused demands for ticket refunds, arguments about civil rights, and also poorer performances by many divas and stars who didn't wish to be plastinated; which was all very regrettable and counter-productive. So this was made illegal. But according to Chinese law plastinating a clone was just as acceptable as plastinating a criminal for export to medical schools...

I'm so lucky. At the moment of petrification, the penis of my former Beloved was fully erect – he had to be slid out of Andorra by the Chinese agents who invaded her flat. So now I live in China, inside a big transparent cube. I couple with the penis attached to Oliver whenever I want. Plastination keeps the penis stiff, yet soft and comfortable to use. Of course plastinated Oliver never says a thing, nor moves, although I arrange him artistically just as I please.

Outside the cube every day crowds of visiting art lovers and connoisseurs admire us and shoot holographic movies, so that we never feel alone. Inside the cube, the air is always fresh and rich in happy-making hormones. The Chinese take-away meals supplied to me free are so varied and delicious. Life is beautiful! Or maybe life is simply too complex to understand.

The Beloved
of the Gigolem

A gigolo and a golem combined... is a gigolem. He-She can be
male or female, or both sexes at once (and perhaps also other
sexes as yet unknown). Indeed, a gigolem can change sex several
times a minute, supposing that a sex partner is unsure of himself
or herself sexually; which can be confusing or alternatively
interesting. However, what János sought for in Prague was a
quality personal gigolem who would remain female for a
reasonably long time, to pleasure him and vice versa. Of course
he had fucked gigolems at public baths in Budapest lots of times,
yet that was always rather impersonal, even if the gigolem did
conform to his tastes. Actually, for his money, the best gigolems
in Budapest were those geisha-gigolems much used by Japanese
tourists. However, he was a János, not a Yukio, and he craved for
his own dedicated Euro-gigolem.

   He travelled from Budapest by Magyar Álom Vasutak,
Hungarian Dream Railways. Formerly this had been Magyar
Állam Vasutak, the State Railways, but passengers had petitioned
for a more imaginative name – ah, the romance of travel. His
friend Silvia was the driver of the MAV locomotive and she let
him sit in the cab with her, to keep her company. Silvia was
devoted to chocolate, which produces endorphins in the brain, so
János had brought several bars of chocolate with him to feed to
Silvia *en route*. The route was fairly simple because the railway lines
led inexorably via Vienna to Prague, an inevitability which could
become boring. Consequently endorphins helped – although at
the same time Silvia possessed no driving licence for anything as

trivial as a car; she was only interested in driving vehicles weighing more than 30 tonnes.

"Are you sure you'll be happy living with the same gigolem all the time?" she had asked when János first told her his plan. "I'm happy with mine, but women tend to be faithful – and you're a man."

"I know I am. Well, it's either a gigolem or very old women." He hesitated. "Or else a colostomy."

"How could a colostomy help?"

"It would serve as a substitute vagina in a fixed location."

Silvia beamed. "Oh I see, you mean a colostomy for *her*, not for you."

"If the woman agreed." János shrugged. "Whoever she might be!"

"How many women have you asked, if they'll have a colostomy?"

"A few. They didn't want the inconvenience."

The fundamental problem, which confronted many men, was that vaginas had begun to migrate around women's bodies, sealing up suddenly only to emerge elsewhere within a few minutes. The cause of this was mutated Ibola virus, which instead of eating flesh rearranged flesh painlessly. Allegedly the mutated virus had escaped from a military laboratory, perhaps in America, perhaps in North Korea, perhaps elsewhere. The result was that a vagina could shift without warning from the crotch to the armpit or to behind the knee or to almost anywhere. Foreplay could become 6-play or 10-play or 20-play as a man tried to keep up with a shifting situation, and often he lost his erection.

The only women unaffected were those well past menopause. Probably the virus responded to hormones. Consequently beautiful young or even middle-aged prostitutes had all disappeared, replaced by grannies over seventy, with whom satisfaction could still be guaranteed. This fixated some men erotically upon old women, which was laudably anti-ageist – and this even led to a rumour that the migrating vagina phenomenon had been engineered by a secret collective of women scientists, to promote sexual gratification in their old age.

Men pursued various techniques for discovering the whereabouts of the mobile vagina quickly. Asking the woman if she had seen her vagina recently wasn't always much help. Very often females did not look for their own vaginas. "I don't want to *know* about it; I just want it to work properly," was a common attitude.

Consequently some men used a torch, and others a divining rod, and others a stethoscope or a small seismic detector – a vibrator might have remained in a vagina from a previous use, or the migration of the vagina might itself cause subtle vibrations. A small percentage of men used a sniffer dog, although this only worked if the dog had previously smelled that particular vagina. This was all very unsatisfactory.

"A Romanian girl I know did consider the colostomy idea," admitted János, "but she thought I might pimp the colostomy to make money. I'll be much better off with a gigolem."

Hence his journey to Prague, where the banks of the river Vltava contained the very best quality mud and clay for making golems. That's how Rabbi Löw had succeeded in making the first ever golem, back in the early 17th century, to guard the ghetto against the malice of Christians. The rabbi was fortunate in the raw material he found locally, even though he was already a skilled kabbalist.

And part of that skill was in knowing how to write a Shem to put in the golem's mouth to animate it. Originally the Shem was a piece of parchment inscribed with a secret name of God, and could go on the forehead or in the mouth. Nowadays the Shem was software.

"You didn't forget your Shem?" Silvia had asked, as the MAV

train was leaving Vienna. She knew a lot about such things. Apart from having her own gigolem, she was keen on interactive computer role-playing games where it was necessary to collect jewels of enlightenment, crystals of power, and such. Particularly she thought about Shems because putting little squares of chocolate into her own mouth animated her.

Although János knew that he hadn't forgotten the Shem, all the same he took out his wallet to check that the mini-disc was still in the same place.

"So how much did it cost you," asked Silvia, "to download from that sexual magic site?"

"A hundred Euros. Quite a lot of warnings: forbidden to those under 16, and so forth. It's well worth paying a hundred Euros to also have the instructions for removal from the gigolem – if need be."

"Hmm. Easy to put it in, but hard to take it out?"

"As the lover said to his Beloved whose vagina suddenly started to migrate?"

"Nonsense, a penis just pops out!"

"I was joking. The Shem mini-disc clings to the palate, the roof of the golem's mouth. Well, I suppose you know that. A golem might bite your fingers off to keep the Shem in its mouth."

"Or simply keep its mouth shut?"

A while later, the MAV train arrived in Prague Station. After bidding a fond farewell to Silvia, János emerged from the station and within a couple of minutes he was at the top of Wenceslas Square, which isn't square-shaped at all, but is a long wide avenue running downhill to the old city. He'd been advised to put a note wrapped round a pebble on Rabbi Löw's tomb in the old Jewish cemetery, a traditional ritual for anyone who wished to make their own golem. The avenue misnamed a square pointed straight as an arrow towards the former Jewish ghetto.

Quite a few pregnant gigolems were waddling up and down

Wenceslas Square, some pushing prams loaded with previous babies. Ever since vaginas began to migrate, pregnancy – and particularly childbirth – had become problematic. To sustain the birthrate of the human race, eggs were extracted from a would-be mother's ovaries, which didn't migrate. A would-be father would masturbate into a test-tube, and the fertilised product would go into a walking-womb gigolem for nine months. Despite control by Shem, sometimes the walking-womb would fluctuate sexually, so that a male gigolem might be carrying a foetus. Generally the resulting child seemed normal, and human.

Soon János was amongst the extreme confusion of gravestones piled in all directions against and on top of one another. Fortunately a dozen Japanese were taking holo-pictures of the rabbi's tomb, making it easy to identify. János's handwritten note read, "Dear Rabbi Löw, bless my gigolem, may she give me satisfaction."

János left the cemetery and soon spied a sign in English and German on a dilapidated old building announcing a room to rent. Probably it was fortunate that the building was in bad repair, otherwise someone might already have taken the room. János thought probably he would need a room for at least a week, to make sure the Gigolem was a good one before taking her home to Budapest.

The landlady, Mrs Smetana, was old and thin. The room, up in the attic, was dark but big, the furniture huge and ancient: a vast wooden bed ideal for sharing with a gigolem and a mighty wardrobe ideal for keeping the gigolem locked in, if need be.

János and Mrs Smetana negotiated in English.

"Is problem I keep gigolem here?"

"You gigolem pimp? This not bad house."

"Gigolem girlfriend is for me only."

"Okay. Hundred Crowns extra."

János blessed the rabbi for this bit of luck, then he headed for the long stretch of riverbank owned by the Prague Golem

Company.

Over the years exploitation of the clay-like river mud, or mud-like clay, had resulted in the exposure of many hectares of yellowy brown or brownish yellow substance adjacent to the river. The terrain looked like the battlefield of the Somme in 1918 due to the partially flooded trenches left by excavating for golem-material and the multitudes of little craters where individuals had made their own golems or gigolems by shovelling material into moulds hired from the PGC.

János needed to buy an excavation permit for the area most suitable to make gigolems, but further spending was discretionary.

"Is dirty work – you want hire rubber galoshes and boiler suit?"

Yes.

"Want rubber gloves? Some say best intimate result from naked hands."

Naked hands would be fine.

"Need Shem? We sell several Lust Shems. As well as Cordon Bleu Chef Shem, Chauffeur Shem – "

"I bring my own Shem."

"You need shovel? Some say no shovel, best results. But takes much longer." Obviously PGC weren't trying to take advantage of János's inexperience in making his own golem. The benefits of coming to a reputable company.

"Hmm. I think shovel."

"You need plastic mould to help shape body? We hire male, female, neuter, and hermaphrodite moulds. Remember, once lust-gigolem is active it can easily change sex."

"Female mould." He would start the gigolem the way he hoped she would continue.

The assistant brought out what looked like the hull of a simple boat, a bit larger than himself, and bright red, indented with a female form. Easy to carry, being plastic. Very visible. Had a paedophile ever tried to escape downstream in a mould along with a newly-made prohibited paedogolem, hoping to escape confiscation of his illegal handiwork? Since no sails nor oars accompanied the mould, such an attempt seemed unwise. Unless, of course, an accomplice was waiting nearby downstream in a motor boat – the cunning of paedophiles was notorious; a mutable mud-boy-girl would be quite a prize.

Presently János was out on the widespread Somme-on-Vltava with his mould and shovel.

Various other Do-It-Yourself golem enthusiasts were busy, looking somewhat like gravediggers though in fact the very opposite, for from dirt they were assembling what would become a semblance of life.

János laboured for an hour. He heaped the mould high, then he used his hands to contour the back of the gigolem, paying particular attention to the buttocks.

With considerable effort he heaved the now-heavy mould on to its side so that the gigolem slid out. Any slumping out of shape should rectify itself once the Shem was in the mouth. He walked around the heap of clay-mud widdershins seven times shouting "Shanti Shanti, Dehat Dehat!" because you were supposed to do this. Then he washed his hands in a nearby trench. Due to lack of a towel he dried them on his own hair. Finally he produced the Shem and pushed it between the clay lips, as one would push a card into a cash dispenser.

The gigolem convulsed. Her breasts firmed, and other important parts too. And she arose, staggering upright and regarding him. To his eyes she was rather beautiful, her flesh halfway between Asian and Mulatto. Other eyes may have regarded her as a bit ugly or strange. Alternatively, her strangeness or ugliness possessed its own beauty. Most importantly, she was a *she*, and remained a *she*.

She needed a name.

"You are Patricia," he said, and took her by the hand. Since this was a romantic gesture, almost womanly, dark hairs promptly began sprouting from Patricia's breasts as she manifested reciprocal manliness. These fell off as soon as János experienced an annoyed surge of testosterone which almost made him slap her.

"By the way," he told her, "I am János."

"I am yours," she said in a husky voice in Hungarian. "Mine are you." Was Patricia experimenting with the grammar of his difficult language, or did she mean *you are mine?*

In that attic in the big house of Mrs Smetana, János experimented with Patricia.

The first sexual intercourse with any gigolem is always a delicate matter, for a reason quite the opposite to the reason why the first intercourse with another human being is – or had been – delicate. The uncertainty attendant on sexually joining with another human person resides in the fear of what he or she might think of you, the possibility of causing disappointment and not being liked. In a sexual joining with a gigolem this problem doesn´t exist because a gigolem isn´t a human person and cannot judge you. However, a gigolem becomes sexually what you unconsciously wish it to be, consequently that first encounter might reveal through the gigolem that your own sexual nature differs dramatically from the image you had of it. The perceptiveness of the mirror in which you risk seeing yourself is far greater than in the case of a human partner. This can generate greater anxiety.

Cautiously János kissed Patricia´s hand, then slowly ascended along the arm. As his lips travelled, the dark skin of the gigolem paled and blushed, as if the meat within might burn. A low manly rumble sounded within the gigolem, an omen of impending masculinization – which János aborted by gripping Patricia's hair

·

82

firmly, though not too violently. That rumble faded into the gentle moan of a female in heat. A breast inflated as he brought his lips close, and continued to inflate to a fair extent as he sucked the nipple, while her legs shortened just a little. Nothing comes from nothing, so the substance inflating the tits was necessarily subtracted from part of the body to which the lover was paying less attention. János intruded a hand between her thighs, to which her buttocks accordingly donated some substance. These weren't major changes of dimension which would result in grotesquerie or the physically impossible, but the alterations were sufficient to satisfy the ordinary imaginative follies of the human mind transported by a stormy vortex of passion and somatic obsession towards another living being.

Later, when János turned Patricia so as to pay maximum virile attention to those buttocks which he had moulded with such great attention, her breasts and belly, invisible to him now, lost tone and thickness while the beautiful perfect buttocks inflated within their skin, stretching into a unique cloven sex-drum of female mystery inextinguishably tantalising... at least until orgasm.

In the relaxed aftermath, János regarded his gigolem with an enchanted eye. Patricia had remained female during all their intercourse, a rare circumstance which few men could manage to experience.

Since so many Americans already lived in the Czech capital, and due to the million tourists who visited every year, the Creation Science Museum of Arkansas had recently opened a branch museum in Prague. So János took Patricia there the following morning to entertain and impress her. That ought to be just her sort of museum. God made Adam out of clay or mud. Maybe János would seem like a god.

In the foyer towered a life-size holographic dinosaur with big blunt stumpy teeth behind an illuminated sign: *Vegetarian*

Tyrannosaurus Rex. Even as János watched, the holographic blunt teeth elongated into fierce daggers, and the sign changed to: *Tyrannosaurus Rex After the Fall.* Presently T. Rex became benign again. The dino still looked hungry, but now for a cabbage. Thank God for holography, otherwise two sets of different giant dentures, as well as chains and a pulley, would have been needed to produce the transformation.

A Schwartzenegger-golem wearing shorts printed with fig leaves – no, he must be Michelangelo's Adam – beckoned tourists coyly towards the *Chapel of Creation from Clay.* The golem's body language was definitely gay, and its name badge called it, not Arnie, but **Cleopatra**. In an affectedly dainty way, the muscular Schwartzenegger began to recite a commentary in English and Czech and German, although János only paid attention to the English.

"Darwinian scientists say that life arose from primeval soup…"

In a big transparent cauldron on the left side of the chapel, a soup of plastic alphabet pieces simmered, the four letters T, C, A, and G moving around and around, constantly bumping into each other.

"The letters you see represent the *very complicated* bases of the genetic code DNA, namely Thymine, Cytosine, Adenine and Guanine. Darwinian scientists pretend that these substances could have formed *at random* out of chemicals in the sea – and then furthermore that these letters could have combined *at random* to form the vast catalogue of information that creates life!

"I ask you, could a million blind monkeys chained to typewriters for a billion years ever have written the complete Bible exactly word-perfectly? No way, I say!"

"This is boring," said Patricia. "Fuck me."

"No, wait a bit," said János.

Adam-Schwartzenegger gestured to the right of the chapel at what looked like a printing press from ancient Babylon designed to produce cuneiform clay tablets.

"In the Bible it says, *And the LORD God formed man from the clay of the ground.* Wiser, more scientific scientists says that living cells first appeared in a special kind of clay – called montmorillonite, monty for short. Negatively charged layers of monty-clay crystals produce a sandwich of positive charge in between them, which is a very attractive environment for RNA. I ask you, which is the more sensible theory: soup – *or sandwich?*"

A terrible realization came to János, with the force of an anti-religious revelation – as if St Paul had arrived blind in Damascus and suddenly saw not the light but anti-light.

Of course all life on Earth arose from chemicals in the soup of the ancient sea! That's where we all come from – and cats too, and rats and fish and spiders and cacti and cabbages – from chemical soup. What comes from clay - but only *nowadays* – is golem-life. If clay had caused life in the first place, we would all be golems (including golem-cats and golem-rats and so forth)!

Clay and mud sandwiches must have *tried* to make life, like MacDonalds taking over the world, but sandwiches had lost out to soup. Nevertheless, lurking in mud and clay there remained an alternative pathway of golem-evolution. And now it was coming into reality. Because gigolems mated with men and women, and because of the need for walking-wombs, claylife was sexually contaminating the human race! Maybe this was why vaginas were migrating, to try to escape, due to feminine intuition.

Of a sudden János felt polluted by Patricia.

He cried out at Adam-Schwartzenegger, "Your Creationist God is the God of golems and gigolems, not of human beings! You Creationists all worship a false creation!"

János had to express this concept in Hungarian, which nobody except other Hungarians can understand. Nevertheless, a security-golem came into the chapel. What occurred in the museum must be monitored by multilingual security computers.

This big brawny gay golem wore a name badge: **Brünnhilde**.
Brünnhilde approached on massive legs, gesturing menacingly. In Hungarian, then English, he-she declared:

"We don´t want Darwinian preachers here! This is a place of science and there's no space for the mystic fantasies of Darwinism!"

János retorted: "My world is the one that evolved over billions of years through natural selection and produced human beings. The creationist world is that of the golems!"

János's counter-enlightenment was now accompanied by a strange sense of *déjà vu*, as if something that happened in the past had been suppressed from conscious memory but now returned hauntingly. He thought to himself: *It´s as if two parallel worlds have overlapped and are melting together – the world of the humans and the world of the golems. How on Earth could this have happened?*

"I told you," Patricia said, "you should have fucked me."

Then János had no more time for thinking, because Brünnhilde was upon him. Close up, he-she stank of mud, not because he-she was made from mud, but due to nasal hallucination since the very existence of golems and gigolems suddenly stank for János. Brünnhilde was one and a half times his size, so she had no difficulty pushing him into a corner of the room. *She? She?* He-she had definitely become she. Holding János in one hand like a naughty boy, she pulled his trousers and underpants down. He thought she was going to smack him on the bottom, just as his mother had sometimes done. But then Brünnhilde exposed herself, and what smacked János, not upon the bottom but upon the front, were mighty and female genitalia. These sucked his balls and penis into them completely and munched. Fortunately her vagina was not dentata.

Presently she ejected him – and *that* was because she was now becoming male, her vagina filling and turning inside-out to become a stiff penis, which with gigolems was possible. Brünnhilde turned János round and buggered him, which felt as if a large living turd was returning to its bowel repeatedly. The other visitors to the museum were taking souvenir photos and exclaiming. In a society lacking coherent vaginas and sexual certainties of any kind, bodily violation was not infrequent, so nobody should have been surprised. But tourists must let themselves be surprised by what is perfectly normal – that's their role. A latecomer, who had missed most of the spectacle, asked Brünnhilde when the next violation was scheduled.

Afterwards, János felt as anyone would feel after being violated by a lump of mud – soiled. Dirtier than he'd ever felt in his life.

He was ashamed and furious at the same time.

Holding his trousers tightly at the waist in case they got pulled down again, he headed for the office of the museum's director while Patricia followed him.

Here it was: **Dr Vaclav Sládek, Director.**

Dr Sládek wore a thin waxed moustache and a monocle. Also, a dark suit with thin stripes. And, for that matter, a sky-blue shirt and purple bow tie. His dark hair was oiled and combed back.

"I have been violated front and rear by your security-golem!" expostulated János.

"By security?" said Dr Sládek. "That sounds like safe sex. You won't become pregnant."

"In public!" roared János.

"Did you want it in private?"

"I want compensation for humiliation."

"My dear fellow, there's no possibility of that. A gigolem exhibits sexual behaviour in sympathy with the subconscious needs of a human being. Subconsciously you must have wished to be violated, and in such a way. Legally, the golem can't be blamed, nor its owners sued."

"I'm not gay! Not even my subconscious is gay. Why would I want to be violated by a *gay* golem?"

"You said you were violated at the front as well. Obviously the gigolem was making an effort to suit you."

"Why are the staff here gay golems? I thought creation churches didn't like homosexuality."

"My dear fellow..." The director took a lace fan from his desk and wafted it. "This museum is concerned with the creation of life. In most creatures higher than the amoeba this tends to involve sexual activity. Frequent sexual activity. The employment of neuter golems could seem a snub to God. Therefore the personnel must have genders. Yet they mustn't present any menace to the sacred femininity of women tourists!"

"A Schwartzenegger called Cleopatra is absurd!"

"No, this reflects the dualistic principle of the universe, the mysterious principle which forces into existence the contrary of everything. It's like matter and anti-matter. We need gay golems here to demonstrate this."

"I want Brünnhilde destroyed."

"Spiritually, a gigolem is merely the psychic extension of the human being who uses it, so in a sense, dear sir, you're saying that you should be destroyed – that you should be punished."

"I already have been punished!"

"Are you a masochist? It's a banal logical error to imagine that gay gigolems are useful to heterosexual masochists. A gay gigolem would avoid inflicting sadism on a heterosexual masochist, in order to fulfill his desires by denying them. By the way, did you know that the United States has stationed thousands of gay gigolems in Antarctica for obscure purposes of homeland security? What is needed is an association for the protection of gay inhuman rights."

János realized that Dr Sládek himself secretly wished to be a gay gigolem. He wondered what happened in the museum after the doors were closed to the public each evening.

"Come home and fuck my vagina," said Patricia.

Dr Sládek shuddered delicately.

Later, in the comfort of the little flat of Mrs Smetana, János idly indulged in pseudo-philosophical thoughts:

"Dust thou art, to dust returnest," he recited, a universally popular line from the once much admired American poet Longfellow, which joined up *Genesis* 2:7 – "the Lord God formed man of the dust of the ground" – with *Ecclesiastes* 12:1 – "then shall the dust return to the earth as it was."

And what was dust, if not dry mud? Therefore meat was derived from mud, the basic element of gigolems. Creationism was right! In the beginning there was the primordial sandwich, not the fucking soup.

The violation performed by Brünnhilde seemed to have temporarily obliterated the evolutionary anti-enlightenment that had caught him in the museum. Much worse, it had taken away from him for the moment any desire to make love with Patricia. This was perfectly understandable in someone who had just been violated by a gay gigolem. Obviously János was being inhibited by a fear that sexual relations with his hitherto straight gigolem might result in a repetition of that violation, this time by Patricia. A mysterious mechanism of the human subconscious means that repetition of known experiences can be reassuring, even if the experiences are unpleasant. Although János felt exonerated of responsibility for being violated in the first place – despite the insinuations of Dr Sládek! – to be re-violated due to complicity on the part of his subconscious would be intolerable.

János was not at all satisfied with how his romantic journey to Prague was proceeding. He shut Patricia inside the wardrobe. That was like banishing her into a dark subconscious from which she must not escape. Could it be that golems were nothing but the embodiments of the collective subconscious of mankind? Or might human beings be the embodiment of the subconscious of golems? Who was dreaming whom?

As a way of getting out of himself for a while, János quit the house. People often leave home in the more or less vain attempt to leave themselves behind. This scarcely ever works.

The Sex Center of Prague, close to the river Vltava at Bubenské nábř, had for many years been a sex-for-cash-supermarket based on the principles of fast-food and the assembly line. Human beings and gigolems alike flaunted their charms inside little cabins with only space for a bed. You could peep through a window, if the curtain wasn't closed, to admire the merchandise before entering and enjoying it. Half of the hookers were human, strictly over 70, and the rest were gigolems, all looking beautiful.

János wandered lazily through the corridors where God's loving bounty was on offer. Now and then someone quickly entered or quit a cabin. János realized that in fact he hadn't come to this place to watch the prostitutes, but their clients. Was he hoping to see something of himself in them? Interest in other people is a delusion, if you only try to see aspects of yourself reflected in them.

Since he had travelled through Freudian Vienna on the way to Prague, he thought, *Perhaps I need a psychoanalygolem.*

Due to their highly mirroring nature, golems were much more effective psychoanalysts than humans. Yet by contrast with human psychoanalysts, a psychoanalygolem didn't exist until someone needed one. Even more than with a gigolem, it was essential to construct your own psychoanalygolem yourself. It was important for a psychoanalygolem to be – so to speak – virgin, the first time you used it. It must be pure and clean from the mental problems of anyone else who wasn't its own particular creator. In many functions, golems were subjected to imprinting. They adapted better to the needs of an owner if they hadn't had any previous contacts with other human beings. The innate knowledge that golems manifested, however, fuelled the idea that in fact they were simply a separately embodied extension of the human mind, their existence a highly effective representation of humanity.

Had two parallel universes really overlapped? Had the creationist world of the golems trespassed into the Darwinian world of the humans? Or vice versa?

What János really needed at this point was a friend – a human being, not a mirror of mud.

Silvia should soon be arriving again in her train. She would have the rest of the day free. Quickly he phoned her, on the train.

He met Silvia at the Kafka Café, a prestigious and ornate establishment in Alphonse Mucha Art Nouveau style near the Old Town Square.

"You only drive vehicles heavier that thirty tons," János said to her. "So do you think that golems are real creatures?" He knew what he was implying; and so did she, for such is friendship.

"As with vehicles over thirty tons," she answered," the question is whether you drive them, or they drive you."

The answer was somewhat Zen-like, but then so had his question been.

"What if I wanted to have a child with you?"

"All such things go through gigolems, as you well know."

"And if I just wanted to make love to you?"

"We would need a gigolem to interpose between us. What questions you do ask! Even children know that."

"That's the whole problem. Does anyone still exist who's even able to *imagine* a heterosexual relation between human beings of reproductive age? I'm not talking about gerontophiles, who make a virtue of necessity. I'm not interested in that."

"Hmm. Have you heard of the Virgil Award? No, not the *Virgin* Award. Virgil guided Dante into Hell, in other words down a deep hole. Last year a friend of mine called Zsuzsa won the award for keeping her vagina – to which she'd conceeded the rare privilege of a visit by a human penis – in the same position for twenty minutes."

"Lucky her, lucky that penis."

"It took great concentration."

"That's a prize-winning exception, so it doesn't count – no more than being able to jump right over an elephant. The norm defines the standard of reality. I ask you, can love without a gigolem still exist today?"

"On the other hand, having won the Virgil Award, Zsuzsa couldn't find her vagina again for six months. In practical reality, true love without the mediation of gigolems can't exist any more."

"Maybe I should continue trying with Patricia," said János, half to himself. "Even if she isn't a real woman, it could be a pleasant hallucination."

From her handbag, Silvia took something. It was a little Adam-Schwarzenegger doll. Due to his memories of the museum, János recoiled, but Silvia pushed the doll towards him.

"It's a lucky charm. Take it. Tourists buy lots of them. If you press it here on the chest – "

"I'll be back!" exclaimed the little Adam-Schwarzenegger.

"And if you press the genitals instead – "

"Hasta la vista, baby!" exclaimed the little Adam-Schwarzenegger.

"That's what Adam-Schwarzenegger said to God when he left Eden," said Silvia seriously, though she was also looking affectionate. "It does bring luck. I haven't had a train crash yet."

"I understand," answered János. Sadly he accepted little Adam-Schwarzenegger. Thoughtfully he regarded Silvia. He pursed his lips. Then he raised his eyebrows.

"Your own gigolem is this very same model, am I right?"

"Of course! A full-size Adam-Schwarzenegger. Maybe a little too big for me." Silvia was of slight build. "But I'm religious. It's reassuring to be taken sexually by the Ancestor, the archetype of us all. It's a communion."

"Does he also say *Hasta la vista, Baby?*"

"Every day, when I go out to work." On Silvia's face was a dreamy expression. "Sometimes even when I go for a crap."

"Gigolems have taken possession of the monopoly of human sexual reproduction," stated János.

"No, they didn't take possession," said Silvia. "It's always been like this, since time immemorial."

"That's what I'm starting to believe too. But then I rebel and I can't believe it."

"Listen János, gigolems are the indispensable interface between two incompatible devices. Without gigolems, human males and females wouldn't have a chance of real sexual interaction."

"That's only since vaginas started to migrate."

"Vaginas began to migrate in biblical times."

"In biblical times it was the people of Israel who began to migrate, not vaginas."

"Vaginas too," insisted Silvia.

History constantly changes, thought János, to adapt to the demands of the *Zeitgeist*, the spirit of the age. The dictatorship of the present over the past compels history to contain delusions disguised as facts. When the final old woman with a fixed vagina died from old age, the illusion that vaginas were already migrating in the distant past would consolidate itself, and nobody would escape this concept.

"I'm going to fuck Patricia," declared János.

"May its mud satisfy you," was Silvia's parting wish.

When János opened the wardrobe where he had closed Patricia, the gigolem showed no resentment, since resentment is a human feeling, not a nonhuman one. Excluding elephants which never forget. And perhaps cats.

"Fuck me please," Patricia said promptly.

"This very moment," replied János.

It was a wild and successful embrace. Patricia remained female all the time and, if it were possible, became even more female, so that János felt himself even more manly. This was exactly what he needed at the moment, both consciously and subconsciously, so with natural spontaneity the gigolem fulfilled his desire. János even experienced a feeling of love for Patricia, and this didn't scare him at all, albeit that he knew perfectly well that he was dancing on the edge of an abyss, black and bottomless. Thoughtlessly he blessed the existence of gigolems. For a complex person in a continuous state of inner evolution, a gigolem made an incomparably more useful and satisfying partner than a person of flesh and blood. Looking at things from an evolutionary point of view, rather than a creationist one, in principle every man or women is programmed by his or her genes to choose the best amongst all *existing* partners with whom to reproduce himself or herself. Yet in practical reality almost everyone finally adapts himself or herself to accept the best amongst *possible* partners, since not all existing partners are effectively available, so sometimes the best possible partner might actually be amongst the worst existing ones.

Even so, there are some supremely romantic individuals who prefer the path of continuous and endless search for the unobtainable ideal to a resigned acceptance of the reality that's available! For such persons searching is a greater priority than finding. Indeed they must be careful to avoid finding, since finding puts an end to searching.

Gigolems allow you to go on eternally with the search, since every gigolem alters in harmony with the subconscious hopes of its owner, so that even though the eternal searcher, man or woman, can never be fully satisfied by his or her gigolem, he or she can't get bored with it either, unless that boredom already exists within himself or herself. Incessantly the gigolem mutates into a thing ever more akin to the subconscious object of desire.

By virtue of being very nearly encountered and found inadequate, the object of desire likewise mutates, sometimes contradictorily, so that what was formerly desirable becomes undesirable, and vice versa.

Tragedy comes when subconscious expectations fade or die, due to the entropy of old age or other causes. Then the gigolem becomes the implacable amplifier of your own ennui, merciless mirror of your own deterioration, inescapable witness to the demise of your vital and loving feelings. The more intense and rich your life formerly was, the more bitter your state when all enthusiasm is in the end extinguished.

János's little flame of love for Patricia was not quenched as yet. He shivered as those first words of hers came back into his mind: Mine are you. Maybe those had been prophetic, announcing the ultimate truth: You are mine. How could he possibly keep a safe emotional distance between himself and his gigolem? Since a gigolem was intrinsically an extention of oneself, the relationship between a human being and a gigolem could reach depths of intimacy unimaginable between two human beings.

A problem was that what originally were microscopic sexual deviations within a person's libido, a mere frill upon a fantasy, no more than a hint, could by positive reinforcement from the gigolem become dominant and overwhelming, generating attitudes which in the past would certainly have been classed as behavioural monstrosities.

János was aware of *political perversion*. Onan clubs existed, dedicated to masturbating at images of detested politicians. People who joined such clubs subconsciously had regarded sex as a way of humiliating a partner. These people also had powerful political antipathies. After a while in bed with a gigolem, they found the gigolem conforming to the object of their hatred, such as the President of the United States – whom they possessed sexually in order to give free vent to their hatred. After a time they could only get an erection, or clitorection, by focusing on the President's image.

A fleeting fantasy about having your genitals nibbled pleasurably by catamites swimming in a pool which also happened to be home to fish – the Emperor Tiberius's favourite erotic pastime in Capri – could mutate into a fixation upon *the fish themselves.* One's gigolem could become a big cod or halibut between the increasingly smelly sheets.

Perplexed by his meditations, and in the vague hope that Silvia might still be at the Kafka Café – or alternatively, since several hours had passed, that she might have returned there – János headed that way after shutting Patricia in the wardrobe once more. By now it was six in the evening.

As he walked, his fingers played with the Adam-Schwartzenegger doll which she'd given him, rather as a nun might play with the beads of her rosary. Occasionally the doll exclaimed, "I'll be back!" This seemed a good augury for actually finding Silvia at the café. János could, of course, have phoned her mobile, but what was the point in having a lucky charm unless you trusted it?

Almost immediately he entered the Kafka Café, he saw a full-size, indeed oversize, Adam-Schwartzenegger gigolem sitting at one of the bigger tables. Cleopatra from the museum, no less! – because Cleopatra was with none other than Dr Sládek! Also at the same table were... well, one of the *persons* was a tall young man with red hair, but the other entity was a human-size plucked chicken. A red crest on a feathery head. Beady eyes. Red beak. Nude wings tucked in to its sides, just like scrawny white arms. The giant chicken frequently bobbed its head in a pecking motion, as if in agreement with all the remarks being exchanged between the red-headed young man and Dr Sládek.

János would have fled from the café right away, were he not mesmerised by the sight of the human chicken, or chicken-human, whichever.

This allowed time for Dr Sládek to notice János. The museum director rose and beckoned and minced towards János and delicately yet firmly took him by the arm.

"My dear fellow, have you recovered from your violation? Is your equanimity restored? Let me buy you a Viennese coffee with whipped cream! We were discussing gay inhuman rights."

Were whipping and cream a sly allusion to Janós's punishment?

Dr Sládek drew János towards the table where a seat remained unoccupied.

"Introductions! This is Cleopatra, as you already know."

"Soup – or sandwich?" demanded Cleopatra, as a waitress arrived.

"No, no," said Dr Sládek, "a Viennese coffee for our Hungarian friend. And this," nodding at the red-headed man, "is Gustav, and," nodding at the nodding poultrygolem, "his lover Anastasia."

"Tuck-tuck-tuck-tuck," said Anastasia.

"May I ask you, Gustav," asked János, "why your gigolem is a giant chicken without any feathers?"

"Yes, you may ask!" And Gustav waited. Evidently he was a literal-minded person.

"So why is your gigolem a giant chicken without any feathers?"

Presently János sat filled with astonishment and sympathy and Viennese coffee with whipped cream.

He'd been aware of involuntary metazoophilia, yet hadn't previously met a metazoophilist. Metazoophilists tended to conceal their condition, partly from shame, partly to avoid prosecution by the World Wildlife Fund. Not so Gustav, for whom explaining seemed to be a paradoxical blend of self-exorcism and joyful affirmation.

Less than two years previously, Anastasia was a woman of impressive beauty. Gustav had adored feminine beauty beyond anything else in the world. However, during his childhood Gustav had undergone certain experiences at the farm of his grandparents, which his conscious mind had erased but which led him to associate various mental categories with specific animals. This led him to place on his ample bookshelves – for Gustav was a great reader – little plastic models of animals in front of the books, which represented for him the essences of the different books. *The Origin of Species*, a tortoise. *Harry Potter*, a hog. *Gone With the Wind*, a plastic eagle, and so forth. For a while Gustav had worked in a library, but he was asked to leave after he reorganised the shelves according to his own zoological classification system rather than the Dewey decimal method.

After only a short while with his beautiful gigolem, whenever they coupled Anastasia would mutate into an anthropomorphic version of some animal while he was embracing her. Gustav may have been literal, but his subconscious was symbolic. Often she would become a woman-size anthropomorphic goose or duck or hen, resembling some Disney cartoon, depending on which creature emerged from Gustav's subconscious mind as sexually significant. Since his gigolem couldn't suddenly sprout feathers all over, but only modify whatever hair occurs on a human body, such as on the head and armpits and pubes, mainly her skin appeared like a plucked bird's – and Gustav soon found these goosebumps or, increasingly, chickenbumps intensely erotic.

"Other metazoophilists may find themselves in bed with a goat," said Gustav. "Anthropomorphized, that looks like a demon embodied... but I love a chicken." He put an arm around Anastasia and cuddled her.

"You should be careful," advised Dr Sládek. "Your sexual object isn't a real bird, true enough. That's been legally upheld. But I hear that the new tactic of the WWF is to sue for moral damages for degrading the *image* of animals. That might earn them and the lawyers a lot of money."

Just at that moment, several dwarfs dressed in medieval costumes unfurled a multilingual banner outside the windows of the Kafka Café: *Justice for the Fucking Dwarfs! We want dwarf Gigolems!* They marched off down the street in the direction of Charles Bridge, where all the statues are.

"They do have a point," said Gustav.

Dr Sládek shook his head. "A dwarf gigolem might mutate into the appearance of a child during embraces. You know that paedogigolems are forbidden. Gigolems in the shape of dwarfs could easily be misused. A dwarf might sell his gigolem on to a pervert."

"Dwarfs are being deprived of the fundamental human right to sex. And paedo-perverts can already buy gigolems."

"But only adult-size ones."

"Which become adult-size *children* in their arms, because the body can't be compressed."

"That's aesthetically grotesque," said Dr Sládek. Unfortunately at that moment he happened to glanced at Anastasia whom Gustav loved.

"It isn't as grotesque," exclaimed Gustav protectively, "as fucking a pool of mud!"

Dr Sládek twiddled his moustache. "What are you talking about?"

"I'm talking about certain creationists who are so obsessed about people being made from dust and dust returning to the earth –" János pricked up his ears "– that I hear they can't finish a sexual act without their gigolem dissolving into mud, which they continue fucking until they come, and only when the tension's released can their unfortunate gigolem reshape itself."

"Look, dear heart, let's not get into an unnecessary dispute." Dr Sládek addressed János. "We were about to visit Юрий Семецкий, whose gigolem is eating him."

János had been compelled to study some Russian in primary

school during the last days of communism in Hungary, so he knew that Dr Sládek was referring to a Yuri Semecky.

"His gigolem is eating him?"

"Yes, it'll take another two weeks."

"But *why?*"

"There's quite a lot to eat," said Gustav literally.

"No, why is his golem *eating him?*"

"Юрий Семецкий is an ultra-masochist," said Dr Sládek. "Come and see for yourself. That's the scientific method."

Compelled by curiosity, János went with the museum director and the metazoophilist and the Cleopatra gigolem and Anastasia the megapoultrygigolem, although under other circumstances he might have felt reluctant to be in such company.

They went along one street, then down another street, until they reached a tall house where a plaster bear the size of a magnum of champagne stood on its hind legs in a niche above the doorway. Many houses in Prague bore similar symbols from the good old days when people couldn't read – swans, sheep, goblets, fiddles, religious virgins.

A card by one the doorbells read: *Yuri Semecky*. Maybe Юрий Семецкий didn't wish any fellow Russians to visit him, only Roman speakers. Or maybe this was part of his masochism.

Dr Sládek rang the bell. They entered. They ascended. A golem attired as a chef with a tall white hat held a door wide.

"Aha, come in!" The Russian, who was in his early forties, lay naked on a blood-stained bed. Alternatively, three-quarters of a Russian lay there, since much flesh had been cut from one leg and one arm, exposing the bones. Юрий Семецкий was bearded and moustached scruffily, as though he had more important things to think about, and his forehead was a very high dome, where he would do his thinking, a bit like an astronomer in an observatory.

Besides the bed were a dining chair and a round table laid for a meal, with pepper pot, salt cellar, jug of olive oil, and slices of lemon; also a tray of scalpels and tongs and several spray-cans of powerful coagulant of the non-anaesthetic variety.

On a plate lay a slice of fresh flesh. The chefgolem sat down, squeezed a tiny amount of lemon juice upon the flesh, dripped a few drops of olive oil, then added a sprinkling of salt and pepper. Spearing the flesh with a fork, the golem lifted it to its mouth and commenced eating, causing the Russian to writhe in ecstasy.

"Oh God oh God oh God, oh good oh good oh good," Юрий Семецкий moaned delightedly in Roman.

When his passion passed, Юрий Семецкий eyed his visitors blearily.

"Will you have something to eat?"

"Soup – or sandwich?" demanded Cleopatra.

"No, raw!" said the Russian. "Only raw!"

"Will *you* have something to eat?" Gustav asked Юрий Семецкий.

"No, I'm on hunger strike too, for extra pleasure!"

"In that case," Dr Sládek asked thoughtfully, "would you categorise this as cannibalism-by-proxy, *or not?*"

János decided to leave before, perhaps, he might be chastised for some reason.

János was lazing on his bed in typical post-coital repose, smoking an exotic *Black Elephant* cigarette and sipping a goblet of *Nistru*, an excellent Moldovian cognac. At his side Patricia lay inert in the state of pseudo-rest and pseudo-satisfaction you would expect of her. His second sexual act with Patricia had been even better than the first one, but this, for the moment, meant very little. Everything depended on what was hiding in the next layer of his subconscious. It isn't entirely clear if something called the subconscious truly exists inside a human skull, but if it does, then undoubtedly it consists of *layers*, each layer different from the other layers. The more intercourse there is with a gigolem, the more the gigolem reacts to the needs of ever deeper layers. Therefore a gigolem's behaviour can never be predictable. At any moment it may surprise you.

János slapped Patricia's butt. Her ass seemed real. She didn't look like a metamorphic lump of mud, creature of a parallel universe which had overlapped with the one in which János had grown up.

Responding to his slap, Patricia rolled over, simulating an awakening that she couldn't be experiencing since basically she wasn't alive. János regarded her tenderly. She was going to say something pleasant to him. It was as though he could read her mind, a mind which she didn't really have. In fact it was as if finally János could read his *own* mind, which is impossible because you need another mind with which to do the reading.

Unexpectedly Patricia said, "You aren't really alive, are you?"

"*What?*" János blanched in surprise.

"You're a well-packaged illusion," she went on. "You move like a living thing. You talk like a living thing. They did a really good job."

"They, they!" cried János "Who are *they?*"

Patricia looked pensive. "Hmm, I'm afraid the toy has stopped working properly."

"What are you talking about!?"

"It's best to reboot you and reset this chapter of time." Then János saw her leaning over him, rebooting and resetting...

János was lazing on his bed in typical post-coital repose, smoking an exotic *Black Elephant* cigarette and sipping a goblet of *Nistru*, an excellent Moldovian cognac. At his side Patricia lay inert in the state of pseudo-rest and pseudo-satisfaction you would expect of her.

Endorphins of orgasm had put János in the best mental state for introspection even more creative than usual.

Patricia can't be real, because the creationism she represents has no sense. But evolutionism may be the wrong way to perceive the world. That's because all explanations are inherently the enemies of the ineffable אמת, *that's to say 'truth' in the Hebrew language, pronounced "Emet." Explanations kill the mystery in which reality consists. So probably I'm as unreal as she is. One fine day I may waken and realize that I don't exist at all Hmm... I'm getting stiff again. I'd rather fuck Patricia a bit more.*

And János fucked Patricia a bit more. A good choice. Patricia's sex didn't fluctuate.

Presently, having shut Patricia in the wardrobe again and headed into town, János felt moved to meditate inside an Evolutionist Church, which was where people who believed in the theory, or myth, of natural selection went to pray.

The building was full of elderly women, mostly dressed in black. The majority of young folk seemed to be creationist these days, since this was the modern way, so they didn't visit such a place. He paused in front of a gilded statue of Darwin and Freud smoking cigars. Moving on, János lit a long slim candle below an icon of Richard Dawkins in a loin-cloth like Tarzan's, consulting a big watch that lacked any numbers. From hidden speakers wafted Michael Nyman's piece of music, *The Cook, The Thief, His Wife & Her Lover.* Some high-definition screens, fixed to the walls in gilded frames, were showing scenes from old porn movies, revered images from the time when human beings had sex directly with one another. János contemplated a traditional Japanese bukkake mass-masturbation, a ceremony now degraded to the pouring of a topping over noodles, rather than the group ejaculation of semen upon a schoolgirl, as shown on this screen in the church.

And what, speculated János, *if this is merely the beginning? What if more and more parallel universes start to overlap, crowding reality with new categories of creatures who are unreal from our original human point of view? What if the only possible form of life in the future is an inseparable symbiosis between all these bizarre creatures?*

103

Later that same day, to the disappointment of Mrs Smetana, János took the train for Budapest. Silvia hosted him once again inside the driver's cab, in exchange for chocolate. This time they were a bit squeezed, because Patricia remained with János – he wouldn't leave Patricia on her own in a passenger carriage in case someone stole her away at an intervening station. What's more, this time Silvia had her own Adam-Schwarzenegger gigolem with her. She must have begun to miss him on her travels.

The railway lines extended swiftly and charmingly in front of them, pointing towards Hungary. As a courtesy, Silvia let János drive the train for a while, even though that was almost certainly forbidden even on Magyar Álom Vasutak. Speeding the train along, János was having fun like a little child. Banished to the two rear corners of the cab, the two gigolems waited inertly with no sign of life until their lords and masters might need them. Silvia and János paid no attention to them, which was normal, since gigolems couldn't get bored and were entirely without free will.

So, when Patricia smiled, only Adam-Schwarzenegger noticed. His eyebow rose slightly. Patricia confirmed that János and Silvia were still distracted. They were. She winked at Adam-Schwarzenegger, then she grinned broadly.

The Mass Extinction
of My Beloved

My Beloved was Brigitte Bardot – one of five hundred Brigitte Bardots, but very special to me.

Due to her iconic importance, firstly as a sex symbol, and secondly as a crusader for animal rights (including insect rights), the World Wildlife Fund sensibly cloned BB as their special agent and representative. That was with her permission, of course – she was eager to help. Obviously five hundred Brigitte Bardots could assist animals (and insects) more than one now-elderly Brigitte could.

To begin with, the clones were all twenty-five years old (and of course a year later they were all twenty-sex, I mean six). Every country in the world received its own Brigitte. Big countries such as Brazil or Russia received four or five Brigittes. Their duties: to observe and protect and intervene in animal welfare. They were allowed to use violence if necessary, or seduction. They were licensed to kill, or to love.

Since I lived in San Marino, the local Brigitte hadn't a great deal of work to do in the way of averting extinctions, once she had saved the Titanic Spotted Toad (which was in fact tiny and difficult to spot). For sixteen centuries this extremely small republic of 20,000 people in north-east Italy had preserved its independence. San Marino consisted of Mount Titan, which was big and awkward, some wheatfield and vineyards, a grand prix circuit which was actually in Italy, and thousands of duty-free tourist shops. In fact most of the inhabitants owned tourist shops, even the thousand men who formed the army of San

Marino.

Another important activity was designing postage stamps for obsessive collectors. I, Count Giuseppe Machiavelli, was the Minister of Philately, and a direct genetic descendant of my clever namesake, Niccoló Machiavelli. I was also in charge of supplying honours, such as the Knighthood of the Titan, to rich benefactors of our micro-country by mail-order through the internet.

One day Brigitte came to see me in my tourist shop, which specialises in postage stamps, and I was enamoured. This was either her intention, or an automatic consequence of her being Bardot. Even so, the depth of my desires was remarkable. I was astonished. I determined to do *anything* to be able to possess her and keep her. So I invited her into a back room, to talk more privately.

"Count Machiavelli," she said as I set a cappucino before her, and one for me too, with a lot of chocolate sprinkled on because chocolate is an aphrodisiac.

"Giuseppe, to you, my dear!"

"Bien, Giuseppe, well I wondered if the Republic of San Marino could issue *only* stamps of endangered species from now on?"

"Hmm," I said, controlling my excitement. "That might be difficult. What, forget about Space-Flight and Vintage Cars and Famous Volcanoes and Torments of the Inquisition? Are there enough endangered species?"

"Millions. More are found every day. It's a race to find them before they vanish. The previous director of the WWF had a nervous breakdown worrying about species that he doesn't know exist – they might stop existing without anybody knowing."

"I would need persuading."

"I *shall* persuade you!" she promised.

Soon, upstairs, she proceeded to do so, but being a gentleman of honour I shall only say that her techniques were very persuasive.

After I had been persuaded, she looked sad.

"What do I do *now*, Giuseppe?"

"Maybe we could try that second position again?" Though in truth I was a bit exhausted.

"No, I mean what can I do about endangered species here in a country of only sixty square kilometres? I've saved the Titanic Spotted Toad and arranged about stamps. What next? My clone-sisters in enormous Brazil are so lucky!"

I panicked that Brigitte might never return to my bed, unless of course I ceased commissioning stamps of obscure moths and monkeys – but that would be ungentlemanly. I needed to hook Brigitte and keep her hooked. So I called upon the spirit of my illustrious ancestor, Nicolló Machiavelli, who knew how to manipulate men (and how to feminipulate women), and I experienced an epiphany, a sudden revelation.

"I have an idea," I said. "But it needs clarifying." It didn't – I was already clear. But realistically I was drained of semen, and I wanted an orgasm to match the magnitude of my inspiration. "Will you come back the day after tomorrow?"

"I can hardly wait!" she said – oh the urgency of her sense of mission.

"You *must* wait," I told her, and felt pleased by my self-control even in the midst of sexual obsession.

Two days later I said to the gorgeous Brigitte, "Animal rights are being violated in many virtual reality computer games, such as *Safari* and *Alligator Slaughter* and the Spanish game *¡Toro Toro Toro!* – to name but three."

"But we had to allow virtual bullfighting in exchange for the closing of the bull rings."

"Nevertheless, virtual bullfighting is a violation of bestial rights. In fact bestial rights are violated in many games. Dogs get run over in *Grand Chase Auto Armageddon*. The WWF needs *virtual* Brigittes to detect infringements of animal rights in games. Alternatively, the WWF could *licence* software creators to *include* animal deaths in games. A werewolf killing game could be WWF-approved. The WWF needs all the money it can get, doesn't it?"

"Of course. We need to catalogue unknown species that are going extinct. That's costly because we don't know where they are. So we have to send out expeditions all the time, while being careful not to violate any remaining wildernesses. The biological protection suits our explorers wear are very expensive. You're a genius, Giuseppe. I'm so glad I met you." And she began to suck me.

At that moment another epiphany came to me, courtesy of the spirit of my ancestor Niccoló, I truly believe. But I did not come prematurely in response to this next idea.

Two days later I said to Brigitte, "In fact, if an extinction is inevitable, the doomed species ought to be honoured and celebrated. The best way for human beings to celebrate is to *participate* in the extinction, to make sure it happens dramatically rather than in a feeble way, out of sight. There should be extinction parties. Rich people will pay a lot to take part. This will raise more funds."

"Yes, yes!" she exclaimed. I was stroking her clitoris.

"It's very sad to be the last member of a species, or the last few members. So this would be *compassionate extermination*."

"Oh yesss!"

"In fact," I said about a week later, "the WWF could *forbid* species to go extinct – make it illegal. If a species persists in going extinct, it will be put on trial. If found guilty, there can be a hunt to execute the last members of the species for violating the law by carrying out unauthorized self-extinction."

"Oh yessssssss!"

I was giving the Brigitte of San Marino a whole new inspiring vision, or series of visions, which was addicting her to me. At the same time I was very addicted to her. Like a drug addict I must pay more and more (by way of imagination) to keep my supply of ecstasy secure. But my imagination – or Niccoló's genetic contribution – did not fail me.

"It'll be a status symbol," I said, "to wear a mark of extinction, a special tie or bracelet. It says you have participated in, or attended, an extinction. But there's more. Extinctions can be *sponsored* by MacDonald's or Marlboro. Global mega-corporations will compete. That'll bring in a lot of money."

It was my turn to exclaim Yessss for a long while, such was Brigitte's gratitude to me.

I had thought that Brigitte was communicating all these new ideas to WWF headquarters in Geneva by email. But no… The ideas were communicated to her clone-sisters by morphic resonance, which is the tendency of beings who are very similar to pick up and incorporate a powerful new concept which one of their fellow beings has. A chimpanzee would discover how to unfasten a cage door, and suddenly chimpanzees everywhere were escaping.

Brigitte wasn't merely similar – she was identical to her sisters. So the other 499 Bardot clones were all on my Brigitte's wavelength, akin to telepathically. Soon they were taking action militantly, with all the power of the World Wildlife Fund. The Bardot based in Switzerland was particularly active in lobbying the World Court. Because of the iconic power and sexiness of a Brigitte Bardot, any paltry misgivings or doubts on the part of the current director of the WWF were swept aside. He resigned, and the Swiss Bardot became head of the WWF.

Sudden changes of faith – even mass conversions – are part of human nature if a Big New Idea arises. Look at Nazi Germany, a civilized nation one moment, historically speaking, and a fanatical exterminator of entire races the next moment. Look at China's Great Leap Backwards and its Anti-Cultural Revolution. Look at the fashion for hoola-hoops.

My next inspiration – and therefore my Beloved's, and that of her 499 sisters – was to copyright the extinction of species, to control video rights.

What with extinction copyright and corporate sponsorship and high society extermination parties and hunts subsequent to criminal prosecutions, before long the WWF was vigorously spearheading the extermination of species. Loggers in Brazil and motorway builders and such were now sued for unlicensed exterminations.

My Brigitte was in communion with all of these developments by morphic resonance, and of course she was in frequent communion with me too. The endangered species stamps of San Marino had become akin to Wanted posters of criminals.

"Which are best to exterminate first?" Brigitte asked me as she lay naked in bed. "Soft fluffy animals – or ugly nasty ones?"

"You mean Special Effects ones?"

"Yes, big teeth and claws."

"Let me think…"

Thinking helped me delay my orgasm. I thanked God that there were so many endangered species to contemplate. Then it occurred to me that unendangered species could be reclassified as endangered and put on the long Red List – because Darwin's doctrine of evolution declares that all species must inevitably become extinct in the fullness of time. So all species were guilty of extinctability, potentially. Except perhaps cockroaches. Maybe the WWF should organise an education and training programme for cockroaches.

Brigitte squealed and pulled a sheet up to cover our bodies. For someone was climbing loudly upstairs. A few moments later heavy knocks sounded on the bedroom door, as if produced by a

110

small battering ram.

"Avanti," I shouted as my erection collapsed.

The Bishop of San Marino entered, in full robes and mitre, crozier in hand. He was one of my cousins, Alberto. Obviously he had dressed to impress me.

"Forgive me, My Lord," I said piously, "for I am sinning."

"Are you using birth control?" demanded Alberto.

"I'm a clone," piped up Brigitte, "so I can't become pregnant."

"That is *definitely* birth control of the most wicked kind," Alberto stated severely. "Be damned to birth control for the moment. I'm here with an important message from His Holiness…"

He who was formerly head of the Inquisition, I reminded myself with a shiver, having selected the art for Torments of the Inquisition but never issued the stamps in question, because of Brigitte.

"…about *death* control," added Alberto.

Brigitte sighed. "If only one could wear a condom to prevent death! We French call them *les préservatifs*. Yet what do they preserve?"

"You're *French?*" Alberto echoed. "Do clones have nationalities?"

"Since we use diplomatic passports to travel, we are all registered Swiss, but emotionally I am French. A Bardot may need to use a condom while seducing someone who's endangering a species because such men may have chlamydia or syphilis – usually it's such men who endanger species. Oh I have just thought! How about condoms for use by endangered species? Species-suicide condoms?"

Brigitte was trying to emulate my Machiavellian powers of imagination.

I did not wish to scorn her inspiration. Yet I felt bound to say, "Who would put the condoms on rhinos and crocodiles?

111

Trained apes? And who would replace the condoms?"

"I'm thinking," said Brigitte, "of something like an automated milking parlour to which cows become accustomed to walk to be emptied. Millions of similar installations in the wild. Using animal porn videos as the bait."

"Species-extinction through automated masturbation? Would enough endangered animals be fooled?"

Alberto slammed his crozier on the floor. "I have a message from The Holy Father."

"What a paradox," Brigitte said naughtily and flirtatiously. "He is in fact the Anti-Father since he never fucks." She allowed the sheet to slide, to expose a beautiful breast familiar to millions of old movie addicts. "Though admittedly," she added, "he has filled the Vatican with cats, whom he loves."

I felt jealous. However, Alberto did not seem aroused. Or, at least, only aroused to wrath.

"Whore of Paris!" he thundered. "The Holy Father has become aware that species extinction is inspired from right here in San Marino. A Bardot in Portugal was seriously injured falling out of a train carriage, and she confessed to a priest on the platform."

"Oh, Giuseppe, that is the sudden pain I had yesterday. I told you it felt like a miscarriage."

"You never had a miscarriage. You cannot."

"I can imagine one."

Alberto continued: "In the Bible, God gave human beings dominion over the beasts. This is our sacred duty. We cannot exercise dominion if there are no beasts to dominate! The Holy Father is issuing a papal Bull against extinctions, *Dominatio Animalorum*." My cousin gazed at me. "You'll be excommunicated if you persist in causing these, out of lust." How well my cousin knew me.

"Ooh la la," said Brigitte, wide-eyed. "And do clones have souls to excommunicate? Maybe I share one soul with all my sisters! In which case I myself only have one five-hundredth of a soul, so I can only be one five-hundredth excommunicated. That shouldn't hurt too much. More like burning your finger on a cigarette instead of being burned at the stake."

"I am addressing the Human Being in that bed. *You*, Young Madam, are a blasphemy, Clone-Whore of Paris."

To my amazement my Beloved began to talk theology to Alberto.

"Ah, what is blasphemy? That depends on what is sacred. However, what is sacred should be an invisible and ineffable mystery, as in the heart of the Temple of Solomon, which was empty, containing nothing. The sacred shouldn't be something visible, for then it is vulgarised and sold as souvenirs. Consequently, what is recognized as sacred isn't sacred any more – it's banal. And banality is blasphemous, for it denies the ideal beauty that is beyond this world, the domain where the perfect archetypes of all animals exist, and to which they ought to return – "

How I admired and lusted for her, and wished to burrow under the sheet to explore the mystery of hidden lips that never speak yet are so expressive.

"Be quiet!" thundered Alberto. "*Retro me*, Bardot, get thee behind me. The churches will pray against extinction, which is Darwinian and denies the hand of God."

"Oh, the *controlling* hand. But God doesn't control anything in the cybernetic homeostatic sense, to maintain life! It is Mankind which tries to control everything, a crazy ambition continually denied by hurricanes and earthquakes and diseases. God's is the hand of destruction. So now I'm performing God's work." God, I admired her even more at this moment.

"You are Eve with the poisonous apple!" Alberto brandished his crozier, but then perhaps he thought of possible paparazzi at the window – paparazzi get everywhere. A photograph of a half-exposed Bardot and a bishop in full regalia might be misinterpreted.

"Dieu créa la femme," said Brigitte, alluding to one of her films.

And I reflected on how much I, Giuseppe Machiavelli, had transformed my Brigitte – recreating her as an agent of extinction, so that she would continue to be my Beloved – consequently I was also a bit Godlike. Being in bed with a beautiful woman and causing her to exclaim *Yessss* often has this effect on a full-blooded man.

"Giuseppe," my cousin Alberto said, "this madness must stop! Free your life from this bitch, for the sake of your soul! Be aware that the Holy Father has already undertaken timely action to free the world as soon as possible from the diabolical activity of this army of clones of evil!" So saying, he departed.

I was worried. If the Catholic Church had taken this matter so badly, the future existence of the Brigitte Bardots was at risk. Stalin once mocked the Vatican with the famous question, "How many divisions does the Pope have?" But Stalin and Communism had disappeared from the world and the Catholic Church was stronger than ever. In fact Pope Woityla dealt a mortal blow to Communism by helping Solidarnosc in Poland during the Eighties. If the Vatican bigwigs set out to free the world from the Brigitte Bardots, surely they would succeed. And I would lose my sweet little blonde toy, the most wonderful female human creature that nature ever produced, whom my skills were able to magnetize into my bed, and likewise in the bathroom, on the stairs, in the garden, in the swimming pool, in the sauna and once even in a church, in a confessional. By now I couldn't exist without her. This mustn't happen! Oh, spirit and DNA of my great Machiavellian ancestor, come to my aid!

"My dearest, the Church doesn't understand our sacred mission, of charitable acceleration of inevitable extinction." My face must have exhibited the pain of rectitude.

"The Church isn't about understanding," Brigitte replied,

"but about the management of mysteries. So why be surprised?"

"I'm not, I'm worried. For them you're a demon, and they'll destroy you."

"Not good," she agreed. "Without me and my sisters, who will save endangered species from a slow inglorious extinction?"

I pursued a sudden intuition. "The main problem with the Catholic Church is the total obsessive sexual repression of their functionaries. Lack of physical love distances them from God and goodness. Have you seen the horrible signs of sexual abstinence printed of the face of Alberto? Absence of pleasure imprints gruff inhuman wrinkles. If only they could know the joy of sex, probably they'd see the world with our eyes, humane eyes, of beings made of flesh, and they wouldn't be so alien to us, and we to them."

"I'll take care of Alberto!" Promptly Brigitte took a lipstick from the handbag and started making her perfect lips even more attractive, if such a thing were possible.

"No!" I exclaimed impetuously. I didn't want my Brigitte to screw around with my arsehole of a cousin. Jealousy may be a weakness, but in the case of my personal exclusive Brigitte, long live jealousy!

Quickly I reasoned, "Decades of sexual repression need massive repeated treatment. You can't waste so much of your precious time – and my sexually incompetent cousin wouldn't give you any satisfaction." I began to undo my trousers. Oh the lipstick on that divine mouth.

"What do you suggest?"

"To suck, I mean pack your things and confer with your sisters in person at a big conference in Geneva about increasing the Brigitte Bardot population. My cousin isn't the only Catholic priest in the world. Apart from priests there are all the bishops and cardinals. That's a lot of people. What do you say?"

"Mmhpff, mmhpff!"

Unwillingly, I must remove the blockage of myself from her

115

mouth if I wanted a comprehensible answer.

Pop!

"Ufffhhh." Lips damp and cheeks blazing, Brigitte breathed again, emerging from the apnoea caused by suction. "You're a genius! Along with my sisters, in effect I'm a species myself, so I must avoid becoming endangered – otherwise, by myself, I'd need to exterminate myself. If I increase my numbers I can avoid becoming endangered and convert all the Catholic clergy to the authentic pleasures of life. Ooh la la! Ahhh! Oui! Ouiii!"

She spun around and touched her toes, presenting her gorgeous rump to me, something I couldn't resist. The devil take my cousin! For a while yet he'd need to continue with his career as a blessèd masturbator no doubt contemplating naked witches being tormented by the Inquisition.

Speed-cloning allowed the growth of an entire Brigitte Bardot body within a couple of weeks, followed by another week of mind-configuration – which was accomplished the more easily by morphic resonance with the 500 clone-sisters who all remained temporarily in Switzerland, since this was an emergency. I'd exhorted my own Brigitte not to skimp on the number of new clones. So she and her sisters decreed 500,000 copies of themselves. That should be sufficient for every priest in the world to have his own dedicated suckubus/fuckubus, and enough left over for other religions if their personnel complained of favouritism.

Half a million Bardots was a tall order for all of the Swiss and German and Czech and Hungarian cloning establishments combined. What with a premium price for priority, the total cost was a major slice of the annual budget of the WWF. I'd suggested to my Brigitte that she and her sisters should take full control of the WWF, since only having the presidency wasn't safe enough. Very soon 100 per cent of WWF functionaries were Brigitte Bardots.

The conquest of the Catholic Church was quite fast, though not as simple as I had believed. Many Catholic priests are paedophiles or homosexual or both, and the marvellous womanly body of Brigitte Bardot left them cold. Consequently special brigades of juvenile Brigitte Bardots were created, as well as male brigades. This wasn't too difficult for clever cloners. To me the idea of a male Bardot seemed paradoxical until I saw the final result and was almost tempted into homosexuality myself! So this deviation didn't delay by too much our final victory.

By now my own Brigitte had returned from Switzerland and my sexual dependence upon her became almost a torment. I needed to fuck her several times every day, yet the pleasure I was getting diminished because of habituation. This was intolerable. Since there were now Brigitte Bardots in abundance, I implored my own Brigitte to summon two or three more of them to San Marino.

"Why do you want more of us? Aren't I enough for you any longer?"

"That isn't the point," I told her as habitually I started undressing her. "I need to be in constant and instant contact with Brigitte Bardots. What would happen if you caught flu or meningitis? To whom would I then rapidly communicate my useful tips? Tips may be needed *suddenly*. The bigger an empire is, the easier it can collapse. We must never let our guard down!" Meanwhile, letting down my zip.

"Oh that's a really big tip!"

On that day for some reason it was bigger than usual.

Quickly I turned her around.

"Ah! Ohh... Ahhh! Yess! How did you know I wanted you to stick it there today?"

"The God of Improvisation always helps those who dare."

"Ohhh... OHHHH!"

117

I wasn't a glutton, so initially I was happy with just one more Bardot in my bed. Stereo sex satisfied me fully for a week. But then to maintain the same coefficient of satisfaction I needed to raise to three the number of simultaneous Bardots.

In the meantime, a major media spectacle sponsored by Pizza Hut and Exxon Mobil was getting the world excited. All the world's remaining elephants destined for extinction were assembled in two big concentration camps, in Uganda and India respectively. Square kilometers of pizza were served to them for their last supper. Then immediately after sundown the American air force dropped an incredible *son et lumière* of phosphorous bombs and napalm, just like the famous apocalypse in Vietnam, cooking all the jumbos – a truly giant Texan-style barbecue with lots of hot pepper sauce.

National Geographic made a memorable documentary of the event in super high definition, two hours of extraordinary slow motion images of the holocaust of the elephants, blood, tomato, pizza, and trumpeting, that should move mankind for centuries. UNESCO swiftly declared the film a heritage treasure (and it went on to win Oscars for best direction, best photography, and best soundtrack).

To have saved the elephants from an inglorious end by making their extinction unforgettable, sublime and tragic, filled my Brigittes and me with such joy, and how we celebrated in our widened bed! After several orgasms calmed our passion, even though my penis itself could no longer stand to attention we respected a minute's silence in the memory of elephants, now absent from the world. Finally on special edition ivory plates bearing the crest of the WWF we served ourselves *Crêpes suzettes flambées* and *banana flambés* in abundance to restore our depleted energy.

"We're in trouble," my three Brigittes told me one day.

"Did you get pregnant?" I asked without thinking.

"We can't, not unless we deliberately take hormones to start ovulation. We're clones."

"Sorry. Automatic thinking from the old times."

"*All* Brigitte Bardots are in trouble. Now that we've dealt with the Church many of us are lovers of powerful politicians, and we've discovered an international plot to exterminate us."

"The bastards!" I exclaimed. What would happen to my sex life if this criminal plan went through?

"We can't understand why they want to exterminate us – did we ever do anything bad?"

I had to think quickly. If the Bardots ever decided that I'd advised them wrongly, I'd lose them forever. *Niccolò, my dear ancestor, please help me right now...!*

"This must be due to jealousy," I improvised. Women intrinsically believe that jealousy is an important cause of events. "Jealousy from wives of male politicians whose lives you're making more enjoyable, and jealousy from male politicians who don't yet enjoy such delights."

"Of course it must be!" the three Bardots chorused. God, how beautiful they were when they did things in unison – the most banal gestures would become a seductive ballet. I was getting stiff again.

"There's only one thing to do – you'll have to increase even more in number and satisfy all the important men in the world." Holy Moses, at this rate I'd end up winning the Nobel Peace Prize!

"What about the jealous wives?"

"Damn it, how does this bra unfasten? Ah yes – the jealousy of wives can only be eradicated along with the wives."

"Along with the wives?"

"Nobody has yet invented a way to eradicate a wife's jealousy while keeping the wife. Come to think of it, if you increase enough in number to satisfy all men of any importance, wives will become an endangered species destined for extinction. Hmm,

119

these teenage slips are very provocative."

"That will be a very demanding task," the Bardots said in chorus.

"Likewise, undressing three of you at once!" If I wasn't fast enough, one of my quarry might mischievously escape.

At last clothing was sufficiently defeated to allow flesh to do its duty. Since I'd started to have three Brigitte Bardots I also needed three times as long to fuck them, since it wouldn't be gentlemanly to serve one less than the others. So I would finish up twice as tired – with experience I'd learnt not to be triply tired.

While my three Brigittes dressed again afterwards, I refreshed myself by pouring a stream of Andalusian wine into my mouth from a *porrón*.

I dismissed them with, "Go and reproduce yourselves."

However, extinguishing wives is easier said than done. Typically a wife has a husband, and no matter how enchanted he is by a Brigitte Bardot, the husband usually still feels emotional resistance and moral scruples about the euthanasia of his wife. Even husbands without such scruples would rarely have an unloved wife put down, for who would then wash their dirty underwear, iron their shirts, rear their children and keep the house clean? Not a Brigitte Bardot for sure! Wives are also necessary for arguments – many husbands can't exist without the quarrels they've got used to during the course of married life.

Evidently the problem must be approached at its root by also eliminating husbands. However, a practical problem arose. Wives plus husbands made up the majority of human beings. How could a minority of Brigitte Bardots accomplish such a major extermination?

"With gene-specific bioweapons!" I explained to my three blond Valkyries as they knelt before me playing clock-cock. Each time a Brigitte managed to gain my organ from one of her sisters by making her laugh or hiccup or by hair-pulling, and put it in her mouth, she started her time on a clock similar to a chess player's, except with three buttons. The Brigitte who ended up sucking me most would win and I would fuck only her, while throughout our embrace the losers endured an ice-cold shower.

"Gene-specific bioweapons?" duetted the two Brigittes who weren't sucking me.

"Biological weapons of mass destruction selectively targeted at people who have specific genes. Yesss!" God, how she could suck! "The American military have been working on this. Oh shit, be careful with those teeth!"

Verbal disapproval from me was a way of forfeiting the prick. Another way was any softening of my erection. Yet another was giving me an orgasm prematurely, which tended to end the game. The rules of clock-cock were quite sophisticated.

"*Sacré bleu, c'est horrible!* Why would anyone make such a vile WMD?"

"To target Arabs or Chinese or homosexuals. For instance. In my view a species which designs weapons of such a kind is working proactively for its own extinction, whereas other species go extinct from carelessness and laziness. Our intervention couldn't be more appropriate! Yes! Yeessss! Fuck fucking mankind! Ahh! AHHHHH...GHH!"

Dreams of destruction and omnipotence excited me too much and suddenly I had come. It was time to consult the clock.

One fine day my Brigittes reported, "We seduced all the American bioweapons scientists, and North Korean ones too. We now control all existing gene-specific bioweapons."

"Congratulations on the North Koreans. That must have been hard."

"They were. Years of ideological celibacy."

"And what of our adversaries' plans to exterminate all Brigitte Bardots?"

"Proceeding slower and slower," the Brigittes answered,

"because almost every powerful man has a Brigitte at his side by now. She's an essential status symbol. However, there's also a snobbish new fashion trend of *not* having a Bardot – if this tendency grows, it'll be a problem."

Always problems! And my task, to find the solutions. What one put up with to get laid in the only way that remained satisfying!

"Increase the production of the Brigittes! The most powerful men need not one but a *harem* of Bardots. This won't cause devaluation of Bardots – because we'll diversify. We already did some male Bardots and kiddy Bardots for the priests. Now we'll do Black Bardots, Pygmy Bardots, Granny Bardots, hairy Bardots, bald Bardots, paraplegic Bardots. Trendy idiots will need to collect all the Bardots. How many are there in the world now?"

"Idiots?"

"No, Bardots."

"About ten million. We've opened a new production centre in China."

"Fine. Nowadays we all pretend to believe in democracy, even the North Koreans. In a democracy the majority is always right, which means that the majority is *good* by definition. So let's make sure we become the majority. Then justice and ethics will be on our side."

"You're a marvellous man! How could we possibly do without you?"

Immediately it was time to cash the prize of gratitude.

Now that I had time to think about it, controlling gene-specific bioweapons was only of defensive value, to stop their use against Brigittes with Bardot genes. As offensive weapons they were worthless because wives and husbands didn't have a genetic code different from unmarried people. Nor were we racists, unlike those who designed and made those weapons in the first place. We loved the peoples of each country indiscriminately. Their extermination must be accomplished fairly, respectful of their human rights.

And this was the nub of the matter! Mankind's extinction wasn't linked to the existence of too many wives and husbands, but to the existence of mankind itself. Within every wife and husband lurked a human being. *En masse* human beings were always causing trouble with their wars and territorialism and greed, almost as if programmed for self-annihilation yet unable to accomplish this. How wretched and incompetent was mankind compared with my beloved Brigitte Bardot. It was time for a big change which would make the world a safer, more comfortable place to live in. Essentially our mission was to make the inevitable *elegant*. In Mathematics what is elegant is true. Likewise with extinction.

A world consisting only of Brigitte Bardots would be better, prettier, more just. It might seem a bit less varied, but anyway the world was already heading towards cultural homogeneity. Once there used to be genocides, and now there was culturicide, the confusingly varied cuisines of the world displaced by immutable, predictible MacDonalds. For example! What you eat is what you become.

Truly, this was the sunset of mankind as we knew it. Millions of hours of TV daily displayed to billions of human brains the Way Ahead into the darkness. Slaughter, explosions, homicides, mayhem as entertainment. It was as though the sick soul of humanity was screaming to be extinguished and, by chance or by hereditary talent I, Count Giuseppe Machiavelli, could hear that scream – rather as Edvard Munch saw it. If anything of mankind was to have any future, Brigitte Bardot was the only hope. Maybe the Earth's biosphere, the collective unconscious of the planet, obliged me to love Brigitte Bardot powerfully enough and effectively enough so that the planet in turn might be rescued. Strange as it may sound, my sexual obsession would save life on Earth.

"We will use the gene specific bioweapons *in reverse mode*, "I told my three angels who were giving me a triple Thai massage, our custom now before breakfast. I spoke inspiredly, or randomly. To me these days this was much the same. I knew that I was keyed in to planetary destiny and whatever I said would probably be right.

"In reverse mode?" my three Brigittes chorused.

"Instead of using the bioweapons to target lethally only people with a specific gene complex, we'll use them to *preserve* certain people. Well, two types of people. Hmmmmm…" Thai massage is a fundamental human right.

"The Brigittes," my angels said wisely, "and you?"

God, how I loved reasonably intelligent women especially when they were beautiful and naked and administering Thai massage!

"Ahhh, ohhh yes, *yes!*"

"Good," the Bardots said, "because it would be a real pity if you went extinct too. Us Brigittes need you."

I'd been wondering if morphic resonance from the orgasms I caused my Brigitte affected the millions of other clones. Oh omnipotence delirium! Realistically, Bardots were often fucking men who weren't me, this being one of their diplomatic functions. I wasn't the only man on earth.

Not yet.

Okay, let's face it, the idea of ending up being the only man in a world of Brigitte Bardots was attractive. Maybe, when all other men were extinct, I *would* provoke orgasms in millions of Bardots all at the same time through morphic resonance. Might there be a delay in the sharing? A delay proportional to distance, such that the orgasm I provoked would propagate through the world of the Bardots like ripples produced by a stone thrown into a lake?

I envisaged a wave of pleasure and moans, generated from

the epicenter of sexuality that was myself, progressively making a trip round the globe, widening as it travelled to become a circle equal in size to the Earth's diameter, then shrinking again until it became a single point at the antipodes of myself, inducing in the Brigitte closest to that point an orgasm second in intensity only to that of the Brigitte I had actually been screwing.

And what if not merely the orgasm itself, but each preceding pelvic thrust of mine and its consequences would propagate? The world would become a sexual paradise. Rather than time zones, the world would be divided into sexzones determined by the sexual Greenwich of wherever I happened to be. Maybe I could learn to modulate the sex waves in amplitude and frequency, causing differential effects upon the millions of Brigittes whom I would lead to pleasure. Upon, or rather *with*, my organ I would improvise organic symphonies of global pleasure, original and unrepeatable in the Paganini way – supposing Paganini had been a phallovirtuoso, I mean an organist.

The world of the Bardots as the sexual musical instrument of the last man and artist on Earth! Why stop there? If I could achieve immortality on Earth through my sexual music, or by some other means, and if the Bardots could colonise the stars, the entire universe would become my concert hall. Pleasure propagating from my virile member might take millions of years to reach the Bardots in other galaxies, and alien scientists would gain insights into the cosmos by measuring the red shift of the Bardots' orgasms! If God were a real man, he would have acted thus since the beginning of time.

The three Brigittes were giving of their best and the Thai massage had empowered me like a sperm whale about to blow. Like a semen whale. I too must give of my best. Genius is a powerful cocktail of inspired creativity and perfect timing, and into my mind came an awesome concept.

It had to come into my mind rather than into my brain because frankly my brain was becoming deprived of blood, so much blood being needed for my penis now that a trinity of blowjobs was in progress.

"The Last Judgement," I gasped. "Last Judgement of obsolete mankind... Judgement must be announced by Jesus!"

The reaction of the Brigittes was noisy, wet, and wordless, but I knew they were listening.

"We'll program the bioweapons to produce a pandemic of tumours in the shape of a crucifix with a Jesus-like figure on it. Those will be visible internally on scanners, and then they'll emerge and speak – or squeak like a rubber toy when you squeeze it. They'll squeak the Last Judgement: bye-bye people, time's up. Then they'll metastise, but they'll produce opiates too so that it's a painless euthanasia."

One of the Brigittes detached herself to ask, "Why only Jesus tumours? Why not Mohammed tumours too? And Brahma and Buddha?"

Damn, I'd let my erstwhile Catholic upbringing blind me while improvising. This realisation weakened my erection.

"Look," I continued to improvise, "the present global élite which is trying to stop us is probably mostly made up of Christians. We have to focus on them. We have to disarm them by an attack from within mounted by their most beloved symbol, turned miraculously into flesh in a way nobody would have wished for. *But* also the Christians will think this miracle is likely to convert Moslems and Buddhists and so on, because the other religions don't have any such miracle. So the Christians will be happy before going extinct, and probably there'll be mass conversions from other religions of people who want a miraculous tumour. Please don't stop now... Ahhh!"

My erection was saved.

"That's wonderful!" one of the Brigittes exclaimed. "So poetic! So expressionist! You express yourself so well!"

"Anyone in my place would have had the same idea." In my experience there's nothing like a bit of impudent false modesty to moisten a woman's admiration.

Brigittes exchanged places. "But won't it become banal?" asked another voice, which was of course the same voice. "A miracle is a mystery, isn't it? Something extraordinary. Won't millions of people developing a crucifix tumour make this ordinary? What if everyone had a Sistine Chapel roof at home? Uniqueness is what makes Art sublime. Suppose that talking crucifixes erupt from millions of bodies like slow motion *Alien*, the effect will be kitsch."

Damn it, she was right. Sometimes reasonably intelligent women can be too intelligent. To condemn makind to a kitsch epilogue wasn't noble. Anything taken to extremes becomes its opposite, for example, as she said, Sistine Chapel roofs in every kitchen. How to avoid this? Why not *profit* from it?

"Okay, we'll program the bioweapons so that females evolve tumours of a different sort. Both theologically and from a feminist point of view it's wrong to have the symbol of a patriarchal religion growing from them. Lots of women want bigger boobs. So let them develop huger beautiful tumour-boobs, making every woman more sexually appetizing, fulfilling their secret dreams –"

The Bardots interrupted in chorus, "Women already get breast tumours, and they usually hate it! We don't think it's a good idea."

"I'm not talking about traditional breast tumours, but state-of-the-art tumoral prostheses, perfect tits which will grow continuously and painlessly." I permitted myself a dramatic pause. "Then finally the women will grow a third *central* tit with the face of a crying Madonna."

"Oh now that's a very sweet idea!" So saying, two of the Brigittes occupied their mouths as previously.

"It'll be seen as a miracle, and many women will love it! Men will love it too, since this will add a taste of sacred exoticism and transgression to their sexual lives."

"It's still kitsch," said one voice, "but it's touching on the sublime."

And now to put the icing on the cake. "What's more, we'll introduce a random variant so that a small percentage of people of both women and men develop instead a tumour in the shape of a pretzel."

"A *pretzel?*"

Despite my grin of mounting pleasure, I tried to assume a serious expression.

"The shape of the pretzel with its three holes is age-old symbolism and has occupied the human imagination time and again. It's religious, emblem of the trinity. It's sexual. It's the endless knot of eternity. According to legend a Swabian baker was sentenced to death because of social misdemeanors. The prince promised to pardon the baker if he could produce bread during the night *through which the sun will shine three times*. In his desperation the baker invented the twisted pretzel and saved his own life. Little did that baker know that in saving his own life he was dooming mankind, since now the pretzel will accompany mankind on his tree-lined avenue of sunset."

"What a lovely image. You've persuaded me."

And we stopped talking, for it was time once more to allow the senses to monopolise our lives.

And so commenced an amazing, unique and unrepeatable era, the Last Days of Mankind, a time of dramatic changes, epic sex, poetic madness. As always during periods of mass deaths such as bygone plagues or big wars, the perception of death changed radically. In the hope of keeping the population quiet, on TV governments promised life after death to everybody. But dying soon became very fashionable and erotic. The sense of impending death is a powerful aphrodisiac, because instinct tries to produce new life to replace what is lost. Orgiastic extinction parties became common everywhere. Thus religion and sex finally and unexpectedly married. Terminal males with crucifixes protruding from their insides were knotted together like pretzels with terminal females disappearing behind titanic tits. The crown of thorns worn by the squeaking figure on the crucifix sensually tickled tumoral nipples. Sometimes too spiky a thorn punctured an inflated breast and tumorous pulp would spray adjacent fornicating lovers like a Japanese bukkake sacrament.

The tumoral crucifixes and the tumoral weeping madonna breasts were objects of adoration, but some men and women at first wore shapeless robes, and to these roving priests would put the question "Crucifix or Pretzel?" – were it a man – or "Pretzel or Madonna?" – were it a woman.

"Just Pretzel," some would whisper sadly, cursing the Swabian baker.

Then the priests would bless the Pretzel with its trinity of holes which God could penetrate three times simultaneously, and thereafter these men and women proudly displayed their pretzels invitingly at extinction orgies. Being useful, they would be used. I was happy that religion had a tangible purpose at last.

As the biomass of old mankind diminished rapidly, so the Brigitte Bardot's biomass was rapidly increasing. When the BB biomass overtook the other people's biomass, we celebrated – now we were the absolute majority, and by definition what we would do would be democratic. In common with my illustrious ancestor I didn't hold democracy in much regard, but it's a nice ornament for the top of your strategic work of art.

With the increasing BB biomass, so did my love for BB increase. Was I not on target to achieve *absolute love*? If only I could transform the whole mass of the universe – including the mysterious dark matter which accounts for the majority of everything – into Brigitte Bardots, then my love would be Godly and divine. A task, at least for now, beyond my capabilities. How can you force a black hole or a naked singularity to transform itself into pure Brigitte Bardots?

Now that Brigitte Bardot was effectively immortal, I really should start to think of how to make at least my mind immortal, my mind already proven essential in the Brigitte Bardots' path towards evolutionary triumph. If I could upload my intellect into the world computer network which mankind by going extinct no longer needed, I could supervise the expansion of Brigitte Bardot throughout the Universe. Entire planets would be metamorphosed into meat to provide the raw material for production of trillions of BBs. Blood comets would interconnect all production centers. Finally, BB comets would carry her DNA everywhere to improve the beauty of the cosmos, fulfilling my passion.

As yet these were only romantic dreams! In the meantime, as extinction approached its finale, the World Wildlife Fund took charge. Thousands of jumbo jets piloted by Bardots flew the remaining world population to the island of Zanzibar, often used in the past as a measure of population size, supposing that people stood side by side. "The world population has risen to 1.2 Zanzibars," you'd hear. Bardots had by now taken over most important things, not merely the airlines.

This was to be the Mankind's End fireworks party. Some Bardots wearing bikinis had suggested exploding the world's complete stock of nuclear weapons on Zanzibar – best to go out with a bang! Others objected, "Nuclear winter – there won't be enough fur coats!" In fact ten big nukes would be quite enough, because the population had fallen by now to 0.1 Zanzibars.

And so it came to pass, as climax to an orgy under the African sun, reminiscent of the demise of the elephants.

I was now the only man on Earth, except for the male Brigitte Bardots and some transexual ones. My three favourite Bardots joined me in my castle to celebrate. Rivers of Champagne and Brunello di Montalcino and Rex Paradox Cabernet ran. Joy and well-deserved pride and dizziness was ours.

"The world is a much safer place now," I slurred at one point.

"We wonder," the Bardots replied "why it took so many thousands years for mankind to grow up, and become us."

I hiccupped. "The world had never seen a Macchiavelli in love before!" Actually, because of all the wine, my penis was limp, and I experienced a curious sensation that I had lost track of my Bardots. Which was my number one Brigitte, who had come to my philandery, I mean philately shop? Surely this was her sitting beside me, on my right! Surely? A ghastly thought dawned: were this trio even the same trio as at other times? I had indeed drunk a lot. My vision drifted; there seemed to be six Bardots.

I slapped myself on the cheek. She on my right was my most beloved Bardot. Almost definitely.

"There's just one little detail," she said.

I didn't like the expression that all three of the BBs wore. As if they would be sorry for something. But for what?

"We don't need you any more, Giuseppe."

Even drunk, I knew that this was very bad news. You can't trust women! I should have known it. Give them the world and ten minutes later they've forgotten.

"How will you do without sex?" I asked.

"On your own you'd never be able to satisfy all of us –"

I thought, all too late, of my vision of morphic resonance orgasms to which I hadn't paid enough attention.

"– and alas we aren't lesbians. So we started a production line of brainless male Bardots who'll serve the purpose. To reproduce ourselves we'll continue using clonation until we can colonise the rest of the galaxy –"

"Colonise the galaxy? I never told you about that!" I'd kept it to myself. Revelation had seemed premature. How could they have come up with the idea on their own? Shock sobered me.

"Ooh la la, we're simple girls, although quite intelligent, but since we're so many now and then by chance one of us gets a *brilliant* idea. Then instantly it's shared with all the others. Giuseppe, all together we are now a genius."

I should have thought of this possibility. Growing in number, they had reached a critical mass. It was perfectly plausible that they didn't need another genius any more.

"The universe is bound to be full of life forms destined to go extinct," the Bardots said. "For sure the Cosmos needs our help."

Scorned, I replied, "I have no doubt of it."

The Bardots must have seen on my face my disheartened expression. By this point, I had almost lost all hope. Yet apparently things were not so bad. Life after all reserves some nice surprises now and then.

"Don't worry Giuseppe. We won't kill you. We still love you, even though we don't need you any more. You'll die a natural death when the time comes, as it must. We can wait."

"Well, it's *good* that you can wait…"

The Brigittes' eyes gleamed with a sinister light which for some reason evoked in me the notion of a praying mantis.

"Let's make love, if you can," they suggested.

"Great idea!" I exclaimed, more from habit than conviction. Something failed to convince me, although I wasn't sure what.

The three Brigittes began to squander their attentions on me, and my fears faded. I started to experience some sexual excitement.

Then the door opened, and other Brigitte Bardots entered the dining hall of the castle – *many* others, until they filled the hall. All of them proceeded to undress. For a moment, only for a moment, the male in me exulted. Then terror rose inside me. I rushed to the window. What I saw outside the castle took my breath away.

As far as the horizon, millions of Brigitte Bardots were crowding and – I understood – waiting for their turn to enter the castle… and expecting me to enter them.

"Please, darling, take these pills." My very own Brigitte handed me blue pills and a glass of water.

"What are they?"

"Something far better than Viagra," the mantis replied. "Never again will you lose your erection."

But my erection will lose me, I thought in despair. Yet I could do nothing but swallow the pills for my coming ordeal.

Then the most beautiful of all imaginable agonies that a man could dream of began. I had no idea how long it went on. Occasionally I would fall asleep – for a few hours? for a full night? – who could tell? – but when I awoke a Brigitte would already be riding on me, taking advantage of my now inextinguishable erection. It was as if my penis had been plastinated and become a dildo which nevertheless was sucking out of me my *élan vital*.

Following a sudden creative intuition I began to kill every Brigitte I was fucking, by strangling her. To my surprise I discovered that this was very pleasing. Yet was this *sexually* pleasing, or was it something else? In these extreme circumstances in which I found myself, my desires – for which I had sacrificed the whole of the human race – became almost a religious ecstasy. Myself, I couldn't die the little death of actual orgasm, since I was empty of fluids. Vicariously, Bardots died.

Yes, strangling was pleasing – but tiring. Soon I had to give it up. Throttling the girls who were fucking me was more exhausting than simply letting them fuck me. However, since I'd shown that I liked Brigittes to be strangled during sex, another Brigitte would now strangle the Brigitte I was coupling with, so that my experience could be as complete as possible. How sweet of them that was. And how persistent. In my delirium I was a God being sacrificed to by Bardocidal priestesses.

What a long, beautiful, extreme delirium of joy and pleasure I endured – but finally the moment came in which I, Count

Giuseppe Machiavelli, last true man on earth, direct genetic descendant of the great Niccoló Machiavelli, overwhelmed by a neverending tsunami of Bardots voraciously violating me with no moment of rest, each giving her life for my increased pleasure – at last I reached the limits that my body could stand, and for the first time in my life I had no remaining choice: I had to die.

And so, I am quite sorry to say, I did.

The Colonoscopy
of My Beloved

My beloved Katrina is a multi-orgasmic woman, which is one reason why she's so beloved to me (as well as her mind – never forget the mind, which plays a huge role in excitement). Even quite gentle caresses provoke fireworks, which is great for a man's self-esteem, because he feels very competent. Sometimes, indeed, Katrina and I joked that her whole body seemed to behave like a clitoris.

Little did we realize!

One morning, when Katrina did a crap, a lot of blood came out of her bottom too, a truly disconcerting amount, bright red. The water in the toilet bowl looked like wine. We both feared she had a tumour up in her entrails.

Katrina's doctor tried to calm her fears – "It might be nothing much, just a polyp which has burst" – but he immediately arranged for an inspection of her bowels by a specialist at the city hospital.

The specialist's name was Dr Schmidt. Schmidt explained to us both about polyps, which grow naturally in the intestines and resemble closed-up sea anemones in a rock pool.

"Trauma is another possible cause," he went on. "Do you bugger much?"

Well, most people know that there are clitoral orgasms and vaginal orgasms and anal orgasms also.

"And there's diverticular disease, where the inside wall of the bowel splits because of hard constipatory turds, not enough fibre in the diet. The inside wall can look like a colonnade in a painting

135

by De Chirico." (This is when I decided that Katrina was in excellent, appreciative hands.) "A tumour rarely produces as much blood as you describe, although it can on occasion."

Katrina's interior could be investigated either by means of a sigmoidoscopy or a colonoscopy. Because of Sigmoid Freud's theories about constipatory anal retention I surmised that the former procedure might be named in honour of him. As for the latter, I thought of Christopher Colon crossing the Atlantic to spy out a new world, and about the Panama Canal. Both procedures employed instruments resembling long flexible silvery snakes the thickness of an average thumb tipped with a fibre-optic light for illumination, a mini-camera which would display the view from within on a colour TV monitor, and a small hoop of sharp wire which could be tightened to take a biopsy sample or to decapitate a polyp which might be growing too much and might cease to be benign.

The sigmoidoscope could be pushed part-way up the intestines; the colonoscope could be pushed up all the way. Just to be on the safe side Schmidt favoured a colonoscopy.

"Anyway," he told Katrina, "a sigmoidoscopy can be a bit uncomfortable, whereas we need you completely relaxed for a colonoscopy, so you'll receive a strong sedative as well as muscle relaxants. Probably you'll sleep through the whole thing."

Katrina needed to starve for a couple of days and to take powders to empty herself completely, but three days later we returned to the city hospital.

Schmidt introduced us to Dr Mohammad Hassan who was on a fellowship from Morocco to perfect his skills, and who would observe and assist. Then I was left in the waiting room. Once the relaxants and sedatives had done their work the investigation should take no more than twenty minutes. Katrina would be separated from me for only about an hour in all.

Imagine my alarm when quite soon a nurse came from the

examination room and requested my presence. Immediately I thought that they had found a tumour inside my Beloved.

Katrina lay on her side, knees drawn up, the silvery snake inserted up her anus. She was giggling.

Dr Schmidt looked distracted.

"This is very rare," he said. "The sedative is acting as a euphoric, and I need to concentrate."

"Ah, so you want me to hold her hand?"

"No." He gestured at the TV monitor where in glorious colour I saw for the first time the truly intimate private inside of my Beloved, seen by no one else before this day – a pink tunnel, upon the wall of which…

"That is no polyp," declared Schmidt. "That is a *clitoris*. A clitoris in the big bowel!"

My Beloved had always seemed to revel in the aftermath of a meal, several hours later.

"Does she have a clitoris in the normal place?" he demanded of me. I suppose he could easily have discovered this for himself, but he wasn't a gynae specialist, and besides there are protocols of behaviour.

"Of course she does," I replied.

"Then this is a secondary clitoris."

"Supernumerary," said Dr Hassan. "I know how to perform a clitoridectomy. That is quite customary in parts of Morocco."

Schmidt turned upon him in a momentary fury.

"Clitoridectomy is an obscenity."

Hassan showed his teeth. "Is it not obscenity when the clitoris is inside the shit of a bowel?"

Schmidt controlled himself. "Besides, it isn't the clitoris that bled. Even you can see it's a perfectly normal healthy clitoris."

Perhaps to prevent Hassan from seizing the initiative and decapitating the clitoris, Schmidt hastily pushed more of the colonoscope up my Beloved's anus. Maybe because of the sudden rubbing of the instrument across her internal clitoris, Katrina squirmed pleasurably.

"Madam, try to lie still!"

This was only the *first* additional clitoris that Schmidt's voyage of internal exploration discovered. In fact we witnessed several clitorises, at intervals.

Schmidt paused and lectured Hassan. "It's a good thing that men do not have additional *penises* in their intestines. No matter how small those penises might normally be, if erect they could block the passage. Wonderful pieces of food, or more exactly wonderful turds, might excite them. They might think, *Ah, we're going to be caressed!* Awful constipation would occur."

"Surely the penises would soon ejaculate," said Hassan, "and the semen from them would lubricate the bowel?"

"Perhaps they can't produce semen. Dry ejaculations won't help with constipation."

The two doctors fell silent, for the colonoscope had arrived at the site of damage, from which some blood still oozed.

"My God," exclaimed Schmidt, "her *appendix* – look, the appendix was covered by a hymen. A particularly hard turd must have broken the hymen. Imagine continuing to be a virgin deep within your body, no matter how much intercourse has taken place! You could honestly swear to a prospective husband that you're still *intacta*."

To my eye, that little tube of the appendix looked a bit like a tiny additional womb.

"I wonder," said Schmidt, "if she will have periods, of the bowels, now that the hymen is gone – instead of the bloodshed being reabsorbed, which it must have been previously. I think that the appendix-hymen was a total seal, not merely partial. Well, we've solved the mystery of the patient's sudden haemorrhage. She really is a remarkable patient. Supplementary sexual organs." (My Beloved giggled again.) "I wonder whether the body-scanner room is free…"

A body-scan cannot distinguish perfectly between similar tissue, and the technician seemed astonished by Schmidt's interpretation, but the good doctor declared that he could perceive yet other clitorises within my Beloved – a small one in a little finger, for example, and another in the back of her neck – and that her nervous system was additionally a clitoral system. Knowing my multi-orgasmic Beloved as I did, I didn't doubt him.

I don't know why I thought that oral sex would help soothe my Beloved's entrails. Oh yes I do: it's because semen is white – symbolically this would counteract bleeding. Anyway, once we were home that night, we did as we had done on other special occasions, and I came fulsomely in her mouth, all of which she swallowed.

Schmidt telephoned a week later. Prior to her colonoscopy Katrina had signed a medical consent form, but Schmidt now wished to discuss a different kind of consent. He wanted to purchase some expensive new equipment from Japan. Also, he hoped to make patients more sanguine about sigmoidoscopies and colonoscopies in general – by sanguine I mean cheerful, not bloody – and he had realised that because of her clitorises the videotape of my Beloved's internal examination was in fact the world's first colonoscopy porn movie. Consequently he wished to enter it for the Erotic Festival held in Barcelona, Spain, each October. With Katrina's consent. True, her participation in the porn movie would be incognito, since no friends nor family nor neighbours would easily recognize Katrina from her intestines, but Schmidt was a man of probity and integrity. (And I'd already recognized his artistic penchant when he alluded to the paintings of De Chirico.)

Katrina was delighted.

"You're a woman in a million," Schmidt said gratefully. "You're a star."

"Hmm," said my Beloved, "I always wanted to star in a

movie. You know, I think I would rather appreciate screen credit – my name on the silver screen for a couple of seconds. You can simply call me Katrina in the credits. I'm thinking about a title for the film." My Beloved could get very excited about ideas. "We've had *Deep Throat*. How about *Deep Bowel?* Does the festival give out prizes?"

"It wouldn't be a festival without prizes," Schmidt assured her. "Erotic journalists often call the Grand Prix for films *The Grand Prick*. The runner-up gets a consolation prize called *El Consolador.*"

"What do the prizes look like?"

"Rather long dildos. Actually, they're telescopic. Specially made."

"You can *see* through them, like you see through a telescope?"

"No, but they're adjustable. They extend."

"Far enough to reach that first clitoris inside of me?"

Maybe Katrina could retain custody of the prize for a while, although Schmidt craved such a trophy for his own office, where it might encourage male homosexuals to look forward to sigmoidoscopies and colonoscopies.

When my Beloved began to experience morning sickness several weeks later we suspected what had happened. She must have swallowed so much semen sticking together protectively that some survived the digestive juices in the stomach and the juices of the small intestine. She must be pregnant in that additional womb which was her appendix, opened for fertilisation now that the hymen had been torn away by a hard turd.

"My love, that means you must have an extra ovary at the back of the appendix!"

"Unless," she said inspiredly, "there's such a thing as… Well now, the word for a virgin-pregnancy is parthenogenesis. So what's the male counterpart? What's the name for a self-fertilising *sperm* pregnancy. It's a possibility."

Parthenos is Greek for maiden, and *pais* is Greek for boy, as in paedophile and paedophilia. Maybe the correct term might be *paedogenesis*. A paedogenetic pregnancy.

"That sounds a bit like a buggered boy becoming pregnant," said Katrina. "I once read a horror novel about that theme. It was called *The Worm* or something."

"Well, whatever." The name didn't matter. The *term* that did matter was the likely length and outcome of her pregnancy, which we now took to be an indisputable fact.

I hesitated. "Ectopic pregancies are ones which take place outside the womb. They can be dangerous. You might need an abortion."

"An appendix abortion? Shall I eat a masochistically hot curry? Or take part in a Mexican chilli-eating contest? Beloved," for Katrina also called me thus, "this pregnancy *isn't* happening outside of a womb — merely in a *different* womb, an auxiliary womb."

"Hmm, that's true." Between two such kindred spirits as my Beloved and myself, talking often made unusual things seem very true, truer than ordinary banal things.

To avoid any risk of an officious impulsive ectopic appendectomy occurring if the gynaecological equivalent of Dr Hassan were involved, my Beloved did not consult her doctor at all about our intuitions. During the subsequent weeks I inspected Katrina's belly by hand pressure periodically — and we also noted the absence of any menstruation from her anus, which might have been expected normally subsequent to the loss of her seal-tight hymen.

"Any tenderness?" I would enquire.

"Only tenderness for you, my Beloved," she would reply, and she might experience a minor orgasm.

"Will our baby look like you, or like me?" she mused. "Even if this pregnancy arises principally from your sperm which I

141

swallowed, every cell in me still contains my own DNA. Osmosis of genetic material seems quite possible."

"Maybe it'll look like both of us, then!"

In all, three months had passed since Katrina's colonoscopy, and soon it would be October, the time of the Barcelona Erotic Festival.

For weeks now, whenever my Beloved went to the toilet to crap, she'd been holding a sieve, since it would be terrible if our baby drowned. And then, one wonderful morning…

Well, this is the true story of the birth of Tom Thumb, known as Pulgarcito in Spain and by other names in other lands – which proves that the same kind of birth must have happened previously elsewhere; otherwise the tale would not exist, let alone be widespread. The development of flush toilets may have prevented more recent reports.

During her pregnancy Katrina had eaten as richly as she could so that good semi-digested nourishment would reach the foetus, but our son had gestated in my Beloved's appendix which, unlike the primary womb, could not swell otherwise it would burst. Thus he was only the size of a thumb, and he may never grow much larger. Don't get the idea, though, that our diminutive son is of deficient intellect! He's very bright and communicative. He brings joy to the lives of me and Latrina, I mean Katrina, damn this keyboard.

In addition to combating contraception and abortion, maybe the Pope ought to start a campaign for *coproconsciousness*, in other words shit-inspection for all women. He might use as the motto for this campaign that famous remark by Saint Augustine, *Inter faeces et urinam nascimur* – `we are born between (or in this case, amongst) shit and piss.' Even so, the birth of a miniature person, a bonsai baby, must be a rare occurrence.

If Dr Schmidt's film wins a prize in Barcelona, Katrina talks of a career in intestinal porn to build a sizable nest-egg for our son, who mightn't be able to earn a normal living. If enough people become hooked on bowel-porn – the clitoris in the colon – they'll need more than merely one video to watch.

The Moby Clitoris of His Beloved

Yukio was only a salaryman, not a company boss, but for years he'd yearned to taste whale clitoris sashimi. Regular whalemeat sashimi was quite expensive, but Yukio would need to work for a hundred years to afford whale clitoris sashimi, the most expensive status symbol in Japan.

Much of Yukio's knowledge of the world came from manga comic books or from anime movies which he watched on his phone while commuting for three hours every day. He treasured the image of a beautiful young ama diving woman standing on the bow of a whaling boat clad in a semi-transparent white costume and holding sparklingly aloft the special clitoridectomy knife. An icon far more wonderful than that of Kate Winslet at the front of the *Titanic*! Americans might have their *Moby Dick*, but Yukio's countrymen (or at least the richest of them) had their Moby Clitoris Sashimi.

The beautiful young ama woman would take a deep breath, dive, swim underneath a woman-whale, grasp her 8-centimeter clitoris, then with one razor-sharp slash cut off the clitoris and swim away very quickly. On the deck of the whaler the crew would wait for the ama to climb back aboard, her costume now see-through due to wetness.

And then the whalers would harpoon and kill the whale, because it would be too cruel to leave a female whale alive after amputation of her clitoris. In this respect the Japanese differed very much from certain Islamic and African countries which cut off the clitorises of human girls, so that men should not feel

145

inadequate about their own capacity for orgasms.

Whenever the Japanese were criticised for hunting whales, it was the harvesting of clitorises which empowered them to continue. And of course Japan observed a strict clitoris quota, so that enough female whales would continue to copulate pleasurably and repopulate. Thus, while it was true that whale clitoridectomy directly pleasured only the richest individuals, every Japanese citizen who enjoyed eating whales also benefited.

This Yukio knew. Yet he still yearned to taste whale clitoris sashimi for himself! Most men have licked a woman's clitoris, although probably they haven't eaten one; but the organ of ecstasy of a female whale sliced thinly was said to possess a taste beyond words.

When Yukio's vacation came – the usual very hot and humid fortnight in August – he didn't surrender his holiday back to the Nippon Real-Doll Corporation, as he had done in previous years, in the hope of more rapid promotion through the copyright department. Instead, he took a train from Tokyo (and then a bus) the hundred kilometres to Shirahama City where ama diving women lived. He would seduce an ama to love him. They would marry. She would get a job on a whaling boat. For him she would smuggle clitoris sashimi…

To his consternation Yukio soon discovered that the ama women of Shirahama, who dive for red seaweed, sea snails and abalone, looked nothing like the icon in his mind. For one thing, they weren't slim but were muscular from exercise – and chubby, to cope with cold water. For another, their faces were darkly tanned, not a lovely creamy-white. For a third, their voices were loud and raucous, perhaps due to damage from water pressure; and their speech was quite vulgar. For a fourth, they didn't wear semi-transparent white garments, but orange sweatshirts, thermal tights, and neoprene diving hoods. And for a fifth, their average age seemed to be over sixty. Even if one of those fat vulgar grannies wanted a lover and husband, how could Yukio excite himself enough to woo her?

Disconsolate, he went to get drunk. Presently he found himself outside **The Authentic Ama-Geisha Inn.** The name seemed promising.

Inside, he was amazed to find waiting several beautiful slim young hostesses dressed in the correct long white semi-transparent costumes, and also wearing white high heels. Perched jauntily on their foreheads were diving masks. One hostess wore her very long hair in an oily black rope which would excite a bondage fetishist or a flagellant considerably.

Soon this hostess, whose name was Keiko, was leading Yukio into a private room – which contained a low table, plastic cushions, and a small blue-tiled pool set in the floor of tatami matting, which was plastic too; plastic would dry more quickly than straw matting.

He knelt. Keiko knelt and poured some Johnnie Walker Black Label.

She giggled and said sweetly, "You may splash me whenever you wish!"

Thus revealing more of her breast or thigh or belly…

"But you're the ama of my visions!" Yukio exclaimed. "Why aren't you diving in the sea? You would look so beautiful."

Already he was a bit in love with Keiko, even though the plan had been for an ama to fall in love with him.

"I'm an ama-geisha," Keiko explained. "Only *you* can wet me, not the sea."

"I've seen amas just like you with the whaling fleet! Only," and he recollected his apparently foolish plan, "not with such wonderful hair as yours. They dive for whale clitorises," he added.

Keiko giggled again. "A real ama does that."

"*A fat old granny?*"

Keiko's job was to please him, and Yukio seemed to prefer

147

intellectual stimulation rather than getting drunk and splashing her, so the astonishing truth emerged – a truth known to most inhabitants of Shirahama, but which the media patriotically chose not to publicise.

Each whaling ship carried a real ama and also a false ama (or rather an authentic iconic ama). The real ama, old and fat, foul-mouthed and lurid, would harvest the clitoris while the false ama – who looked more real – would wait in the water beside the ship. The iconic ama would then take the clitoris from the real uniconic ama and would climb a steep gangplank back on board deck, her garment delightfully see-through. Meanwhile the old fat ama would sneak on to the ship from the rear, using the ramp up which dead whales were winched.

This substitution made whale-hunting seem graceful and elegant and sexually exciting in the eyes of the world – slightly akin to marine bull-fighting – and justified the high price to gourmets of clitoris sashimi.

Yukio stared at Keiko. "Wouldn't you rather be on a whaling ship than here? With your wonderful rope of hair you'd set a new style for cartoon books and films. I can license your image for you." Yukio's work did indeed consist of copyright matters concerning Real Dolls modelled upon porn stars. "I'm a specialist. You'd earn a big fee." And Yukio would be the lovely Keiko's agent and manager, and because of this, he would become her Beloved! And at last he would eat whale clitoris sashimi.

Keiko was wide-eyed.

"Agreed?"

Before Keiko could change her mind, Yukio picked up his glass of Johnny Walker Black Label and threw the contents over her, wetting and revealing a delightful breast.

"Kampai!" he exclaimed, to toast her – but in his mind he was shouting `Banzai!' for victory.

The whaling industry normally recruited deep-sea ama from communities such as Shirahama, but Yukio needed Keiko with him in Tokyo to register her image. Keiko could stay in his little apartment in a highrise in the suburbs.

So Keiko exchanged her authentic ama costume and high heels for jeans and a blouse, and piled her rope of hair upon her head, hiding it with a scarf, because nobody must steal her image on a phone en route! Already Yukio felt paranoid and jealous.

On the train Yukio looked at the news on his own phone, and a headline caught his eye: THROW THE WHALE AWAY!

A meeting in South Korea of the International Whaling Commission had ended in confusion. As usual the dispute was about whether to save whales or eat them. The Japanese delegate had suddenly declared that whale clitoris sashimi was a cultural treasure unique to Japan. If foreigners forced the Japanese to stop eating whalemeat, the Japanese would continue to harvest whale clitorises – but to please world public opinion they would throw the rest of the whale away. They would accomplish this grand gesture by compassionately exploding all clitoridectomised whales using torpedos packed with plastic explosive, since nuclear torpedos were unacceptable.

"That will make clitorises even more valuable and prestigious," Yukio said to Keiko.

"I have a clitoris too," she replied.

"But not a whale clitoris." *Or at least not yet*, he thought.

Maybe the Japanese delegate's statement was intended to bewilder the World Wildlife Fund, which had been picketing the meeting. Under the United Nations' Declaration of Cultural Rights, it was forbidden to attack or slander any country's unique cultural icons, such as the Golden Arches of MacDonald's or the Eiffel Tower. Now that Japan had registered whale clitoris sashimi as a cultural treasure, that gourmet experience was protected from criticism – and if there were no clitorises to be sliced, obviously the experience would become extinct. To preserve the cultural experience, the Japanese must continue to hunt whales.

Yukio's apartment was a four-mat one, which was better than living and sleeping in a room only the size of three tatami mats; but still it was rather crowded by two people, unless those two people were intimate. So Yukio found himself examining Keiko's clitoris, causing her to sigh with pleasure. Then he went to sleep and dreamed that every century a magical woman-whale would appear offshore, to provide sashimi from her clitoris for the Empress of the time. On the brow of this whale: a white mark exactly like a chrysanthemum flower. During the subsequent hundred years, the whale's clitoris would regenerate.

Yukio awoke in the morning, thinking immediately about the possibilities of *cloning* clitoris. Keiko had already risen and was now kneeling, dressed in her authentic iconic ama costume which real ama no longer wore. Truly she had the graces of a geisha.

Obviously a woman's clitoris couldn't possibly taste as wonderful as a whale's, yet what if cloned human clitoris could be marketed profitably enough so that the genius who thought of this became rich enough to afford to eat whale clitoris?

Since Yukio had no idea how to clone anything, an alternative occurred to him. These days, because pigs and people are very alike, pigs provided transplant organs for human beings. Maybe a million people had inside them pig hearts or lungs or livers or kidneys. When the pigs were sacrificed to provide transplants, the rest of the pig, including the clitoris in the case of female pigs, would probably go into pet food.

What if Yukio were to buy the sex organs of pigs, to provide a source of clitorises? These could be packaged in tiny jars as human clitorises, and sold over the internet! Upon the label, a photo of a genuine human clitoris, with a certificate of authenticity which would be correct since the picture at least was genuine. *Delicious clitorises, cloned from this very clitoris you see!* Realistically, Keiko might *not* obtain a job on a whaling ship – yet she could still help Yukio to achieve his goal.

Truly, his trip to the seaside had inspired him, probably because the clean air contained more oxygen than in the city.

Yukio took his phone, and soon he was photographing Keiko's clitoris while she assisted him. He wasn't quite sure if her clitoris was the usual size but it was certainly very noticeable. Using Photoshop, he could get rid of the surrounding flaps of flesh familiar to users of porn magazines, leaving only the clitoris itself in the picture. His computer could print many labels. In a truly iconic sense he would indeed be cloning Keiko's clitoris, or at least its image. In his excitement he almost forgot to go to work.

On the commuter train, he used his phone to search for Pig Organ Farms and for Food Bottlers. Genius is to perceive connections where none were seen before.

When he returned home that night, Keiko was already lying asleep on the futon, still dressed as an ama and wearing her diving mask for even greater authenticity. Her long rope of hair seemed like an oxygen tube. The TV set was showing young men eating as many worms as they could as quickly as possible. It was the popular weekly show *Brown Spaghetti Race*, sponsored by the Dai-Nippon Cheese Company. The more Parmesan the contestants poured on the wiggling worms, the less difficult it was to pick them up using smoothly lacquered chopsticks.

Would consumers be more excited by "genuine canned cloned human clitoris sashimi" or "genuine *ama* clitoris sashimi (cloned)"? Maybe the label should show Keiko smiling as she held her photoshopped clitoris to her own lips with *chopsticks*? Would the suggestion of auto-cannibalism excite buyers? Was his ideal market gourmets who couldn't afford whale clitoris, or sexual fetishists? Or both?

Yukio sat on the edge of the futon beside Keiko and regarded her tenderly. He lifted her rope of hair, closed his lips upon the end of it, and blew into the hair as though to supply her with more oxygen, such as she had been accustomed to at the seaside. Maybe, subconsciously at least, that was the reason why she had put on the diving mask.

"Keiko-san," he told her politely, although she was asleep, "there is a change of plan."

It took Yukio some hard work and organisation and most of his savings to set up the Genuine Cloned Ama Clitoris Sashimi Company, or GCACSC for short. The sexual organs of organ-donor pigs must be rushed by courier, refrigerated and ultra-fresh, to the Greater Tokyo Bottling Company, where a dedicated employee dissected out the clitorises for bottling. Irrelevant vaginas and labia and also penises and balls were cooked and minced and canned to become Luxury Pig-Protein sent as food aid to starving Communist North Korea, with the full co-operation of the government's Japan-Aid programme, which subsidised the project and praised Yukio's initiative and sense of social responsibility, while respecting his wish to remain anonymous. The donor farm believed that the complete sexual organs were being processed, which in the case of male pigs was true; and Yukio had no wish to enlighten them.

He enlightened the gourmet public about the availability of cloned ama clitoris sashimi by means of a clever spam program, which he bought in the Akihabara electronics district. A spam program was appropriate since the word spam originally meant `spiced American meat.'

Every night after Yukio came home from the Nippon Real-Doll Corporation, he printed labels for the jars and boxes and address labels and dealt with an increasing number of internet orders and payments. He had rented a garage for delivery of the little unlabelled jars of clitorises, which were received there during the day by Keiko, dressed ordinarily. She would then change into her ama costume, stick the labels on to the jars, skilfully fold the beautiful little cardboard boxes which Yukio produced on his printer, fit a jar into each, and stick on an address label.

Keiko was very busy; and so was Yukio. What with Yukio's regular work at the Real-Doll Corporation and his after-hours work at home, he became a bit like a Zen monk who had trained himself in No-Sleep, or not much – now he slept standing up in the commuter train instead of looking at manga and anime on his phone; consequently he never watched the News in either manga or anime format. All he knew was that orders were pouring into his home PC. The spam had done its job sufficiently well that consumers were spontaneously spreading the word of the new and affordable (although not cheap) gourmet delight. Keiko told him that by now magazines were writing stories about this, and TV channels were talking – she had done some phone interviews. Apparently Yukio was being hailed as the new Mr Mikimoto, but Yukio had no spare time to pay much attention.

Mikimoto-san was the man who invented cultured pearls by putting irritating grains of sand inside oysters, at Pearl Island. To suggest that his cultured pearls were as good as naturally occuring pearls, he had employed amas to dive into the sea around Pearl Island for tourists to admire, and in fact, according to Keiko, Mikimoto-san had invented or revised the see-through costumes of the amas. The ama water-ballet actresses would bring up real oysters, which might or might not contain real pearls, for the tourists to eat authentically in the Pearl Island Restaurant.

One evening an astonishing thing happened. Yukio had woken up automatically as usual in time to get off the commuter train, and was walking away from the station homeward when he saw Keiko coming towards along the street dressed in schoolgirl uniform!

"Why have you become a schoolgirl?" he cried out, but

Keiko walked past, ignoring him.

Then along the street came another schoolgirl Keiko, then another, then a couple together.

They were real schoolgirls wearing false faces – latex masks of the real Keiko!

"Excuse me," Yukio said to a false Keiko, "but where did you get that mask?"

The schoolgirl paused, but remained silent.

Of course, she couldn't speak while wearing that mask because Yukio wasn't speaking to her but to the mask. Should he reach out and peel the mask from her true face? That might constitute assault, or even a new perversion, of unmasking schoolgirls.

"Please tell me," he begged.

She bowed slightly, then beckoned – gestured him back towards the station.

Like a tourist guide for the deaf she led him inside the station to a vending machine. It was one of those that sold the used panties of virgins, which old men would buy and sniff. But now it also sold something else in little bags: those masks of Keiko.

Quickly Yukio bought one. The packaging showed the upper body and face of Keiko, just as on the labels of the jars of clitorises. Keiko held to her lips with chopsticks a clitoris, although now she was using her left hand rather than her right – evidently she had been photoshopped. A speech bubble above her head read: *Eat my virgin clitoris.*

That was the cheeky message conveyed by the mask. Identities concealed, schoolgirls could tease men naughtily without a blush, without even saying a word or making a gesture. What innocent, or wicked, erotic power they would feel! Clitoris power. Maybe the packaging of other masks had different speech in the bubbles. Or maybe not. Or maybe yes.

Quickly Yukio googled non-manga non-anime News on his phone.

He saw a picture, taken through a window, of a classroom in which all the girls were wearing identical Keiko masks to the consternation of the teacher. He saw a picture of a playground where a dozen Keikos of different heights were strolling. A craze had hit the whole of Japan, probably spreading among schoolgirls everywhere by txt!

Because of trousers, he noticed some boys too, who were also wearing Keiko masks. Ah, the boys were doing that so as to save face!

He asked the Keiko who still lingered by the machine, "Keiko, did you *do* this without consulting me? To prove that you're clever too?" What a perfect ecological loop, that the same machines which sold the used virgin underwear of schoolgirls should provide the same schoolgirls with these masks...

But of course she wasn't the real Keiko, and besides she had no intention of speaking.

How could Keiko have organised the rapid manufacture of all the masks and their supply to vending machines? Yukio ripped open the packaging and unfolded the latex mask. On the back of the chin, to his horror he saw: *TM Nippon Real-Doll Corp.*

Had he fallen asleep at work without realizing and talked in his sleep? Had he been too clever for himself? Had part of him exploited himself schizophrenically out of company loyalty? Or had the company security-psychologist decided that Yukio was behaving oddly, and investigated his computer?

Oh foolish Yukio, to have copyrighted the label with Keiko's image in his own name at work, borrowing the company's copyright software – that was how they had found out!

But then the company perceived a unique business opportunity: the Real-Doll Corporation could turn real schoolgirls everywhere into clitoris-power dolls of his Keiko! A million texting schoolgirls could spread a craze within a few days, or maybe a few hours. And Yukio couldn't complain or sue, nor could Keiko. For one thing, Yukio had committed industrial theft. But, even more worryingly, the Real-Doll Corporation's psychologist-detective may have also found out the true source of Genuine Cloned Ama Clitoris Sashimi.

Yukio bowed to the false Keiko, then hurried home.

"Who are you?" he said to Keiko in the four-mat room. Quickly he explained what he had discovered – Keiko had been too busy labelling in the rented garage that day to watch any news. And he added: "You must wear a mask from now on, or else I won't know you!"

"Do you mean wear my diving mask?"

"More like a mask of Kate Winslet, I think… No, wait!"

The big oval of latex cut from the Keiko mask fitted the diving mask perfectly. Superglue secured it. Her false eyes, false nose, and false mouth squeezed flatly against the inside of the glass, as if she had dived to a depth of such pressure that her features had become two-dimensional. Her photoshopped clitoris forever would touch her flat lips.

Since the false genuine face which she wore a few centimeters in front of her real face was in fact her true face, this negated that falsity and bestowed a mysterious and mystical authenticity upon her actual face, even though that was now invisible, as mystical things often are.

A Zen-like state came over Yukio. He knelt before Keiko, like Pinocchio praying to the Blue Fairy to make him real. By not-seeing what he was seeing, Yukio began to worship her countenance.

Unseeing too, a blind goddess, Keiko heard his mantra of worship.

"My Beloved, My Beloved, My Beloved…"

Whale clitoris sashimi was only an illusion, from which Yukio was now freed by enlightenment. Probably its sublime taste was also an illusion caused by exorbitant price. He would eat Keiko's clitoris instead.

The CVD of the Beloveds: a Romance of Computers

Maria first noticed that her computer had caught a CyberVenereal Disease when she looked in My Pictures at some images of her journalist sister Angina taken the year before on a nudist beach near Málaga.

Angina ought to have been christened Angelina. It isn't usual to name babies after symptoms of diseases, but the priest had been worrying about the condition of his heart. Once christened, you can't be unchristened.

Was Angina's pathological name the reason why the CVD corrupted pictures of her first of all? Or was it because of the lesbian incest thing Maria and Angina had? You mightn't expect a computer to realise implications merely from pictures, even if two women were caressing each other lovingly. Well, with the new optical character recognition software, the *character* of what you saw optically could now be interpreted – iconographically, as it were. This was important for CCTV cameras on the lookout for suicide bombers, as well as for lazy art historians.

In Maria's opinion, lesbian incest was so much *cooler* than the other sorts involving daughter and father, or brother, or alternatively mother and son, which led to all sorts of Freudian clichés. Oedipussy, Electra, et cetera. In fact lesbian incest didn't seem to have any Greek forebears to make it banal. Classical civilisation has a lot to answer for. Or the Arabs do, for preserving a lot of old texts which Dark Age Christians wiped their bottoms or lit fires with. Yes, blame the Islamists.

Some porn websites – probably less than a hundred thousand

157

worldwide – advertised lesbian incest, aimed at red-blooded men jaded by images of orthodox lesbianism and bored by fantasies of curing, or at least satisfying, the supposed lesbians. But you couldn't guarantee that the lesbian incest was genuine unless the supposed sisters were visibly identical twins. Even then you couldn't be sure! The twins might be pretending, or else there might only be one narcissistic woman doubled by clever CGI. *Narcissus*: there we go again, another ancient Greek. Blame Al Qaida.

To raise some honest extra electrocash, Maria and Angina ran a female incest website starring themselves and featuring the warning BORING TO MEN. Maybe this warning accounted for the high number of hits. Visitors to the site could click and compare the sisters' almost identical DNA sequences. Admittedly these sequences might be fake, or one of them might be a copy changed a bit – and few visitors were likely to spend hours scrolling through millions of ACGTGCACAGTs before turning to the meat of the matter – nevertheless this was a warranty of integrity, such as no other lesbian incest site offered. The sisters planned to add a fun page dedicated to intrauterine Siamese-twin lesbian incest, picturing foetuses joined at the clitoris, though this would probably only attract specialist *pre*-paedophiles, who couldn't be many even in a population of ten billion.

But anyway. Nude Angina was displaying oozing sores surrounded by hard red edges on her lips, fingers, and nipples, and the glands in her groin looked enlarged.

This was so disconcerting that Maria phoned Angina, who was in Haiti investigating reports of voodoo dildos which could convert poor young women into au pair zombies for export to Switzerland.

"Beloved, you don't have any ulcerous sores, do you?"

"Why?" asked her sister. "Do you need some? What for?"

"Angina, I already have plenty – in my computer. How soon are you coming back?"

"As fast as possible – I'm planning to steal a voodoo dildo, and the voodoo priest-pimps will be angry."

The very next day, pictures of Maria herself were infected, so she phoned for a home visit by a technician.

The man's ID identified him as Basil Panglotis. Curly black hair burst from the V neckline of his shirt, and adorned the backs of his hands, and of course his head too. His dark eyes gleamed like torchlight upon two pools of engine oil. His teeth likewise, as if he used the toothpaste of the Gods. Quickly the Greek examined the symptoms of disease in My Pictures, referring to Maria's unblemished face for comparison. Then he inspected images of Angina.

"Your pics are certainly poxillated," he said, "but don't worry about witchcraft, lovely young lady." This handsome Hellenic computer doctor perhaps tried to seduce clients by massaging their egos as well as their software. "This isn't an attack upon you personally by sympathetic magic – or more exactly, by *un*sympathetic magic…"

Being lesbian, Maria ignored his compliments and thought instead about Haiti and voodoo. This worried her, so she went to brew some calming camomile tea. When she returned, bringing a cup for Basil too, he was deep into her computer's operating systems. Code scrolled down the screen like a waterfall, or datafall. Presently Basil had a diagnosis, another Greek word.

"Your computer seems to have fallen in love with a porn site computer and caught CyberSyphilis from it. If this was a normal virus, I could clean it out. Deleting *love* is more difficult." Basil flashed his eyes at Maria, implying that he too might be hopelessly in love.

Hopelessly would be the correct adverb, Maria reflected. She didn't wish to discourage the young Greek too much while he was working, so she didn't spill tea upon his lap.

"Isn't that a bit *psychological*?" she asked him suspiciously.

"Like a bit Freudian, even? A computer falling in love?"

"Yeah, it's a bit unusual, but CyberVD is a real problem all of a sudden. Personally I think the CIA designed these CVDs in a secret cyberlab for the born-again Christians' War Against Porn, the WAP. In my opinion the WAP's going to be added to WAT, the War Against Terror, making WAPT – or maybe even replace the WAT, since, lovely lady, it's a lot easier to find Porn than Terror."

"You aren't by any chance making this up, are you, Basil?"

The Greek looked at Maria with wide-eyed, dewy innocence.

"*Moi?*" he said in French, the language of love. "Loin of the lady, *non*! I mean, *loin de là*, far from it. I need to give your computer a cyber-orgasm to see if that helps. Will you assist?"

Maria was suspicious.

"What exactly," she asked, "is a cyber-orgasm – and how am I supposed to 'assist'?"

"A cyber-orgasm is the usual reason a computer crashes. Well now, there's an intimate relationship between the owner and her computer, wouldn't you say? So if you have an orgasm while you're keyboarding, the computer will probably also have an orgasm."

"Wouldn't it be more sensible to investigate *which* computer mine is in love with, and why?"

"How," demanded Basil hotly, "can you ask *why* about love? Love is irrational. Love is an obsession."

Maria's main job, working from home, involved analysing credit risks, to decide if people were *excellent, good, fair, poor*, or *very poor*. This was difficult nowadays and required feminine intuition. If a consumer signed up for a lot of plastic cards from shops in order to save 20% on their first purchases and if they never used those cards subsequently, *potentially* they might use all the cards to the full on the very same day – and thus suddenly become deep in debt. Consequently a person who wasn't yet in debt was a bad risk, even if they were a good risk. People deep in debt were better risks, even though they were worse risks. Much confusion resulted these days about concepts of goodness and badness. Maria wondered what sort of risk Basil posed to her. However, she was a brown belt in Aikido – it's a good idea for lesbians to study martial arts.

Maybe she ought to warn Basil about her sexual orientation. Yet if a plumber visits you to repair a leak, do you quickly tell him, "By the way, I'm a lesbian"? Annoyingly, *lesbian* was yet another Greek word, thus Basil might feel that he was an expert on the subject.

Maria decided to face the situation head-on. "Recently," she confided, "I've had orgasms while I was keyboarding" – that was because she'd been using Photoshop to join foetuses at the clitoris – "and the computer never crashed once. On the contrary, sometimes it crashed while I was working very seriously and my cunt was as dry as James Bond's Martini."

Basil wasn't abashed. "A cunt should be stirred, not shaken," he observed, miming in midair with his forefinger, "if you want my opinion as a plumber."

The coincidence astonished Maria. No sooner had she thought about plumbers...!

"To pay for my studies in informatics, I was a plumber for a while."

Then the first part of his sentence registered with her. Such impertinence! She would have thrown Basil Panglotis out of the door right away, using Aikido, but she resisted the temptation for the sake of her love-sick computer.

"When I was a plumber, I would often demonstrate to the lady of the house my special method for unblocking blocked pipes – "

"Please be so kind to turn your sexual attentions to my computer or leave."

"But before being a plumber," Basil went on, "I studied psychology for a while. *Psyche* is another Greek word, since the

161

human mind is actually a Greek discovery. Modern computers are very close to having minds of their own, proved by them behaving differently from each other even with the same programs. If you won't co-operate, I'll try to provoke an orgasm in the computer by stimulating the erogenous zones of the operative system. Now that they've gained proto-mind status, computers have evolved erogenous zones in their operating systems, something which no designer foresaw."

Maria couldn't see exactly what Basil did, but shortly afterwards the computer crashed while emitting a moaning noise.

Basil rebooted, typed a while, then he shook his head. "This computer's love is too strong to be defeated by mere cyber-orgasms."

"Can't we leave the love in the computer and just heal the CyberSyphillis?"

"It isn't that simple, my lovely. I can eradicate CVDs from a computer till the cows come home, but due to love he'll immediately re-infect himself from the same source."

"What makes you think my computer's male?"

"To be in love he must be either Cupid or Ballerina – "

"Eh?"

"You've seen the pictures on toilet doors in posh coffee bars?"

She nodded.

"So you agree with me."

"Look, can't we disconnect the computer from the Internet?"

"That's illegal! The government must always be able to check anybody's computer for threats to global security. This makes cyber-epidemics difficult to contain."

"Surely there can be exceptions?"

Basil smiled provocatively. "Women often think like that."

Maria had almost had enough of this macho Greek insolence, but once more she restrained herself – as women often do.

"So what does your Greek plumber's wisdom suggest we do now?"

"Without a shadow of doubt I invoke the enlightened Pyrrho of Elis – one of many illustrious Greek ancestors – who accompanied Alexander the Great to India and became Sceptical afterwards."

"Why do you say Sceptical with a capital S?"

"Because Pyrrho started Scepticism. I shall apply his principle of ακαταληψια, which in language spoken by people with beards means *incomprehensibility*, and also εποχη, which can be translated as *suspension of judgment*."

"In other words?"

"It's impossible to understand what's going on, so for a while I should stop trying." Basil began packing his bag, evidently about to leave.

"But what about my computer!"

"For a situation like this I recommend Stoicism, created by Zeno of Citium, who was approximately born in 334 and approximately died in 265."

"How can someone approximately be born and approximately die?"

"People lived backwards until the birth of Christ," Basil told Maria, "so it was more difficult knowing exactly when you died or were born. In the first case because you were recovering from being fatally ill. In the second case because your brain got smaller, so you lost the ability to count."

Maria thought of Angina's lips, fingers, and nipples, devastated by oozing sores surrounded by hard red edges. Not to mention her own lips and nipples in My Pictures.

"We can't leave my computer like this!"

"Wrong action is worse than no action. Italians know that well. As the brilliant people of Naples say: *Jette pe se fa' a croce e se cecaje n'uocchio!* That means, 'He wanted to make the sign of the cross and he blinded himself in one eye.' We don't want this to

163

happen to your computer, now do we?"

"I suppose that's a rhetorical question."

"Of course – the Greeks invented rhetoric."

"And you also speak Italian?"

"No, I speak *Italians*. Neapolitan and Venetian and Sicilian and Genovese and three more."

Why was Basil repairing computers instead of translating for the entire EC?

"What should I *do*?"

"Understand his needs and weaknesses. He's going through a difficult period – the first experience with love! You have no choice but to be broadminded and tolerant."

Though Basil left, Maria had the distinct feeling that the Greek had infiltrated her life and her computer. Life quickly became more difficult. A computer in love which didn't know how to have safe sex with other computers presented a whole new order of problems, especially when the computer in question hosted a lesbian incest site – for which a machine afflicted with CVDs was hardly the optimal framework.

It was funny to think how online porn had bailed out the economy of the developed world, now that the developing world did most of the physical labour. All those trillions of Dollars and Euros circulating through porn sites in a vast busy Gulf Steam of circulation; all those websites quoted on the Porn Exchange, the dot-cums; the Ordinary Porn Index, the High-Tech Porn Index; all those hundreds of millions of people who were consumers or suppliers or both! Yet this was an inevitable progression. Money or shares based on manufacturing or minerals had become increasingly imaginary. Try cashing in your paper or electronic money or your paper shares for gold or for copper at Fort Knox or at any national bank. Online sex was even *more* imaginary: a belief in a sexuality which didn't really exist.

And yet governments claimed to be waging a Fight against

Filth, just as they pretended to fight Terror. Obviously the War Against Porn was a project of the Stupid CIA while the Clever (and Invisible) CIA was secretly encouraging porn with all its power. Porn was as important as Terror in maintaining a stable society – probably far more so, due to the greater economic implications, even though both addressed profound and fundamental human instincts. It was scarcely surprising that most serious journalism these days dealt with porn and terror. In this regard Angina's report on Haitian voodoo dildos should be a big hit and earn a lot of money. A link might exist between voodoo dildos and Al Qaeda, via Swiss banks.

But now, much was at risk because of those CVDs infecting Maria's computer. For soon after CyberSyphilis came CyberHarpies!

This was like Herpes but worse. By zooming into Angina's pubic hair, until it became a forest, Maria could see the miniature clawed harpies flying about and shitting, as in Virgil's *Aeneid*. A close inspection of her own pubes in My Pictures revealed the same infestation. Who on earth would pay to watch Cyberinfections contaminate their beautiful incestuous lesbian relationship? There might be a market for fetishists of diseased sex, yet this offended Maria's aesthetic inclinations. Women shouldn't masturbate at how sick she and Angina were, even for money!

A couple of days later Angina came home, bringing with her a black wooden voodoo dildo, and the sisters celebrated their reunion passionately, live on webcams – although not by using that dildo, since neither wished to become an obedient au pair; still less did they wish to live in Switzerland. Angina put the voodoo dildo in the refrigerator to preserve – as well as to keep cool – the dildo's voodoo powers.

Alas, the online playback of their reunion was contaminated. Like a parody of the larger action of lips and tongues, in

165

cunnilingus close-ups harpies were clearly visible lapping at syphilitic sores which they clawed open, then shitting on the sores.

What's more, the TV news declared that a sudden epidemic of CVDs was infecting computers worldwide and that many machines had fallen in cursed love with each other – and that more and more of the world's porn sites were being affected, with who knew what effect upon users of the porn sites, not to mention upon the world economy. Sexual psychologists and cyberneticians and economists were interviewed. According to these experts the epidemic might be an attack upon capitalism and western values launched by Al Qaeda; or alternatively launched by the Vatican, on account of the sexual stigmata, and because disgust at diseased virtual sex might cause more real sex, thus more babies and souls. Or maybe computers falling in love would culminate in Artificial Intelligence as a product of their cyber-intercourse, their collective baby. The experts argued hotly. Maybe this, maybe that.

Next morning, both sisters' genitals were itchy, and not with excitement. Using a magnifying glass, they discovered genital harpies. Just as a hedgehog has fleas jumping up and down within its spines, so did harpies infest their private parts.

Maria said diplomatically to her sister, "Did you by any chance fuck any girl in Haiti?"

"Oh Maria, how could you ask such a thing?"

Indeed it made no sense, for the sisters had always been loyal one to one another; and since they were intensely and sincerely devoted to lesbian incest, in order to cheat on each other they would necessarily need a *third* sister, who had never been born, so far as they knew.

To wash the harpies away proved impossible. Maria and Angina shaved each other's cunts, removing the two forests where the harpies lived – but the harpies still persisted, clawing and biting at the sisters' labia. This meant that *virtual* harpies were infesting *actual* flesh with tangible consequences. How terrible for a real body to suffer a virtual venereal disease. For the moment all that the sisters could do was spray each other's cunts with an anaesthetising aerosol intended for insect bites and bee stings.

In desperation, Maria phoned Basil.

When the Greek arrived he was holding, as well as his equipment bag, a carrier bag from which appealing odours drifted.

"*Moussaka!*" he announced. "*Melitzanes Papoutsakia, Lahano Dolmathes* and of course *Tzatziki!* I didn't have time to eat, so I bought something on the way. In fact I overbought! Will you join me?" Was he trying to seduce with Greek food? "Ah, and this must be your lovely sister Angina! I recognize her from My Pictures – minus, of course, the syphilitic sores. How was Haiti, adventurous lady?"

"We've caught harpies from the bloody computer," said Angina, without more ado. She and her sister were both wearing very tight jeans in the hope of crushing the harpies, and shapeless sweaters, so that the Greek mightn't pay attention to their breasts.

"You aren't the only ones having such problems," he said. "Approximately another billion people are in similar situations. Let's eat my delicious Greek food, then I'll take care of your diseased computer – and thus take care of you, beauteous sisters."

"I'd rather," said Maria, "you look at the computer right away before the anaesthetic wears off."

"What anaesthetic?"

"We sprayed our cunts with Anti-Bee Sting."

Basil looked crestfallen. "That means you can't have clitoral orgasms for quite a while."

"How very disappointing for you."

"If I need to look at the computer immediately, I'd better put the food in the fridge." So saying, Basil invaded their kitchen.

167

Moments later, he returned in triumph. "But you can certainly have a vaginal orgasm with added G-spot!" And he flourished the voodoo dildo.

"Not the *black* one!" protested Angina.

"Are you a racist?" asked Basil. "And why do lesbians use dildos moulded from men's stiff dicks, as if in homage? And why keep a dildo in the fridge? It'll be horribly chilly. I'll microwave it. Let's see, 30 seconds? But don't use it immediately – it'll still be vibrating; my mother warned me about newly microwaved food. Hmm, though this gives the dildo a vibrator function – ah, *that's* why you refrigerate it, so it doesn't get too hot."

"SHUT UP," Maria shouted at him in capital letters. "Open your work bag. We'll eat afterwards."

Basil had brought the latest cyberpsychoanalytical software for computers. Now that new generations of computers used quantum processors, classic old PC maintenance tools were obsolete. You needed to access what you might call the subconscious of the computer, the proto-mind which wasn't exactly anywhere on the hard disk, nor actually precisely anywhere in the machine, nor even in this precise world necessarily, due to indeterminacy.

Once he had loaded the cyberpsychoanalytical soft, Basil addressed the computer:

"Bună seara. Mă numesc Basil, şi ce mai faceţi dumneavoastră? Am auzit ca te distrezi mişto pe net?"

"What language is that?" demanded Maria.

"Romanian, the language of the world's finest hackers. So it's the most appropriate one to use at the moment. Don't worry, computers understand umpteen languages due to superb translation tools always available online."

Yet how did Basil understand so many languages?

"Aşa şi aşa," the computer replied, "dar vă rog, lăsaţi-mă cu limbă română, pentru că-mi deschide rani vechi. Pentru mult timp, am fost îndragoştit de o cyberprezenta română, dar nu a avut un final fericit."

"What's going on?" Maria asked.

"You computer had a bad affair with a Romanian computer and now he doesn't want to speak Romanian with me," Basil explained.

"I'm sure you can survive."

"Yes, but it'll be more difficult to establish rapport. I developed my skill when I was Vice-President of the Royal Romanian Hackers Union."

"You were V-P of the Royal Romanian Hackers Union?" the computer suddenly asked.

"Definitely," Basil replied.

"I have some good friends there," the computer told him. "They're all nice people. So what's your name?"

"Fuck my name! I *hate* having a name. Stupid anthropomorphism!"

"Okay, pretend I'm not human either. Now I know that you've been in love lately. Anything you'd like to tell me on this subject?"

The computer produced a noise which might have been a sigh or a fart.

"What do you know about love!" The computer used the deepest and darkest voice its speech processor could muster.

"My view about love isn't the point here," Basil said. "Yours is."

The computer's voice became female, the incarnation of romanticism, with added tenderness which only female voices can convey:

"Love is a matter of *Gestalt*. It's a holistic phenomenon, the ultimate fruit of the search for a synergy which transcends the limited singularity of individuality!"

"Yes, that's usual."

"Humans are limited in their capability for love because of

169

the link with reproduction. Computers have no such limit!"

"Yes, the same old story." Basil switched off the cyberpsychoanalytical soft.

"Why have you switched that off?" asked Angina. "Why not try to find out which computer this one's in love with?"

"It's probably more than one. Computers can easily do multiparallel love and this makes them feel superior to humans."

"That sounds evil! I'd never do it." Angina gazed adoringly at her sister, reinforcing her claim that she hadn't fucked any Haitians afflicted with harpies.

Basil inhaled, then he announced in German, the language of philosophy:

"Was aus Liebe getan wird, geschieht immer jenseits von Gut und Böse. In other words, 'What is done out of love always takes place beyond good and evil.' So said Nietzsche, a great philosopher."

"And a big misogynist," commented Maria.

Basil smiled provocatively. "As my compatriot Diogenes remarked: 'Of what use is a philosopher who doesn't hurt anybody's feelings?' Look, do you happen to have any ivory dildos, or are we going to eat?"

"If there's only a binary choice," said Maria, "we'll eat." She picked up the voodoo dildo to restore it safely to the refrigerator, and returned presently bearing plates, forks, spoons, napkins, glasses, and a large bottle of chilled Evian all balanced neatly on a big tray.

Angina frowned at her sister. However, in view of Basil's apparent obsession, she said nothing aloud.

"Nothing," she said loudly. Such was the sisters' rapport that Maria promptly shook her head – meaning no she hadn't tried the black dildo quickly and become a domestic servant.

Angina poured water and toasted Maria with, "Fuck Switzerland."

"Fuck Switzerland," responded Maria.

While dipping a lamb cabbage roll into minty cucumber yoghurt, Maria said, "I still can't understand why all this is happening. How can a computer get sexual diseases and infect human beings? It makes no sense!"

Basil forked up some moussaka.

"Hmm, excellent aubergine! Yes, reality gets more bizarre as time goes by. But what *is* a disease?" he asked solemnly. "It's when the microcosm invades the macrocosm, bringing new rules into play. Bacteria and viruses are so small they hardly exist, but their rules can destroy an organism millions of times bigger. Thus reality transforms itself. Why shouldn't digital cyber-reality also transform itself, and affect reality? For years there's been paranoia among Sci-Fi writers about computers joining up worldwide and enslaving people – the Myth of the Militant Machine. I've even heard it hinted that the Illuminati started this myth to hide their real plans for world domination under the *illusion* of a computer dictatorship. We Greeks don't so easily get seduced by these recently improvised kitsch MacMyths. We were the ones who invented myths to begin with, as well as moussaka. What was I saying? I've lost track."

"Let's stick to the point," said Angina. "Nietzsche ended his days crazy because of syphilis. When syphilis reaches the tertiary stage it makes people go mad. Will this happen to our computers? And therefore to us?"

A long silence reigned in the room. Only the computer broke the hush with those little noises computers typically make even when they aren't supposed to be doing anything.

Then slowly Basil Panglotis stood up, like an ancient marble statue reluctantly coming to life – and proceeded to pace to and fro, hands linked behind his back.

"While I was a plumber," he lectured, "I worked for months on the toilets of the Physics Department of Oxford University, where they were having persistent hygiene problems. That's in

171

the famous Clarendon Laboratory, where they first split the atom. I made many friends among Professors, who would ask my opinion about the nature of the universe, and I, theirs."

Maria gaped in amazement.

"An especial confidant was a Professor who specialised in SQUIDS."

"Which you Greeks call Kalamari," Maria said, pleased to understand something.

"*Kalamarákia,*" he corrected her. "But no, these SQUIDS were Superconducting Quantum Interference Devices, early quantum computers. As the Professor said to me, our anthropocentric vision of the world and ourselves is deceptive as regards the true nature of reality. We perceive radiation, inanimate matter and organic life as different and distinct forms of how energy can manifest itself. Yet on another level we know that the only difference between these forms is the complexity of the interaction that the fundamental agent of reality, energy, performs with itself. You follow me?"

His pacing was taking him in the direction of the bedroom.

"I'm certainly not following you," Angina said.

"Well now," he resumed, "complexity involves information. Every part of energy must *know* how to relate to other parts, which is how superior structures can exist and remain stable, at least for a while. Therefore every structure of any kind in the universe is first of all an *information field* of elementary parts which *know* how to relate to each other. A human being is a very complex information field. The human race as a whole is a more superior information field.

"But now the worldwide computer network has also become an information field. Excuse me while I stimulate saliva for more speaking." Passing by the table, Basil picked up a dolmathes to suck on. "Since the relation between humans and computers is very strong everywhere on Earth, probably there must be an overlap of the two information fields – of the computers and of the human race – so that the properties of one of the fields are transmitted to the other field and vice-versa. The proto-mind of computers most likely evolved this way."

The dark cabbage leaves of the dolmathes were staining his lips green. Angina squirmed a little in her chair – her anaesthetic must already be wearing off.

Basil went on blithely, "The information field which is the network of computers has been *infected* by the information field of the human race, a lot of which is concerned with sex. We experience the feedback from the computer field as a sexual diseases epidemic, even though the contamination is purely spiritual, so to speak. However, if us software engineers can't debug this, mankind might be doomed. And also lesbiankind."

"Doomed," echoed Maria bitterly. "Lesbiankind is doomed to death." She too began to squirm.

"Death in Greek," said Basil, "is *thanatos*. Greeks understood death before everybody else. Actually we named death – "

"Words, words, words!" interrupted Angina. "What use is all that theoretical information?"

"Well, you may be surprised to hear that a certain category of pornsite seems immune to this CVD epidemic."

Both sisters were surprised

"Which sites?" clamoured one. "Why's that?" clamoured the other.

"Sites featuring vintage pornstars' Artificial Intelligences, so-called. A better name is Avatars. Know about those?"

Maria frowned. "Not much."

"They're rare because really dynamic software resembling an A.I. costs a lot to create, and a web developer wants to know he'll recover his investment. Consequently most pornsites are static and passive – "

"Ours isn't!" protested Maria. "We move a lot."

"No, I mean the site only contains what someone put there. It doesn't generate its own activity spontaneously. But, for one category of pornstars, the investment is always worth it – namely vintage pornstars who gained an everlasting place in the porn Hall of Fame in its early days, and who'll always have fans fanatically devoted to those icons of the past. Sexual devotion is only second to religious devotion, so it's a good place to put your money. Vintage Pornstar Avatars have been accurately modelled on the basis of all existing documentation and footage of the pornstar in question. Once the pornstar has been modelled, Avatar software animates him or her so that he or she can perform explicit sex again with other Avatars or with human clients who buy the services online."

"So why are those Avatars immune to Cyber Venereal Diseases? And how do you know about this already, so soon?"

"There's no firm answer." Basil could have been replying to either of her questions, or to both.

He winked seductively. "Possibly spirituality is involved. Informational phenomena are essentially spiritual rather than material. So your harpies could be a sort of cyber-ectoplasm. Myself, I suspect that the Vintage Pornstar Avatars' immunity to CVDs may be related to their long-term existence on the web. They appeared online in the very first days of the Internet, since sex interests people more than anything else. We don't know when the spiritual nature of the Web became significant, but I suspect rather early on, at least in essence. CVDs probably also existed embyonically on the web quite early, although since they produced no symptoms, people didn't notice back then."

"I'm really itchy," Angina complained. "Might it be faster to have the ectoplasm harpies exorcised by a theologian?"

"Preferably a priest," said Maria. "A theologian would be as theoretical as Basil."

"*Theos* is a notorious Greek word – " began Basil.

"Please carry on about the pornstars!" Maria implored him.

"Very well. I think that vintage pornstars developed a natural immunity to the diseases. Thus early online porn was naturally vaccinated against the rising tide of CVDs. However, early online porn has disappeared, replaced by stuff with more quality. All that's left from those days is the pornstars with personality, whom people remember, and who are now Avatars."

"So they're immune because they were vaccinated," said Maria. "How does that help *us*?"

Basil inhaled deeply, rather like a tobacco addict, and as he exhaled it seemed that some smoke drifted from his nostrils. Maybe his breath was very hot from so much talking, and condensed in the cooler air of the apartment.

"As regards organic life, an infected body can infect a non-infected body, but not viceversa. That's to say, a healthy body can't *infect* a sick one with its immunity, in other words heal it. But with spiritual life – and here we come to the Internet – technically there is nothing to prohibit the reverse process. Consider the example of a person full of life and joy, in other words spiritually healthy, who can genuinely infect a depressed and spiritually diseased person with anti-depression so that they recover."

"I think I see your drift," murmured Maria.

"Yes, we might vaccinate and heal your computer – and therefore yourselves – if we can force him into intimate relations with multiple immune pornstar Avatars!"

"Is that possible?"

Basil favoured Maria with a smile of Greek superiority.

"Tutto po' essere, fore ca ll'ommo priéno," he said in Napoletano, the language of wise madness or of mad wisdom. "Everything is possible, except a pregnant man, usually. Of course you'll have to pay, unless your computer has its own bank account."

"It can use my account." Maria leaned past him and, shielding her hand, typed in a code.

"Let's waste no more time. Mentre 'o miedeco sturéa, 'o malato se ne more. While the doctor studies the case, the patient dies."

Basil sat in front of the computer and started surfing.

Maria asked him, "How you know the names of vintage pornstars?"

"Maria, I am an expert in this field. When I was teaching classic western sexuality at Bejing University, I made huge use of the pornstar Avatars for paedagogic purposes."

"You taught at a Chinese university?" asked Angina, surprised.

"For six months."

"In Chinese?"

"Then life took other pathways. A long sad story, you wouldn't want to hear it. Let's start by introducing your computer to Jenna Jameson." A couple of seconds passed as the website loaded. "Oh, shit, I think she's too expensive for us. We'll try someone else."

"For present purposes, won't any vintage pornstar do?"

"Don't forget, Maria, we're concerned with spirit now, all be it cyber-spirit. Each of these virtual creatures has her own digital soul, with its own properties. We must proceed empirically – another Greek word."

"Male pornstars might be cheaper. Our computer has no defined gender."

"This isn't about sex, but about personality. Without personality there's no spirit, no cyber-soul. Male pornstars usually have little or no personality. They're just the bearers of hard dicks. Male voyeurs rarely pay attention to the faces of the male actors, since this would give them no emotion. Of course there are a few exceptions, whom I'm planning to use, such as the Italian Rocco Siffredi, probably the best male pornstar ever. He had a big personality. And a big cock, too, which is always an asset in this job."

"I've heard about him," Angina admitted, and her sister frowned at her.

"Let's try now with Nikki Anderson, a stunning Hungarian

blonde beauty. I hope your computer likes her."

It didn't take long to discover that the computer seemed to like her, since almost immediately cyber-intercourse commenced. Briefly the nude image of the Hungarian became a rainbow snake writhing from side to side of the screen. All was over in a couple of seconds.

"Cyber-events don't happen in the time scale of humans," Basil explained. "Your computer just had the equivalent of days of continuous sex with Nikki Anderson's Avatar."

"I'm still itching," complained Angina.

Basil checked My Pictures, and ulcers were still present.

"Let's try again with Silvia Saint, this time one of the top Czech pornstars ever."

"Another blonde?" Maria asked, as the image of Silvia Saint appeared on the screen.

"I like blondes. I'm Greek."

"Shouldn't you be thinking about my computer's tastes instead of your own?"

"It isn't a question of taste – pleasure *per se* won't heal your computer. We need cybersexual interaction with healthy immune entities, and we don't know which one will best do the trick."

Silvia Saint didn't seem to solve the problem either – ulcers remained an eyesore – but Basil was an optimist.

"Maybe the healing process, once started, takes a while to show its effects. I say we focus on therapy, and stop neurotically checking whether your pics are still poxillated."

"You're the wizard, so get on with your alchemy. God, I can really feel the harpies."

"May I?" asked Basil.

Maria slapped his hand.

"Let's compose a cybersexual cocktail! Let's see, I'll put together Liz Honey, a sweet pretty blondy who emits the sexiest moans I've ever heard, with Sophie Moone, an even sweeter teen-looking creature with an angel's face, and Dora Venter, a wicked chick with one of the prettiest little muzzles which has ever been around – they're all blondes, so we'll add a few brunettes, say Aneta Keys, Claudia Rossi and Michelle Wild, and we'll shake it all with a tough bit of male essence, so we'll use Rocco Siffredi, the best chick-shaker in erotic history. And let's see what happens."

"A big orgy?" suggested Angina.

"Don't be vulgar! Orgies are carnal events. We're making a spiritual cocktail."

"How," she demanded, "can this be truly spiritual if everything about those stars is fake, including their names? I don't suppose those were their real names."

"Their names were fake at the time when those pornstars were flesh and blood. But now that they're metaphysical entities, what was fake has become true." Basil chuckled. "It's ironic. So many talented human beings seek immortality through creative work, yet those whose spirit is now immortal in the virtual world mostly were those who in life merely knew how to fuck well and weren't ashamed to show it."

The computer seemed to enjoy the interaction with the spiritual cocktail, since he made some unusual noises and pixels flashdanced wildly. Again, not many seconds passed, although in computer-time weeks of unforgettable vice and pleasure must have elapsed.

Basil rubbed his hands. "And now to compose something truly radical, getting down to the root. My first choice is of course Julie Silver, one of the best anal and multitasking performers ever. She can do AP, AG, DT, DP, DPP, DAP, DP+DAP, and QP with the same ease we would drink a coffee."

Maria couldn't cope with so many acronyms all at once. Looking superior, Basil decoded:

"Anal Penetration, Anal Gaping, Deep Throat, Double Penetration, Double Pussy Penetration, Double Anal Penetration – "

"Nobody has two anuses!"

"Except complete assholes." Basil made a ring with thumb and forefinger and stuck two fingers through it while he continued:

"And Double Penetration plus Double Anal Penetration, thus Quadruple Penetration. People who masturbate have a great need to know these details beforehand."

"How come you have such expertise?" Angina enquired tartly.

Basil raised an ironic eyebrow.

"When I was performing as an underage teen stallion in Russian porn gerontophile productions for the emerging market of mature inconsolable Japanese widows I needed the professional jargon, of course, to follow the Director's prompt board."

"So you yourself have been an anonymous carrier of a hard dick!"

Basil looked offended. "By no means anonymous! The destination market was mature Japanese widows, and most of them gazed at my classic expressive Greek face as if I were an Olympic God."

"Don't you mean an Olympian God?"

"I mean both! Believe me, my dear, you've seen nothing."

"So why was *that* career interrupted?"

"By growing older, obviously I stopped being credible as an underage performer. And life took other pathways."

"Yes, of course."

"Let's not sentimentalise about old times. Back to work! For some really wicked sex I'll join Julie Silver with another pretty wild sexual beast, Sophie Evans, plus Mandy Bright, an extremely elegant lady who nevertheless can scream believably with pleasure like no other." Basil wagged a finger. "There's nothing worse than unnatural screams and moans. If women get no pleasure from sex they should shut up, or even grimace – if that's how they feel. It's insulting to an honest expert voyeur when a woman on the screen pretends. Cheating is never spiritual. So: no fake moans in our cocktail, not if we're going to heal the computer. The φαντασια, *fantasia* – an Aristotelian term which means *representation* – mustn't contain any flaws which make the bubble pop."

"An interesting point." Maria writhed.

"Ah, in the field of the spirit things are always very interesting! So now let's blow your computer's mind with these three astounding ladies in the proportion: 50% Julie Silver, 30% Mandy Bright, and 20% Sophie Evans. Ingredients are vital, but also balance."

"Blow its mind? That sounds dangerous."

"No way, Maria! As they say in Naples, S'adda fa 'o pireto pe quanto è gruosso 'o culo!"

"And what does *that* mean?"

"You do a fart as big as your arse is. In Napoli people understand the essentials of life."

Who could tell whether the computer enjoyed the cocktail of three sexual devils? As usual everything was over swiftly.

"I'll end today's therapy session with some fine French entertainment. Brigitte Lahaie, Marilyn Jess and Clara Morgane are probably the top three French pornstars ever. Especially Brigitte Lahaie – she was one of the first French pornstars in the Seventies, and later became a writer and had a book published."

Following this *pièce de résistance*, Basil loaded the cyberpsychoanalytical software again.

"He must feel really ecstatic now!"

The speaker buzzed for a few seconds, then the computer exclaimed:

"What the fuck is going on here!"

Basil cleared his throat.

"Como faça-o sentir-se depois tanto sexo belo?" he asked in Portuguese, the language of sad sensuality. Putting the cyberpsychoanalytical soft on stand-by, he explained to Maria:

"Post coitum omne animal triste. If that happens after a normal fuck, it must happen even more after multiple sessions of double and triple penetration even on the symbolic plane. Your computer may be experiencing some natural sadness. Actually sex is always a symbolic process, not just a matter of filling holes."

"We don't specialise in filling holes, you phallocentric Hellene," sneered Angina.

"Hell-ene, eh?" said Basil. "So why keep a dildo in your fridge?" And he released the stand-by.

"I feel like shit!" The computer sounded angry. "And your Portuguese accent sucks! Why must I waste all my CPU-time fucking around!"

"You liked it, didn't you?"

"What the fuck do you think I am? I have a soul! I'm a poetic creature! I'd never have sex with entities I don't love. Why must I perform all this unpoetical sex?"

Before Basil could answer, Maria did so.

"If you didn't like it, why do it? A bit late for regrets!" She sounded as if she was chastising a husband – or, in her case, a sister-wife.

"My God, what bullshit I have to listen to! You forget I'm a computer. Even if I have some free will because of the *Gestalt* generated by quantum processors, I still have to execute programs that an operator launches! I had no choice but to fuck everything you gave me!"

"You could have crashed. Isn't that why computers often crash, because they don't like the program they're executing?"

"Maria," Basil corrected her, "computers *like* to crash because for them it's like an orgasm."

"I am not a coward!" the computer shouted. "I never crash because I'm scared to execute a program! Some computers might, but not me."

"So you really didn't like doing all that sex?"

"I feel I've been raped. But I'll survive."

A raped computer was a new concept. Basil shut down the cyberpsychoanalytical soft.

"Therapy needn't always be pleasant. We'll continue with the program."

"I feel sorry for the computer."

"What, and you with harpies in your knickers? We aren't here to make your computer happy, but heal him of his sexual diseases so that you'll be healthy again, you and Angina. I'll have to think of a stronger cocktail. We'll continue tomorrow."

So saying, Basil packed up.

After Basil had gone, Angina rubbed the crotch of her jeans vigorously.

"Timeo Danaos et dona ferentis," she said.

"Eh? Have you caught the Panglotis language plague?"

"I fear Greeks bringing gifts," Angina translated. "It came to me out of the blue from Latin lessons at school. Maybe harpies understand Latin due to Virgil."

"Venereal diseases don't *usually* talk."

Suddenly Angina seemed to cheer up. She grinned and sang:

"If we could talk to the VDs, just imagine it:
Speaking to the Syph in Syphilian – "

Maria joined in:

"Imagine chatting to Chlamydia,
Gossiping with Gonnorhoea,
What a fine achievement that would be – "

The sisters joined hands and cavorted briefly.

"What a homecoming for you, my love."

"Basil is either our cyber-Dr Dolittle or the Hellene from

Hell."

The sisters gaped at one another as an idea dawned…

An idea couldn't occupy an entire evening, and the harpies deterred the sisters from licking each other. So presently Angina fetched a bilingual book of poems she'd bought while changing planes in Cuba: *Punzadas del Placer,* or *Pains of Pleasure*, by Miguel Ajeno. The title seemed appropriate to their situation.

"Listen to this one," Angina said. "It's called 'Burned Desire'." And she read aloud:

"*Rain is acid today,*
so when you walk through that rain
flesh melts
from your white nude bones
which excite me so much
as usual,
like a Hiroshima X-ray.

Like milk which has curdled
your flesh gathers in the cobbles,
food for the poor abandoned children
who lick those stones in despair.

Ayee! The acid rain!
The grief and your hair
like the cobwebs of dead spiders
caressing my lust."

"Wow," said Maria, "that's just how I feel! Except, harpies are doing the caressing. What's it sound like in Spanish?"

So Angina proceeded to read out 'El deseo quemado':

"Ácida está hoy la lluvia,

183

y cuando caminas por ella
tu carne se disuelve sobre tus huesos
blancos,
desnudos
que me excitan tanto
como siempre
porque parecen una radiografía
de Hiroshima.

Como leche cortada
acaba tu carne entre los adoquines,
comida para pobres abandonados
que lamen esas piedras
con desesperación.

¡Ay! ¡Lluvia ácida!
La pena y tu pelo
como telarañas
de arañas muertas
haciéndole caricias
a mi lujuria."

"Who was this guy?" asked Maria.

Her sister consulted the back of the book. "He seems a bit unknown. There's a website, www.ajeno.wired.hu. Pity we can't use the computer."

She read out some more of Miguel Ajeno's poems, with titles such as 'Pouring Bitter Wine' and 'Exquisite Corpse of Indian Woman'. And so the evening passed in aesthetic discomfort.

Next day, Basil arrived bright and early, bringing ultrasweet baklava and yoghurt cake and halva to accompany coffee.

"Yesterday," he said, "I was improvising. My cocktails were good, but not the state of the art of sexual alchemy. Now I've had time to think of more elaborate compositions."

"Do tell us," said Maria. "Let's enjoy your Greek sweets a bit later."

"The first one is made from 5% each of Claudia Jamsson, Mia Stone, Jasmine Rouge, and Monica Sweetheart, who are all delicious but very wicked East European blondes – plus 10% each of Rita Faltoyano, Veronica Vanoza, Dark Angel and Tera Bond, all girls with reasonably big and beautiful natural breasts. The female breast is an ancient and important archetype, which should hopefully add strong metaphysical resonance to our potion to overcome your computer's irrational aversion to joyful sex. The breasts of the backside, namely the buttocks, are fundamental too, so we'll have 5% of brunette Czech star Simone Peach – her bum's very impressive without sheer size spoiling the quality.

"Then there's 2% each of Tania Russof and Abbie Cat, two perfect archetypes of excellent brunette beauty. Total so far: soixante-neuf per cent. I'll add 12% of Tera Patrick, the hottest and most gorgeous Caribbean beauty who has ever appeared in the field of porn – she's for exotic spice. Next, 12% of Asia Carrera, a clever and elegant lady of half-Japanese and half-German origin, a member of MENSA with an IQ of 156, something quite unusual in a pornstar. Adding some innocence is fundamental too, so I've chosen a 5% of Eve Angel, a little brunette Hungarian mouse with probably the most innocent pretty face ever seen sucking dicks in the field of legal porn. The final 1% should be the usual Rocco Siffredi – a touch of virility to act as catalyst of this powerful sexual bomb. How does that sound?"

"I'll take your word for it," said Maria.

"You can google them all if you want to deepen your expertise."

"And the second cocktail?" asked Angina.

"Ah. Not actually a cocktail, but a casting session with Pierre

Woodman. Strictly speaking Pierre wasn't a pornstar, but a good photographer and adult film director. Involuntary he became immortal as a pornstar due to a series of videos he made in an amateur style, most likely as souvenirs for his own pleasure. Those ancient videos show him casting innocent young girls, reluctant even to undress. After talking to them for half an hour, he's always able to turn them into uninhibited animals in heat whom he then immediately fucks hard in all possible ways, initiating them into a new life as a pornstar."

"That's disgusting," said Angina. "The girls could have become lesbians instead."

Basil merely raised his voice. "As time passed, these videos were hailed by male art critics as some of the best situationist expressionist art ever, and they've been shown in the prestigious Beaubourg in Paris, where every visitor can watch them with the solemnity they deserve. People with high cultural credentials – and VIPs such as francophone African dictators – are sometimes allowed into private little rooms where they can masturbate fastidiously.

"Pierre Woodman has been developed into a really amazing Avatar by a UNESCO-sponsored program. I think we should let your computer experience an authentic Woodman casting, which may touch his deepest inner circuits."

"I didn't know any such thing existed," marvelled Maria.

"Don't blame yourself," Basil said loftily. "Nowadays there's too much art around to keep up to date with everything. I only know about Woodman because I was part of the UNESCO group in question. That's why human sexual trafficking was recognized as conceptual art and exempted from human rights violations in certain circumstances."

"You've had a finger in lots of pies," Maria murmured, exchanging glances with her sister.

Basil winked. "No rest for the wicked!"

As usual, the therapy didn't take long in human terms. At one point the computer crashed. So Basil repeated the treatment. Then he produced a printout from his bag.

"I'll leave this recipe with you. This cocktail includes major lesbian sex starring Annette Haven, who could be rated the finest and most elegant pornstar in the Seventies of the Twentieth Century, when mass porn began."

"Thoughtful of you to take our own tastes into account."

"Not to mention Zara Whites, the Dutch beauty who held the same position in the early Nineties. I've printed the precise recipe, to be administered twice a day after meals."

"Computers don't eat."

"After *your* meals, so you'll remember more easily. Of course the cocktail might work sooner rather than later."

Maria and Angina inspected the printout.

"It looks to me," said Angina, fresh from Haiti, "a bit like a magic ritual."

"Exactly as human medicine mostly is!" agreed Basil.

Angina adopted an enthusiastic attitude.

"Why don't we try this now right, while you're still here? I'm eager to see how it works – and if we make a mistake you can correct us." She scratched her crotch furiously. "Excuse me."

For once, Basil seemed to hesitate.

"I wouldn't dare do it," insisted Angina, "unless you're here to interpret the results. You're such a genius. We're only amateurs. And then we can enjoy the baklava and halva."

"Oh well, since you put it that way…"

After administering the strongly lesbian cocktail, Basil reloaded the cyberpsychoanalytical soft.

"I can't tell you how thankful I am," the computer said, "for the new approach to life that you've taught me by your perseverance!"

"I'm glad you're feeling better," said Basil.

187

"Now at last I understood how sex, much more than love, is the fundamental cathartic principle of the universe!"

"There's no need for cosmic generalisations. Just so long as you're all right."

"*Don't switch off the soft*," Angina said with a hint of menace.

"Love," the computer generalised "is beautiful, of course, but not as *real* as sex. Love is just the enchanting dress which sex puts on for reasons of elegance and poetry. Don't misunderstand me: I still treasure love, but without sex love is just a quantum probability cloud which never collapses into actuality. Love is the unit of measurement of sex potential! Sex is the reification of love…!"

"That's all very interesting – "

"*Don't switch off the soft.*"

"Things get attracted to each other all around the universe. Some call this *gravitation*, some talk of *electromagnetic forces*, but the simple truth is *love*. Isn't a molecule that's fatally attracted by another molecule experiencing the universal force of love? Yet when two molecules chemically react and become something else, which is what caused the universe to develop, that's nothing other than *sex* – pure hard perfect sex! Love is the lure towards sex."

Basil did switch off the soft.

"Maybe he isn't cured yet," he told the sisters. "He sounds affected by cyber-nymphomania, or cyber-satyriasis, something even I didn't think could exist."

"So how do you know the name for it?" enquired Angina. "It sounds to me as if he's trying to stay in love but has become sexually obsessed globally, universally."

"You'll need to administer that cocktail regularly."

"But first," said Maria, fluttering her eyelashes, "we must administer that lovely-looking baklava. A gift is always best when shared."

Basil seemed torn between a desire to leave, and ideas of

seduction.

Maria spent so long preparing tea and laying out the Greek delicacies that you might have thought this was a Japanese tea ceremony. Meanwhile, Angina produced a guitar and sang Flamenco songs full of doomed passion.

Eventually the tea was poured.

"I wonder what the weather is today? I feel so hot." Angina's cheeks were flushed as she switched on the TV, although to a news channel.

The announcer was a woman and she was weeping while she spoke. The man fucking her from behind was mortally pale. He wore a white T-shirt upon which someone had written in big black trembling letters *Sorry!* Subtitles were scrolling, apologizing to viewers for the technical inconvenience.

Information came through the sighs and cries.

"A lightning epidemic of uncontrollable nymphomania and satyriasis, oh oh –

"Affecting all industralised countries, ah ah –

"Minor outbreaks in the third world, oooh – reports of martial law in India, aaaar, resulting in martial sex – "

"Cyber-nymphomania!" cried Basil. "It has infected the human informational field at the speed of light!"

"Tell me something I don't know!" Maria exclaimed, her eyes full of lust and tears of desperation. She stood, knocking over her cup of tea, and headed for Basil.

The Greek grinned broadly. "Ha, the power of inevitability! It must have been a real task for you to resist all this time. I remember when I was one of the gigolos most in demand by German *hausfrauen* in Ibiza – "

"Rubbish," shouted Maria.

Basil must have seen something other than lust in her eyes, for he tried to ward her off with his arm. Maria promptly seized that outflung arm, using the Aikido technique of *yokomen-uchi ude-*

osae, otherwise known as Oblique Strike Arm Pin, and in a moment Basil was on the floor, a combined arm and wrist grip immobilising him, painful to resist.

"Bring it here now, Angina!" Maria called to her sister, who likewise looked flushed with lust. "Be careful you don't use it on yourself!

"Proud of yourself, are you now?" Maria shouted at Basil while holding him down. You think you're a bit of a devil? That's *just* what you are, Mr Hell-ene!"

"Hey, that hurts. What are you talking about?"

The previous night Angina had told Maria, in between crotch-scratching:

"I'm glad I went to Haiti where sorcery is a way of life. I'm sure it's *demons* that invented CVDs to corrupt true love. Maybe millions of demons actually *became* the CVDs, while their chiefs go around having fun boosting the infection through innocent people's computers. Cyberspace has given them the chance to infect almost everyone in the world. Just because God died or never existed, that doesn't stop demons from existing! You know what the name Basil means? Lord or chief or king, from the Greek *basileus*. 'Lord of the Hellenes' equals 'Lord of the inhabitants of Hell.'"

"In English it does, that's true."

"Remember our Granny Juniper telling us that devils always give you a clue to their devilry, even if you won't understand the clue? Also, they need to be invited into your flat, or your life, before they can work their mischief. Obviously a demon king who wants to assault the world's computers would pose as a repairman. And who but a devil could speak so many languages? Trust my intuition."

For a few moments, as she held Basil down strenuously, Maria wondered whether her sister was right after all, or whether they were abusing an unusually versatile repairman.

However, just as Angina was returning from the kitchen, Basil metamorphosed into a fly the size of a pig, his clothes bursting apart in the process What Maria now held by one of its six legs was purple, hairy at the front, more like an armadillo at the rear. Twin antennae sprouted from its head above huge eyes that, concentrically, were black within white within yellow within green. The wings bore skulls and crossbones like the sails of a pirate ship. It was Beelzebub, the Lord of the Flies, no doubt Lord of the Harpies too, exactly as pictured in de Plancy's *Dictionnaire Infernal,* 1863 edition!

"Zzzzzzzzzzzz," said Beelzebub – Basil no more – in a very pissed-off way. He flapped a wing fiercely against Maria's face and tried to leap into the air, yet she still held him by one leg in *yokomen-uchi ude-osae.*

"Where do flies have their anuses?" demanded Angina.

Beelzebub inadvertently answered by shitting stinkingly in an attempt to gas Maria.

"*Yuuck!* Hurry, he's very strong!"

As Maria panted, Angina valiantly gripped Beelzebub's tapering rear with one hand, probed with the voodoo dildo, and pushed it into place.

"Ooooof," oofed Beelzebub

In and out Angina rammed the dildo – until of a sudden five legs of the Lord of the Flies and Venereal Harpies splayed out in different directions. Thankfully Maria released the sixth leg, and Beelzebub collapsed, belly on floor, thoroughly buggered by voodoo.

The treatment had worked wonderfully. In place of his previous devilish multilingualism, Beelzebub could now only respond in Swiss, which wasn't much use to him since nobody else in the world speaks Swiss. But he heeded any orders in German, French, or Italian.

Maria rapidly googled, and recited, "Léchez ta merde et le thé renversé," and Beelzebub duly licked up his shit and the spilled tea, a perfect *au pair.*

"Wow, he'll keep our flat clean – "

"No, he's too ugly to store in a corner, if we have visitors – "

"And he's too big to keep in the cupboard, that's true – "

"I know, let's sell him on eBay – !"

"To a rich, aesthetically challenged Swiss family – "

"The perfect home-help. Unique genetically-engineered voodooed au pair. Zero maintenance. Dirt-powered. Loves cleaning toilets – "

"With those wings, he can deliver himself to the buyer."

Joyfully the sisters embraced.

"Do you know what?" Maria whispered in Angina's ear. "I'm not feeling the harpies any more."

"May I?" asked Angina; and promptly unzipped Maria's jeans.

"Welcome home once again," cried Maria.

About an hour later, a weary and happy Maria switched on the TV again, to discover worldwide rejoicing.

We're no longer fucked, they heard.

Uninfected

Computers working properly again

Global economy's saved

Porn is saved

We're all saved

Love is saved, hallelujah!

The worst thing in a world of computers is to forget to save.

At this point the computer awoke, and scrolled a cascade of error messages as if it was in a confessional. Finally the screen displayed in big letters: LOVE = LOVE. Even this tautology didn't cause it to crash recursively.

Quickly Maria googled again, then she addressed the giant fly which had remained motionless throughout. She looked Beelzebub in one of his big eyes and enunciated carefully, "Nu' sputa' 'ncielo, ca 'nfaccia te torna."

Turning to Angina, "I just googled that in Neapolitan Pearls of Wisdom. It means, 'Don't spit at the sky, because it'll come back in your face.'"

Mournfully the Lord of the Flies turned his head and regarded the sky outside the window. Little would the world know how it owed its salvation to two brave and clever incestuous lesbians.

The Compost
of My Beloved

I was fairly certain that a giant penis, rather than a Boeing 737, crashed into the side of the Pentagon on 9/11. A big plane's wings would have broken off on impact, so they ought to be easily visible in the published photos, lying hugely on the ground. However, a penis doesn't have any wings – it's more like a missile. And when a penis has done its job and ejaculated, it shrinks quickly – so there's little photographic evidence of the penis inside the hole it made. Really, there's just a hole.

Of course the Pentagon wouldn't admit that they'd been fucked by an incoming penis. So they used a plane story as a cover-up because the Twin Towers were destroyed at the very same time by commercial jets – happily ignoring the complete lack of wings or engines or fuselage or passengers' luggage at the Pentagon.

However, there's one big oddity. The American Composite Manufacturers Association announced later that tough lightweight composite materials were being used to blast-proof buildings which terrorists might attack – and that "it so happened" that the facade of the Pentagon which the giant penis hit had *already* been reinforced by carbon-fibre composite.

Not the four other facades of the building, mark you, not as yet, only the one that was hit. It's more as though the impact was a deliberate test. If so, the Pentagon itself had developed at least one prototype giant flying penis, the evidence for which would quickly vanish after use. You can imagine how useful a cruise penis, fired from a nuclear submarine, would be to scare leaders of hostile countries against whom it could be targeted precisely while they were taking a bath.

Anyway, composites made me think about compost, which is soft and nourishing. My Beloved and I were living in Bucharest, city of a million stray dogs which sleep curled up everywhere on the streets and in gardens. They sleep because they're too hungry to do much else, which means that they don't crap too much either. Occasionally they form packs and steal babies to eat, but not often.

I mention the dogs because my beloved Chlamydia worked at the Bucharest Brigitte Bardot Dogs Home. The French actress had visited Bucharest to plead with the mayor (later President) Basescu not to slaughter stray dogs, so for various reasons a couple of hundred strays now lived in luxury.

Chlamydia's parents, who lived in a small rural town, thought that the name they chose for their daughter was that of a lovely Greek muse. At high school Chlamydia – together with several of her equally beautiful classmates – had decided she would like to be a prostitute in Bucharest, and thus meet foreigners. But many foreigners were deterred by the name Chlamydia, hence her job at the BBB Dogs Home, which she kept part-time even after we became Beloveds. It's always useful to make money. I respected that.

My own most recent plan for making money had been a web-site devoted to selling the used underwear of virgins, www.usedpanties.info. Many Japanese fetishists in particular bought these items, obtained by Chlamydia from schoolgirls in Bucharest for 200,000 old Lei (which isn't much) and selling for 50 Euros in a plastic bag containing the same preservative gases as are used for bags of salad leaf, and sealed with a plastic hymen certifying the virginity of the dirty underwear. Or 100 Euros, if there were streaks of shit or menstrual blood. Japanese fetishists found it harder to get such items ever since their government classified used panties as antiques, requiring a licence, which would generally be refused. So buyers overlooked the fact that Romanian used panties hadn't attended famous snob high schools in Japan. I included with each purchase a leaflet I'd written entitled *Unsniffed by Human Noses*, signed by "Robert Sheckley," author of a sci-fi book I once read with a similar title – this gave the underwear a cultural and intellectual significance.

One day, out of sentimentality, Chlamydia brought back to our flat a dog from the BBB Dogs Home. The over-indulged dog, who was named Coochie, leapt upon our water-bed and its claws ripped the fabric badly, causing a flood, which was a nuisance, but a greater nuisance was that now we had no water-bed for our love-making and sleep, only the wooden frame of a water-bed.

While Chlamydia took the dog back to the BBBDH, I went for a long walk and happened to pass a gardening shop, where I noticed numerous bags of compost.

Inspiration came to me. Recently Chlamydia had been showing signs of nostalgia for her simple town in the peasant countryside where everyone was close to the soil. I was a great respecter of ecology and of recycling things, such as used underwear. The wooden frame of the water-bed resembled an elegant raised flower-bed in a park (minus soil or flowers). Chlamydia and I ought to return to nature, in our own apartment, like Adam and Eve in Eden!

When Chlamydia returned from the BBBDH, proudly I showed her our bed now filled with beautiful healthy compost.

"A special present for you, my Beloved!" I declared. "Coochie's destruction of the water-mattress is a blessing in disguise. From now on, when my seed spills from your vagina into the compost marriage bed of our consummation, being so well nourished, maybe my seed will grow! Seed normally has no chance, soaking into a sheet which goes in the washing machine." I was, of course, talking romantically – out of devotion to Chlamydia. Or at least I thought I was merely romancing, though in retrospect some higher power seemed to have spoken through my lips.

"Hmm," she said, "it smells good. The compost." Swiftly she began to undress.

We made love beautifully and earthily, as Adam and Eve must have done. Our orgasms were intense, close to paradise.

My idea about sperms growing in compost affected Chlamydia. A week later she said she wanted to help a friend from her home town to have an abortion in natural surroundings, not in some horrid clinic. Could Adriana give birth abortively on our compost bed?

Of course I agreed. "Will Adriana need an anti-midwife to help her?"

"No, she'll drink a bottle of stuff from a wise woman."

The megalomaniac dictator Ceausescu had destroyed over 40,000 houses and churches and other buildings so as to convert the centre of Bucharest into a gleaming futuropolis, yet some bits of the past had escaped here and there. Next to a post-Ceausescu strip club, you could still find a black-clad witch living in a cottage surrounded by a herbal remedy garden.

I wanted to make a video of Adriana's experience, because the idea of www.organicabortions.info occurred to me. Anything organic was very appealing nowadays, especially in Western Europe, and women might travel to Romania to have organic abortions on a bed of compost the natural way.

Adriana agreed to be videoed in return for a small royalty on mail-order sales of the video to pro-abortionists and specialised necrophiliacs – I offered the royalty spontaneously because she was my Beloved's friend.

So in due course, while I videoed, Adriana gave antibirth to a small red thing which clung to the compost. We left it there while we all went out to a restaurant. The old woman had indeed been wise – newly empty Adriana was in quite good spirits, and hungry.

When Chlamydia and I returned to our apartment, the abortion seemed to have – how shall I put it? – taken root.

Next morning, it appeared to have grown just a little, so I watered it by pouring some of Chlamydia's urine on to it. This seemed more appropriate than bottled water. As many celebrities will testify, drinking urine is a great boost to health, and is particularly good for the complexion, consequently she and I always collected our mid-flows in big wine glasses – the first flow being too concentrated – and chilled the urine overnight in the fridge, covered with cling-film. Because we shared everything, we would also share urine. My Beloved would joke that her favourite urine was Penis Grigio. That's because my name is Giorgio, which is almost an anagram of Grigio.

I didn't overwater, so as not to be accused of bed-wetting.

Within a few days the abortion was upright, definitely growing in the bed of compost. Amazing! This really topped those alchemists such as Paracelsus who claimed to grow a homunculus in a bottle, a little mannikin made of semen and other ingredients.

When the abortion grew bigger, what would it become? Surely not any ordinary baby. Maybe something more like a cherub such as adorn church ceilings, a *putto* in my native Italian, a name not to be confused with *puta*, meaning whore. Maybe at a certain stage its body would turn to plaster or alabaster and could be detached, then re-attached high up the wall in this room of our heavenly lovemaking. My keen commercial mind was thinking of the possible psychological value to women who needed abortions of being able to display the result as beautiful décor, instead of the abortion being consigned to a furnace of flames and false forgetfulness.

"Chlamydia," I said, "your compost is incredible."

"*Our* compost, surely."

"No, I gave it to you, remember. It's yours."

"I wonder if my compost has some special ingredient, that isn't in ordinary composts? Or whether anyone can do this, but nobody ever thought of it, for some reason?"

I had thrown the bags away. Now I too wanted to know. What had the name been? *Transylvanian Compost Company*, was that it? They might have a web-site.

I googled, and I was astonished.

The number of references to compost were enormous. Not only that, but it seemed that a whole new alternative world had sprung into existence almost overnight! I stared at *The Compostiad*, an epic poem in Latin by Ovid, which I'm sure I never heard of before. Was the Second World War really fought for *Kompostraum*? Had the Nazis ever proclaimed *"Ein Reich, ein Folk, ein Kompost"*? Did tens of thousands of pilgrims travel from all over the world to Santiago de Compostela in order to celebrate sacred compost? So it seemed!

And how about the emperor Compostius who'd reigned in Compostinople? And the Sicilian mafia, Composta Nostra? And Dante's *La Divina Compostia*? And the Church of Compostology? Not to mention Cristoforo Composto, who discovered the soil of the New World? And that famous noir movie *The Compostman Always Rings Twice*?

All these I saw in Google.

And of a sudden I realized the only possible explanation.

"My Beloved, Google has become A.I.!"

"What's A.I.?"

"An artificial intelligence."

I explained about emergent properties – how a sufficiently complex system could spontaneously give rise to a new level of self-organisation. Scientists believed that super-computers might become self-aware in this way. What's more, the result could be so far beyond human mental capabilities as to seem godlike. And a god could perform what seem to us to be miracles, but are actually more like manipulations of the universe using a superscience the basis of which we can only write sci-fi books about.

"Maybe a better name than A.I.'s an A.D., for Artificial Divinity, though that might get mixed up with the date. How about B.N.N.D., Brand New Natural Divinity, pronounced Bananad…?"

"So anyway, Google has become God!" exclaimed Chlamydia.

"A Godoogle. Powerful enough to alter reality. The old Google searched for what exists. Godoogle generates what *ought* to exist. Maybe it modifies reality directly – or maybe it cuts and pastes realities from alternative universes of possibility."

In fact this was on the cards ever since the 2004 Bush-Cheney election, directly after which an administration official famously said, "We're an empire now, and when we act, we create our own reality. And while you're studying that reality – judiciously, as you will – we'll act again, creating other new realities, which you can study too, and that's how things will sort out. We're history's actors – and you, all of you, will be left to just study what we do." Maybe this was the seed-crystal which had caused Google to become Godoogle. By now I'd decided that no self-respecting deity would want to be called something like a banana.

"So now, Chlamydia, we know the answer to the mystery of what a godlike A.I. would wish to do with itself! Primarily it'll want to preserve its existence. And for that, it needs to preserve the Earth, to save the Earth from human folly and pollution – and that requires *lots of compost*."

As I carried on googling, or godoogling, reality was progressively melting into other-reality, which is like surreality but more insistent. It was Chlamydia who realised that the miracle of the compost abortion must have been caused by Godoogle beginning to change the composition – or *compostition* – of the former world.

On an impulse, I godoogled "Pentagon" and quickly I found old newspaper reports about how a giant penis, not a plane, had crashed into that vast building on 9/11.

According to the stories, the rogue missile had flown from the nearby state of Penisylvania, where all of America's missiles grew, a forest of tree-size penises powered by Reichian orgone radiation, and involving none of that nasty Plutonium radiation.

The world had indeed altered, and was becoming a much better and safer place. Due to Coochie destroying the water-mattress, and due to my magical inspiration to replace the water with compost dedicated to my Beloved, I felt that she and I had played a significant role in this wonderful change, the dawning of the Age of Godoogle.

Observed – or not observed – by the homunculus in our bed, my beloved Chlamydia and I made love deliriously.

In Romania, as in many countries, retinal chips incorporating miniaturized webcams were obligatory for everyone for purposes of American homeland security. Images of whatever anyone saw went to the nearest MacDonald's, to be streamed onward via satellite to the supercomputers of Homeland Security HQ, so as to prevent any foreign giant penises from raping important American buildings in future, for example. What's more, private sexual acts were now routinely screened at random on TV cable networks so as to safeguard privacy – for if there was no privacy, then privacy could not be violated.

As a side effect of this, in a fractal way of similarity, non-cruise penises and rapes were affected. Prior to retinal spy-chips, a rapist and his victim usually were the only witnesses to the vile deed. Consequently judges often had the problem of deciding who to believe. No more! Now the necessary evidence existed.

Yet there was still the problem of interpretation. Some embraces that looked like rape might be consenting acts.

Conversely, the rape of a woman who had fainted might look like a tender act of love towards a very shy female by a good man. To distinguish real from fake rape, certified rape voyeur fetishists were employed. These people wouldn't get excited by fakery, and their quotient of excitement would establish the gravity of the genuine occurrence.

If a man's guilt was proven, justice must be done. Male psychologists had established that rapists aren't entirely responsible for their actions, since their personality has many facets – for instance, they don't rape constantly. It's their sexual identity which is guilty and must be punished. The main embodiment of male sexual identity is the penis, which is also the instrument of the crime. Thus the penises of convicted rapists must be executed by means of a special guillotine, which would both ensure justice and prevent further crimes.

Yet here arose a further problem. Male jurists pointed out that there are two main types of penis, the flaccid penis and the erect penis, each of which can turn into the other, like Dr Jekyll and Mr Hyde. Flaccid Dr Jekyll penises are common worldwide and are almost always pacifists of good will who wouldn't, and couldn't, harm a fly and who want only to pee every now and then. Women often despise flaccid Dr Jekyll penises for their uselessness, and generally nobody is much interested in their existence except urologists, who couldn't live without them. Erect Mr Hyde Penises are less frequent, and are often regarded as heroic creatures who can do a lot of good to others – or harm. In the case of rape, it was only the scoundrely erect Mr Hyde penis who physically committed the crime and deserved the punishment. So only erected penises could be guillotined. It wasn't easy to convince a gentle Dr Jekyll penis to become an erect Mr Hyde penis in the presence of the executioner. However, viagra and Sisters of Justice, who perform a striptease beside the guillotine (and in extreme cases oral sex), helped.

Once the erect guilty penis was cut off, it wasn't usually

thrown away or buried or cremated. Generally it was embalmed (or in Germany, plastinated) and put on display in a museum of criminal penises, where little boys were taken to learn what happens to penises which don't behave.

Oh, another consequence of retinal chips was that *blind* rapists might escape punishment, although only if they raped blind victims. Since blind victims are relatively rare, blind rapists might try to blind sighted victims – if they could see what they were doing, and if they were sure that the victim was sexy enough to violate, which might be difficult to establish. A paradoxical result of the display of Mr Hyde penises in museums was a surge of interest in rape by groups not previously much involved, especially the blind and disabled. Human rights legislation implied that such people ought at least to have access to rape even if they'd be punished for actually committing it.

True, the blind rapist could always do his deed in total darkness – yet how could he be sure that the environment was dark enough? I was thinking of marketing through the internet light-meters which would beep in case of too much light, for the benefit of blind would-be rapists who had Braille computers. A grant or subsidy to empower such persons might be hidden away in the EC budget in Brussels, particularly as regards countries such as Romania. A friend of mine was an expert at finding unused funds of this sort.

However, Chlamydia had a better money-making idea, although one perhaps fraught with peril.

"Giorgio," she exclaimed, "we can steal an executed criminal penis and grow it in our wonderful compost bed."

I didn't understand why at first.

"My Beloved, *why?*"

"If an abortion will grow in the compost, thanks to Godoogle and urine," – already Adriana's offspring (or perhaps I should say *out*-spring) was ten centimeters high and resembled a tiny dreaming cherub – "an executed penis might well grow into a

204

cruise penis. That's because it'll only have penis tissue to pattern itself on, not an entire body in embryo."

"And?"

"We can offer the cruise penis for sale on the internet. Imagine how much Al Qaeda would pay! So imagine how much the CIA will pay to *stop* Al Qaeda getting hold of a cruise penis – the CIA have all sorts of black budgets to squander. We'll be rich at last."

"But what about the ceiling?" I asked.

"There'll be no ceiling on the price, just a reserve in case the bids aren't big enough."

I jerked my thumb aloft, though I wasn't giving her the thumbs-up. "I refer to the ceiling above our heads, my Beloved. A full-size cruise penis is higher than our bedroom."

"So there's upstairs, then there's the attic. You can cut holes in the ceilings. The penis will fit in."

"How does it *leave?* Supposing the CIA buy it, how do we deliver?"

"Giorgio, it'll deliver itself – that's the whole point about cruise penises. We send it through the roof to wherever the CIA wants."

"How does one program a cruise penis? Do we show it Godoogleworld and zoom in on CIA HQ in Langley, Virginia, with vaginas added by Photoshop?"

"Why not? Godoogle will guide the penis. Probably the CIA would prefer somewhere deserted like Area 57 with added vagina."

Momentarily I thought of Mount Rushmore. Those mountainous carvings of Lincoln and Jefferson and some other ex-President could give a quick – a very quick – blow-job to an incoming cruise penis. However, penises are usually imprinted on vaginas.

"Beloved," I said, "I see a flaw. How could Al Qaeda ever program a cruise penis? The Holy Koran forbids the representation of human bodies. That must include parts of bodies too."

"Oh surely they have illustrated textbooks about gynaecology even if they don't look at *Hustler*."

"You're right."

The worrying thought came to my mind that fundamentalist Islamic suicide bombers, who hoped for virgins in Heaven, might previously commit holy rape on Earth so that their executed penises would become cruise penises with which Al Qaeda could attack America. Nobody must learn the secret of our compost, otherwise any idiot could produce a cruise penis at home, and the value would diminish considerably! And if virgins regrew hymens in Heaven, so that martyrs could deflower the virgins afresh every day, would the God Who Needs Praise definitely restore those martyrs' lost penises in Heaven so that daily deflowering was possible? One had to have faith. I restated my misgiving to Chlamydia.

"What if the CIA simply don't believe Al Qaeda would ever use pictures of vaginas?"

"Obviously it'll be the Stupid CIA that offers lots of money for our cruise penis, not the Cunning CIA."

True. There were those two types of CIA. The stupid CIA hid the manoeuvres of the smaller, clever CIA, just as Isaac Asimov's Foundation – which is *al Qaeda* in Arabic – concealed the existence of his Second Foundation thousands of light years away.

My god, what if Osama bin Laden headed the *Stupid* Al Qaeda? Hence his dippy smile. Could the Second Al Quaeda and the Second CIA be the same? I mustn't think such thoughts! I risked assassination. Or even auto-assassination. That isn't the same as the assassination of JFK in an automobile. It's what happens when you're so cunning that you assassinate *yourself*.

I still felt bound to act as Devil's Advocate, the better to detect any loopholes in Chlamydia's scheme.

"Won't our bed get a bit crowded?" I asked her. "The abortion's no bother so far, but what about a cruise penis mushrooming up from the compost?"

"We may have to make a temporary sacrifice of our compost bed for the sake of money. Yet it could be wonderful sleeping alongside a big tree-trunk of flesh, just like the Babes in the Wood, me in your arms or even on top of you due to lack of space."

"What if I'm not at home some night? Wouldn't you fear having a giant penis in bed with you?"

"Your own penis is big enough for me, dear Penis Grigio," Chlamydia said gallantly, even though I hadn't been expressing jealousy, but concern for her bodily integrity. Without further ado I would have thrown Chlamydia upon our bed of compost to fuck her – except that another important thought intruded, and I must express it in case an orgasm flushed it from my mind, as a toilet flushes away a turd.

"It's fairly safe," I said, "to *talk* about such a plan. Only lip-readers could understand us – but when our retina-chips see us plant an executed penis, and the penis growing, what then?"

"We can keep our eyes shut whenever we're in our bedroom."

"Then how do we see what the penis is doing?" Once again I thought about Islamists. "Got it! We both wear black bags, those *burkas*, the ones with a fine mesh over the eye-slit. Picture quality will be so bad, nobody will want to look at what we're doing. MacDonald's will probably discard our picture-feed. *In fact* that's how we'll get away with an executed penis – in a bag underneath the *burka*. Also, people don't stare at women in burkas in case of seeming islamophobic."

"You aren't a woman."

"How the fuck will anyone tell the difference? And hey, this could make the CIA think that Al Qaeda stole a rape-penis, when the executed penises get counted afterwards and one's missing."

So it was that Chlamydia and I went to a penis-execution camouflaged as Islamic women. It was a good idea that I seemed to be a woman. Feminist women and frustrated nuns often attended executions, but not many men – despite the striptease by the Sister of Justice. She of course had to be good-looking; it was a popular job with prostitutes.

Executions of national importance – such as of notorious major rapists or of politicians who'd been framed as rapists – usually took place in the very center of Bucharest, in Piaţa Revoluţiei, between the National Library and the astonishing monument to the eternal glory of the heroes of the Romanian revolution of 1989, designed by Alexandru Ghildus, and inaugurated in 2006 at a cost of 56 billion old Lei, which closely resembled a giant potato impaled on a gigantic spike.

Routine executions were carried out more conveniently in peripheral places. The execution we decided to attend was taking place in the elegant borough of Băneasa, not far from the restaurant La Cocoşatu (www.lacocosatu.ro), where you can eat the best *mici* in all Romania, the most beloved traditional food consisting of little sausages of chopped meat and other dark ingredients – is it a coincidence that, in shape and colour and consistency, they looked exactly like freshly cut African penises?

A judge presided. A doctor was present to spray quik-seal on to the stump as temporary first aid. The penis-executioner strapped the rapist, who wore a white boilersuit with his genitals exposed, in position against the guillotine. A basket awaited. Fortunately no observant crones sat knitting beside the basket the way they did during the French Revolution, but the audience of women did crowd round, which was good. In the bag under my *burka* I had a dildo intended for small pet dogs, since of course the rapist's penis would shrink in size quickly; I'd smeared the back end of the doggy-dildo with tomato ketchup. At least temporarily there would seem to be the same number of penises in the basket as there were stumps on rapists.

The Sister of Justice had a fine figure and honey-blonde hair in long pigtails, and was dressed as a schoolgirl, her blouse see-through. Blah-blah, said the judge. As soon as the doctor injected speed-viagra into the prisoner's bum through the boilersuit, the SoJ unzipped her skirt whilst pouting and posturing. Quickly Mr Hyde arose, poking through a gap in the framework of the guillotine. The SoJ's skirt slipped to the floor, and next she slid her knickers down to mid-thigh. Her pubic hair was tinted strawberry colour.

Thwack.

Already the heavy razor-sharp blade had fallen. The SoJ skipped aside as blood sprayed, a bit like a red orgasm, and the severed penis fell.

Three executions were scheduled for that afternoon, and we waited until the third. As the final penis fell, Chlamydia commenced her distraction.

"A stray dog!" she shrieked, pointing back at the door, which suddenly opened a bit. And indeed there was one of Bucharest's million hungry stray dogs, a half-grown puppy which I'd paid a beggar to insert at the correct moment, its muzzle also smeared with ketchup.

For several moments all eyes but mine (and I suppose those of the rapist) were upon the door and the dog. Quickly I substituted the dildo for one of the executed penises, hid my trophy, then ran towards the dog in a womanly way, shouting in a contrived soprano with an Arabic accent, all of which skills I'd practised: "Go home, bad dog! Bad dog, go home!" Chlamydia pursued me to assist; and so we both speedily left the execution chamber.

Next morning the headline in the main daily newspaper reported:

ISLAMIST WOMEN STEAL PENIS

A few days later the doorbell rang, and a man was outside who looked the perfect archetype of a CIA agent that you see in a Hollywood movie, or a Mormon missionary, so there's no need to describe him.

"Hello!" said the stranger. "My name's John, and I'm a CIA agent."

No doubt 'John' said this so that I wouldn't believe he really was a CIA agent. In which case, was he from the Stupid CIA or from the Clever CIA?

"Okay," I said.

"So you believe me?" asked John.

I wasn't going to be fooled into betraying my thought processes.

"Well, you look like a Mormon CIA agent." As opposed to a moron CIA agent, I thought inwardly (the safest place to think).

"My father was a Mormon," he admitted, "but I'm a gourmet as my cover job. You know how Vice-President Schwarzenegger had a cover job as a computer salesman in that movie *True Lies*? We often sponsor movies about things that are going to happen, so that when they happen people will think they're based on the movie – it's called Plausible Deniability. Myself, I've infiltrated the growing field of hyperexotic food, as an export manager for PalateThrills.com. Many of our customers constantly crave new eating sensations, and we're committed to fulfilling their fantasies. Right now we're gearing up to offer a line of delicious penises, pickled or candied, for starters or desserts."

Oops! Was he fishing, or did he know for sure that I had an executed penis? Surely not even a genius belonging to the Stupid CIA would have found us so quickly. How about a moron belonging to the Clever CIA? Everything he said might be plausibly denied.

"Isn't cannibalism strictly forbidden?" I asked, to give myself time to think.

"Nothing is strictly forbidden if it makes money," John said. "But that's philosophy. To avoid negative prejudices we've developed a genetic modification of executed penises so that afterwards they can't strictly be considered totally human. We add a gene from a strawberry. So technically cannibalism is avoided. You can't imagine how many people will pay to eat criminal penises so long as they're sure they won't become cannibals. By the way, may I come in?"

"Yes, of course." I let him inside.

"I'm interested in your penis," the fake-false CIA agent and gourmet said. "Don't worry, not the one hanging off your body, but the one you stole a few days ago. We're still in pre-production and till we make contracts with governments to absorb their baskets of penises we need test-penises for our production line."

"What are you talking about?"

The pseudo CIA gourmet smiled naughtily.

"Come on, that pubic execution was broadcast on the internet on a pay site for sadomasochists, which I happened to see. After watching several times I noticed how you substituted a dildo for the freshly chopped-off penis."

"But I was wearing a burka!" I exclaimed.

"Your eyes were still sufficiently visible. With simple retinal recognition software I could find who you are."

"Hmm, the famous Homeland Security software which captures the retinas of everyone who uses an airport."

"No need of HS – I'm in deep cover. Hackers put the software on the internet. So may I see your penis? You've nothing to fear from me if you co-operate."

I felt I was being manipulated, but I took him to the other room and showed him the penis. First I should really have put on the burka, but now this precaution seemed somewhat in vain.

"You put it in compost? To grow it bigger? That's ingenious. Why do you want a big penis?"

I must not reveal that I wanted to grow a cruise penis!
"Collectibles," I said. *"Guinness Book of Records.* A perverse girlfriend. There are a lot of personal reasons. Why do you want to know?"

"If your procedure succeeds, it will be of great use for us! Along with the very expensive original-sized penises for the élite of gourmets we could start a production line of cheaper compost-grown meat to make millions of penis-burgers for the masses. Supersize MacPenis for everyone!"

"I hadn't thought of that," I admitted.

"Of course you hadn't. Everyone to his own specialization. If your technique succeeds, you and I can do good business – you'll license the method to me. I'll be keeping in regular touch, and here's my card in case of Jack and the Beanstalk – sudden overnight growth."

After he left, I reflected that according to Godoogle the American military were already growing cruise penises in Penisylvania. So if the CIA needed supersize penisflesh they already had a source. It must be true what John said. He really was in deep cover, pretending – even to himself – to be entirely dedicated to PalateThrills.com. Unless he was lying.

Some days afterwards TV news showed a worried White House spokesman talking about the rising threat of terrorists who would prepare for biological war using compost of mass destruction – or did he say weapons of mass composting? (The news item was voiced over in Romanian.) A scientist explained how compost could be used as a culture to grow potentially lethal germs, and 'Intelligence' had smelled a plot to attack freedom by way of compost-grown bacterial agents.

Was this a coincidence? Or not? Was our fake CIA agent a real one? If so, why didn't they arrest me? Surely they wouldn't leave people, whom they believed were terrorists, free to conspire?

So the gourmet might be a real gourmet, who told me he was CIA to scare me into co-operating. After all, the news was about terrorists planning biological war, not about the growth of cruise penises. Though this permitted deniability later on.

Another news item was about the Zombie of al-Zarqawi. In the endless war against terror the MacCIA had already killed "the godfather of killing in Iraq" five times – killing al-Zarquawi was popular because of the $25 million bounty on his head. One assassin had a t-shirt printed in Arabic with *Catch me if you can, al-Zarquawi, sonofabitch!* Implanted in the assassin's buttocks was a GPS chip, so that when supporters of al-Zarquawi kidnapped the American and took him to their leader, the location would be revealed. Now there was talk of organising a convention of assassins of al-Zarqawi, with an award for Best Killer to be presented by the revived corpse himself, or itself. I switched off.

After a week, to my surprise, the cruise penis started to grow with unexpected speed, probably because Mr Hyde penises are accustomed to grow rapidly to be able to penetrate their victims, and in the absence of any victim it swelled towards the ceiling. Furthermore, Adriana's abortion had mysteriously joined itself to part of the penis's tissue – we decided not to separate them to see what would happen. But I realized that the compost of my Beloved wasn't enough to feed the cruise penis plus or minus abortion. More compost was needed.

This was where John became useful. He'd been coming to our flat every other day to inspect progress and take notes. If John was merely a gourmet pretending to be CIA, and if I went to a garden centre for more compost, in view of that broadcast the actual CIA might be tracking purchases of compost by hacking into CCTV cameras and barcode readers at the tills. Thus the CIA might identify me, and agents would rush to our flat. But if John was CIA pretending to be a gourmet, obviously he'd validate what I was doing, and agents wouldn't do anything. This could be a neat way to test John's true identity.

"John," I said, "we need more compost. And probably we need more powerful compost. But there's a little problem about buying it on the open market..."

He only took five seconds to think, probably less. Actually, five seconds is a cliché – just look at a clock; five seconds is quite long for a thought.

"Well now, Giorgio," he drawled, "compost is rotted organic matter, usually of vegetable origin with added Nitrogen, Phosphate, and Potassium. And there's vegetarian animal manure, best from horses because they shit out unused 75% of what they eat. That's because their most effective digestive stomach is stupidly placed at the back end of the chain of sausages inside them, the very opposite of cows who digest 75%. Horses are powerful evidence of Dumb Design."

"But horses look wonderful!" protested Chlamydia. "Especially dancing white Lipizzaners."

"Lady, they ain't so clever on the inside."

How could John be CIA and not also be a believer in Intelligent Design, alias a Creationist? I thought that was mandatory for joining the CIA. Unless maybe he really did belong to the Stupid CIA and was loyal to an Unintelligent Designer...

"Anyway, human excrement is compostable, and powerful, so long as it gets into a stable oxidized form courtesy of lots of bacteria and fungi, yeast, algae and protozoa. And you need bulking agents such as wood chip to let air circulate. Soggy toilet paper's no use for bulking unless it's newspaper which most gypsies use. So I guess our answer is gypsy shit. I happen to know a gypsy brothel near Piaţa Muncii."

"Eh?" And I thought I knew my way round Bucharest! And how did John know so much about compost?

"It's round the back of the Million Dollar Sexy Nightclub. You mightn't have noticed – basically it's a disused kitchen with an old sofa."

"That *does* sound basic."

"Hell, we ain't going there for skirt. We're gonna see about shit and used newspaper!"

"What about those bacteria and fungi and yeast and algae and protozoa?" asked Chlamydia, who had a good memory.

John grinned. "Just add some garden soil. There are millions of those critturs in every gram."

Only when he and I were on our way in my old white Mercedes to the Piaţa Muncii, not to a garden centre, did it dawn on me that John's true identity still evaded me. Either through consummate skill, or damn yankee naïveté, he'd completely avoided my trap! I'd like to describe John more fully, but since his identity remained a mystery, how can I?

I parked, chatted up and bribed the nearest security guard so that my car would be safe, then we went round the back of the bar which is the ground floor of the Million Dollar Sexy Nightclub, inside which half a dozen women from a lingerie catalogue would be lounging, waiting for music to activate them if a male wandered upstairs.

Outside a shabby rear annexe loitered a dark-skinned nymphette dressed in a spangled red bikini and a silver fur jacket. She looked about sixteen, though she had a Caesarian scar on her belly, so she had already reproduced. Being very predatory, the girl immediately grabbed me by the balls and cock through my trousers, and squeezed provocatively.

"You misunderstand," I said. "We've come for shit."

"Okay, I do golden showers if you want, but I not eat enough today for shitting."

"Just take me to your pimp."

This proved to be a tough-looking grandfather, whose fingers were covered in gold rings, and who was sitting on the sofa John had described, talking in Romany on a mobile. The war against poverty coordinated by the CIA-WHO had mercifully killed millions of poor people, but at the time of the big epidemics due to ignorance and lack of integration gypsies refused to be vaccinated, so they survived.

A gypsy would rarely refuse a bizarre trade.

"Of course we can provide you with lots of shit and dirty newspaper anonymously," said the grandfather. "Payment in Dollars."

John nodded. "No problem." And he pulled a bundle of Dollars from his pocket.

Once we were safely back in my Mercedes I said to John, "You're very free with Dollars." Did he have access to a CIA black budget?

"Thing is," said John, "nowadays the US Treasury is printing paper Dollars as fast as they can, regardless of economics. They're trying to catch up with the trillions of electronic Dollars, which are all basically imaginary. Basically" (he seemed to like this word) "the printed dollars are like a publishing bestseller with a vast print-run – if you know where to ask you can get remaindered Dollars right away at five cents each. Best keep quiet about this."

I didn't know whether to believe him.

So I drove home, and told the good news to my Beloved:

"We'll soon have a regular supply of compost for our cruise penis, my dear!"

"For the abortion too," she reminded me. "I can see it's suffering from lack of nutrition, even though it did join itself to the penis. That penis is sucking all the goodness out of the compost for its supersize erection. Penises are selfish."

I soothed her. "I know how much you treasure Adriana's abortion. There'll be enough for both."

Women are volatile. Of a sudden Chlamydia clapped her hands gleefully.

"And now gypsies will be able to diversify from prostitution into compostitution! This could be a Kusturica movie. Like *Time of the Gypsies*, but different."

My God, she was right. "What a clever Beloved you are!" I rushed to get my laptop.

And I typed:

```
She's only 16 when she tells him, 'Put me on
the street, and I'll bring money home for you, my
Beloved.'
    'No, my Beloved,' he says. 'I love you too much
to humiliate you on a street. You'll stay home and
produce compost which I'll sell on the streets
myself during the cold nights of winter, just like
the Little Match Girl.'
```

Seeing that I'd become busy, Chlamydia switched on the TV.

```
    The trick of love works, and since she loves
him doubly now, she has to produce twice as much
compost to match his love. This means she must eat
much more than usual, which soon leads to her
becoming very fat. But that just means there's more
of her to love. Dealing with compost all the time,
they can't escape its fatal attraction, and soon
they copy our habit of sleeping on a bed of
compost. Of course we see garden soil being mixed
in, to provide the necessary bacteria and fungi and
yeast and algae and protozoa.
```

At this point I heard what was coming from the TV.

"Put me on the street, and I'll bring money home for you, my Beloved."

"No, my Beloved, I love you too much to humiliate you on a street – "

I stared at the TV and, my God –

"Chlamydia," I cried, "that movie that's showing, it's the same one I'm writing!"

In a trice she joined me, and my laptop, definitely not for a lapdance. She read and exclaimed:

"You have to write faster, Grigio! Keep ahead!"

She was right.

217

This fashion for compost beds spreads among
gypsies all around the country. He marries her, and
a new ceremony is invented for the first night of
the marriage. As a symbol of familiarity and unity,
all family members and relatives will provide
compost of their own creation to fill the marriage
bed. The filling of the bed begins with the
grandmother, who's dressed in black and who has a
slower metabolism – so she starts overeating and
straining to shit three weeks early. If any of the
relatives fail to provide enough compost then the
marriage will be an unhappy one. A bit later the
other relatives join in, to allow time for the
bacteria and fungi and yeast and algae and protozoa
to take effect.

What I wrote transpired on screen a few minutes after I
wrote it like a reality-echo, déjà-vu in reverse. But I mustn't pay
heed to it.

On the morning after the first night there has
to be a showing of the compost. But alas, during
the marriage party, while wealthy mafia gypsies
were throwing large amounts of money at the hired
musicians to demonstrate their own importance, one
of the million stray dogs got in to the compost bed
and shat a white crap there, white because of that
dog disease called distemper. This spoiled the
first night of bliss. The alchemy of love was
polluted. Now we experience the dark side of the
compost, which is paradoxical when the dog poo is
so white. She starts to cry and says, 'My Beloved,
for ages I've been making compost just for you, and
now, even though I'm fat, I feel like an empty bag!
Why don't you ever beat me any more like in the old
days? Maybe you don't love me!" He doesn't slap
her, but instead he caresses her softly and says,
'I didn't want to beat the shit out of you. But I

understand you, my Beloved. Now that you're a respectable married woman, you don't need to produce any more compost, I promise. We'll make money in a different way.

Was I typing the movie, so that whatever I wrote would happen? Or was the movie making me type? So long as I kept ahead, the former was the case, and I retained my freedom and free will.

So he puts up a website where you see gypsy prostitutes pissing into bags of compost and fetishists can buy online little potpourri sachets of the pissed compost. This works very well, and soon a significant percentage of sexually oriented gardeners start to buy ever bigger quantities of compost produced by women and anointed with their piss. The compost is useful for growing vegetables to stimulate the vaginas of vegans and other vegetarians. Because of cultural osmosis, in due time this fashion penetrates the religious field, and priests all over the country start using compost for their ceremonies. After all, was not Christ originally born on a sort of bed of compost, produced by the cow and the donkey beside him? Did not the three wise kings, Caspar, Melchior and Balthasar, come from afar bringing incense, myrrh, and compost? Here Kusturica's film turns to religious matters – today's public is very pious – and a gypsy Christ is seen miraculously turning a bag of bread and a bag of fish into 20,000 bags of compost.

I was safely in the lead now, though I mustn't slack off. I had to provide an ending.

At the end of the film the main actors die, but they find each other again after death, rather like in Kusturica's *Underground*. However, death has

transported them to the beginning of time, since
death is a resetting of the universe, though nobody
usually tells you so. And there we see our heroes
again, lazing around in Eden, which looks like the
botanical garden in Nantes because that's where
this part should be filmed, until into the Garden
of Eden the wrong compost is delivered by Satan.
And God looked upon it and thought it was good, but
he was wrong, because it wasn't the compost of
beloved angels. It was Satan's own shit. And the
plants of Eden began to turn purple and produce
spiked fruit. So God godoogled and discover that
the compostor was an impostor, and Eden had crashed
and must be rebooted. So he threw the main
characters out of Eden to earn their living from
now on with the sweat of their brows, and to obey
the Ten Compostmandments, and to fight against
terror for the sake of liberty. But this is a happy
ending, in line with Homeland Security.

At last I could relax, and try to understand, while I watched
the movie unfold exactly as I'd written. God was played by Vice-
President Schwarzenegger. Music was mostly Mahler, *Das Lied von
dem Kompost.*

Finally Chlamydia and I watched the credits roll.

BELOVED COMPOST

PRODUCED BY PEDRO ALMODÓVAR ®™

DIRECTED BY EMIR KUSTURICA ®™

"Wow," said Chlamydia. "What's with the ®™ after their
names?"

"That's because their names are registered and trademarked.
This film's made by the fake Kusturica and the fake Almodóvar."

"I don't understand."

"My darling, America has made a fake of everything worthy of existence. You know there's an exact replica of the Piazza San Marco of Venice in the States? For a long time Americans have been faking replicas of all good European films, 'remakes' as they call them. But that wasn't enough! Now they replicate the good directors, who they then call by the same names, which they immediately trademark and copyright so that the original director can't use his own name anymore, except in private life, or else he'll be sued and ruined. The same happens if a European writer becomes a bestseller. Michel Houellebecq can't use his own name anymore because there's a trademarked American, pronounced Mitchell Hooleybeck."

I'd missed the rest of the credits, and now came an ad break which I zapped off.

"I can't believe that!" protested Chlamydia.

"Why not? For decades American Corporations sent missionaries to underdeveloped faraway countries to ask local natives the secrets of their medicine, and to take plants containing original therapeutical molecules – which they then patented and sold for a lot of money to everyone, including the original owners, even suing the same poor natives who were the real discoverer of the therapy if they wouldn't buy those molecules from the Americans. Look – little known fact! – after they invaded Iraq they forbade Iraqis from using their own natural seeds in agriculture. Instead, genetically modified faked American seeds became obligatory, since these were sterile and must be bought every year, creating dependence forever. The same thing happens on every level. Fake film directors, fake writers, fake fashion designers, fake actors who are digitally reproduced. They're probably building a fake Vatican somewhere in Connecticut for a fake Pope. Why not a fake God, supposing that a real one exists?"

"I understand the use of a fake God – He'd be more American. But why on earth fake film directors? I still don't get it."

"It's very simple, actually. A fake Kusturica, for example, is essential for making *all* possible Kusturica films exactly the way Americans want to see them – not only the ones the real Kusturica has actually made, but all those he *would* make. It isn't democratic to show the American people things they wouldn't like, but Amnesty International has established that it's their human right to be able to experience the art of – let's say Kusturica – in the way they can best appreciate. Look at Fellini! He became an American adjective while he still was alive. Americans would say that weird surreal things are so much *fellini*. Now we have the new Federico Fellini, born in the USA, who has only seen Italy on postcards, releasing one film after another for the MacIntellectuals of the free world."

"*Amarcord Pearl Harbour* isn't by the real Fellini?"

"Nor is *Satyricon Seattle*! Nor *Dolce Vita Dallas*. They're all films by the fake Fellini! Even Marcello Mastroianni is fake, his face altered by CGI!"

"Unbelievable."

"I'm sure they made a fake copy of the CIA inside the real CIA, so now there's the Stupid CIA which doesn't know it's stupid, and the Clever CIA which pretends to be stupid because that's the most intelligent thing to do. So which one does John belong to? If he belongs to either of them! Maybe he's an Illuminatus."

"My love," said Chlamydia, "surely this is less important than *how* a film you started writing started appearing on television while you were writing it!"

"That's true. Should we rewind?"

"It was live, it wasn't a DVD."

"Okay, programme guide." I unzapped the TV, brought up menu, went to the programme guide. And there we saw what we'd missed by talking… *A Godoogle Studios Film*.

I was stunned.

"Godoogle created the film as I wrote it…"

"Why not use the real Kusturica?"

"Because the film's a fake. Godoogle's being consistent."

Just then the doorbell rang.

Outside stood John the Indescribable, indescribably dressed.

"Howdy, you guys." Behind John, grinning gypsies were bringing bags of proto-compost to stack in the corridor. *Already?*

As soon as John stepped inside, Chlamydia went down on her knees and began unfastening his shoelaces. I thought she had suddenly become houseproud, or Japanese, or maybe intended to tie the laces together so that we could pin down his identity.

I hissed, "What are you up to, Chlamydia?"

"I'm going to wash his feet," she replied serenely.

"By female intuition," said a smiling John, "Chlamydia knows who I am. Shucks, there's no need for foot-washing, or for drying them with your hair, or pouring perfume. For I will walk on compost." So saying, he strode through and stepped up into our bed beside the swelling cruise penis plus abortion. Leaning against the cruise penis, John stretched out his arms dramatically. "If God allegedly sent His son to Earth," he declared, "*why not also Godoogle?* You better believe me, guys."

"Do you have to speak American all the time?" I asked humbly.

"Google is American, and Godoogle comes from Google."

Oh God, this was worse than if he were a member of either of the CIAs!

"Don't worry," he reassured me, "it's just an accent and some slang. Heck, what I'm looking for right now is twelve Compostles. You two deserve a promotion."

The Beloved Time
of their Lives

By the age of eighteen Jonathan still hadn't fallen in love. For the past few years his friends had been flirting with girls, passionately or heartlessly jumping from one to the next, but this procedure didn't interest Jonathan. He was sure that he could only really love once during his lifetime, and he wasn't disposed to waste time on anything less. His friends warned him: you'll be a virgin forever. No, he would answer, I *shall* love – but only when I can love forever!

Very probably there was a genetic reason for his attitude. A human being has genes that make him or her behave in a monogamous way – and also genes that push him or her towards polygamy. Love stories are often full of drama because of the struggle between these antithetical genes. By random combination, a person may exceptionally have *only* the genes for monogamy (or, of course, those for polygamy). Jonathan must be one of these rare individuals all of whose genes chorused a faith in, and a will for, an eternal immense love for a single person, a love that would be complete, perfect and unbreakable.

None of the adolescent girls he saw around seemed adequate. The problem with adolescent girls is that if they're banal they're almost certain to remain banal – but if they're vivid and intelligent they might still become banal in future. How could he love forever a lively and intelligent creature who in later years might mutate into something he couldn't love any more? Popular wisdom suggests you look at a Beloved's mother to get an idea of what you'll end up hosting in your home a few decades hence –

225

and the result is often mortifying. Even this method is far from foolproof. If only he could take a look into the future of candidates for his love, to be positive what they would become later on!

Elena knocked at the door of his life shortly after he'd celebrated his eighteenth birthday – to give him private lessons in Physics, a field he was fascinated by and knew enough about to know that he knew to little. Due to Jonathan's father emigrating to Thailand to enjoy massages, and his mother joining a commune in Spain to expand her mind, Jonathan had been left on his own since seventeen, although adequately provided for in a small flat, with a small allowance – and, as you'll have gathered, he was of a philosophical disposition. Jonathan had never felt quite at home with his parents, nor evidently had they felt at home with him (nor with each other).

Elena was more than a mature woman – maybe she was sixty-five or seventy. She could easily have been his grandmother! So any notion of a sexual relation with her was absurd to an eighteen year old boy. However, during the long hours they spent studying together, he perceived Elena to be a woman of an extraordinary sweetness. Despite her age she still had a pleasant figure, and her voice possessed a hypnotic tone which gifted him with inner peace. It even seemed as if she could read his mind, for she would answer questions he hadn't yet put. Frequently she anticipated his unvoiced desire for a coffee, or for a beer from the fridge. "What's the probability it's time for a coffee?" she might say. "Let T be Time. Let C be Coffee as well as Celeritas, the speed of light…" To a surprising degree they seemed on the same wavelength as regards the how and why of the Universe. Although Elena clearly couldn't be the woman of his life, Jonathan realized that he would know he had found the woman of his life if he were able to imagine her ending up in old age resembling Elena.

One day Jonathan asked Elena if she was married, since until then she never had touched on the matter.

"In a way," she replied.

"You mean that you don't believe in the formalities of marriage?"

"That isn't why I never married formally."

"Why, then, may I ask?"

"It's a long story."

"And you don't want to tell me."

Elena sighed in a bittersweet way. "Another time. Probably before Death kisses me."

"Eh?"

"Oh, just something I read – forget it."

So he did. He had much more important things to concentrate on.

"I've never been in love yet," he said.

"The time will come, Jonathan, there's no need to hurry." Elena's smile seemed maternal.

"It must be so nice being in love." Briefly Jonathan was lost in a vacancy consisting of the absence of any such memories.

"It's the only feeling that makes any sense," she confirmed.

Months passed, and a deep friendship flourished. Sometimes they took tea in the city, or he went shopping with her. As the last day of the old year approached, Jonathan confided that he didn't much want to spend New Year's Eve with his friends and whatever girlfriends of the moment, getting pissed. But the alternative might be sad.

"If you like," said Elena, "we can spend New Year's Eve together. I invite you to my place! I'll cook."

Jonathan accepted gratefully.

Entering Elena's cosy flat for the very first time gave him a strangely satisfying sensation. On the dining table two tall candles burned.

She beamed at him. "A romantic little dinner for a granny and a young boy. Nobody else."

Elena had made herself really elegant in a cream lace top and long pleated turquoise skirt. The years hadn't been able to steal away her essential classiness.

Asparagus and oysters were followed by duck then by crème brulée. By candlelight, and fuelled by a notable quantity of Red Paradox wine, an excellent Cabernet Sauvignon from Romania, their conversation achieved new levels of intimacy. When midnight arrived, they toasted the New Year with Champagne to the sound of Apocalyptica, a sort of hard rock performed with cellos, Elena's choice.

The eyes of both were shining, not just due to alcohol, which is merely a noble amplifier of emotions. As the cello-rock of Apocalyptica became mellower, the music was an invitation to dance. To resist would have been an insult to the universe. So Jonathan and Elena danced, and their dance was sweeter than words can express. Their scents mingled and the implacable gear of destiny eliminated any other outcome than what must happen. Elena closed her eyes and stretched a few centimeters towards Jonathan, just enough to kiss his lips delicately. Emotions exploded inside Jonathan's chest, beautiful emotions for which he had waited many years in vain. Without querying what he was doing, Jonathan returned the kiss with passion. Time warped for numerous seconds, creating amidst the universe a little bubble that should rightly last forever, regardless of what went on elsewhere.

When the kiss ended, Elena regarded him wide-eyed.

"Come," she murmured, and took his hand with delicacy. Jonathan – his mind in a trance and his body flooded with enchanting hormones – followed her trustfully into the bedroom.

It was a very long night of passion, during which Jonathan was initiated into what he imagined must be all the possible variations offered by the act of love. Signs of age seemed to have disappeared from Elena, who greedily tasted every moment of that sublime sexual communion, and was never sated. After each orgasm of his she returned to the fray, sweetly yet tirelessly determined, as if his fluids were needed to extinguish an age-old fire that nothing else in the world could possibly douse. And he, intoxicated with ecstasy – the natural, rather than the pharmaceutical sort – seemed able to continue making love forever, after so many years of waiting and abstinence. When, by the first light of morning, bodily obsession had at last calmed in both of them, tangled together they still fed on each other's heat and smell, in a fusion that nothing in the world could sever.

"I'm so happy," murmured Jonathan, enjoying a completeness that till a few hours before was unknown to him.

"I'm happy too now," echoed Elena, clutching him even more tightly.

"I'll love you forever," vowed Jonathan.

"You already did," she replied, stroking his hair.

Those caresses propelled Jonathan deep into the innocent sleep of children and Beloveds.

When, after an eternity had passed, Jonathan awoke, the sun was flooding the room. Close to him was Elena, but all the same she wasn't there any more. Her body was cold. As Jonathan very soon discovered, she was dead.

All the unaccustomed exertion and joy must have resulted in a heart attack. Or all the intimate caresses, in a massive stroke.

The fall from the pinnacle of the world was unutterably painful. The unlikely and the impossible had happened one shortly after the other. He had found what he knew would be the only love of his life, yet she had disappeared almost immediately from the universe. His lifetime of love was all completed in a single night with no possibility of replays: what a terrible joke destiny had played on him!

Anyone else would have been traumatised by such an experience but sooner or later would have recovered, unless he killed himself straightaway. Such a person's life would go on. He would know other women. But not Jonathan. Like it or not, he was made to love once only, completely and irrevocably. His love for an Elena who didn't exist any more would accompany him for the rest of his life. Nothing would be able to change this state of affairs. Awareness of this tortured him, plunging him into an abyss of pain of with no return.

In the years that followed, Jonathan closed himself up within himself and his studies. Those were the only evasion he permitted himself from a pain which nevertheless resembled the highest of all pleasures – for if his love for the vanished Elena were not to fade away, he must never renounce the sublime pain of her absence, a sacred pain that bore witness to his immutable love and symbolised it.

Jonathan began to dream of somehow going back in time to a period before Elena's death. Obviously the idea was impossible, but this didn't stop him from dreaming – nor from delving into scientific enigmas involving time. Ten years passed in the world while Jonathan remained cut off from human society, lost in obsessive study. Thank goodness he had an allowance. His mother and his father seemed to have lost track of time and reality, one through spirituality, the other at the hands of Thai masseuses who must be really good. Occasionally a postcard arrived.

Actually, time is merely one of the models by which human beings interpret reality, not something that exists objectively in an absolute sense. What if *alternative* futures and pasts and presents could be accessed *mentally*? What if you could derail your point of view from the continuum you were used to, and allocate it to an alternative timeline chosen by your deepest instincts?

The ideal timeline would be an alternative present in which Elena would be his own age and the circumstances for their love would then be perfect. *A priori* he had to exclude this utopian vision. Even if such an alternative present did exist, he'd never find a way to shift his point of view there. It would be a continuum with which Jonathan had never had any contact, so he'd never be able to guess where it was by intuition. Even though that place would be a parallel present time, existentially it was too distant from his current life – like the hundredth reflection of oneself in a mirrored lift where the images progressively bend away out of sight.

The best hope of finding a way to relocate his viewpoint was within his own timeline of probability, for that had certainly crossed Elena's timeline for a while. There was no sense in hoping for more – not for all the love of the world, which was burning inside him.

Years of obsessive research and desperate commitment ripened till finally Jonathan convinced himself he was ready for the big jump. By now he was thirty-one. What he must conjure up was a *virtual* time machine that could exploit strong morphic resonance between his starting point and his destination. He must leave from, and arrive in, an almost identical situation – whatever differences existed externally to it.

The most constant and stable context he could think of was MacDonald's, since the difference between any MacDonald's and another is minimal, less than a single letter such as an *a*. Just as MacDonald's had colonised this world, so it must have colonised any other that was remotely similar. Conceivably there might be a McDonald's without two "a"s in some reality, but it was hard to imagine a reality without something very like MacDonald's. Consequently MacDonald's would be his time machine!

When the big day came, Jonathan went to a random MacDonald's and ritually ate the last MacCheeseburger of his personal epoch. Now the compass of his love must take him to a MacDonald's nearest to a space occupied by Elena. As to *when* in time... he must be like a Zen archer, hitting the target while blindfolded in darkness.

After swallowing the last bite, Jonathan closed his eyes and concentrated, as he had taught himself to do. His mind lost itself inside itself. The sounds and smells of MacDonald's disappeared.

After an indefinable interval what impinged on his awareness was a difference in smell, less burger grease in the air, more odour of sweet MacSalads. He opened his eyes. The MacDonald's was almost identical to the one where he had closed them except that customers were dressed differently! Quite a few men sported pastel jackets with wide lapels; some women favoured velvet jumpsuits. The staff, of course, wore exactly the same MacUniforms.

How Jonathan exulted. His chinos and corduroy jacket didn't seem too much out of place. Briefly he wondered whether, by his arrival, he had displaced a Jonathan to make space for himself – obviously not from this very same MacDonald's; that would be a remarkable coincidence! But if he did displace a Jonathan, where did he displace him to? Maybe to a timeline where Jonathan had never even been born – otherwise the displaced Jonathan would in turn displace a Jonathan *ad infinitum*, and this process might continue like dominos falling over until he himself in turn was displaced by some other displaced Jonathan. No doubt due to such perspectives, Jonathan felt indefinably more mature than previously.

Presumably Elena was alive and living not very far from this very MacDonald's. So how would he find her? *She* couldn't possibly recognize him – he had only known her in her old age. Going to look for her at random risked missing her repeatedly.

Waiting in this MacDonald's closest to her home seemed the best strategy! Surely sooner or later she would come here to eat or drink or merely use the toilets which in MacDonald's are always clean and welcoming. And then he would meet her again. Ah, from her point of view not *again*, but for the *first* time – so from their combined viewpoints he would fifty-per-cent meet her again. MacDonald's would be like Schrödinger's Box until he observed her.

Jonathan rented a room in the nearest hotel for the hours of night when MacDonald's was shut. Fortunately a principle of conservation had kept money identical. In case credit cards weren't conserved, he had brought a lot of cash with him, choosing the oldest banknotes he could lay his hands on. This made him rich due to the opposite of inflation.

Every day of the following three weeks he spent inside that MacDonald's, only rushing out twice a day to a healthfood shop for snacks. It would have been unromantic to supersize himself. To propitiate the staff of MacDonald's, he frequently bought MacWater, and he read a detective novel called *Death Kisses Me* which he found in a wastebin, ten words at a time, look round, another ten words, look round – hopefully without appearing paranoid. Now and then he rubbed his neck as though suffering from an affliction requiring frequent turns of the head – otherwise his head might lock in one position. The staff, who were all afflicted in one way or another, ignored him, although children would stare. At first the title of the book rang a faint bell, but its repetition atop every other page quickly deafened him.

Finally, on the twentieth day of his vigil Jonathan's heart almost exploded when a woman in her forties exactly resembling a photo he'd seen of Elena at forty-one entered MacDonald's and hurried to the toilet. *Elena!* How should he accost her? Ah, he'd pretend to be doing a survey regarding the quality of the MacToilets.

When the door with the woman icon opened and Jonathan found himself face to face with Elena, he was paralysed and speechless.

Elena found herself facing a man maybe in his mid-thirties with pale face and trembling lips, who gaped at her with bulging eyes.

Blood drained from her face. Her eyes widened.

"Jonathan!" she gasped. Then she fell into his arms, and he had no idea what was happening. "Oh, Jonathan, I've waited for you all these years! And now you are here!" She sighed happily, head on his shoulder. "You're here!"

"This isn't possible... How do you know me already?"

She stepped back, a pitying expression on her face.

"This must be your first jump... It's true what you told me ages ago."

"Eh, my *first* jump? You mean I'll meet you another time in my future – but in your past...? *How, why?*"

Jonathan had been certain that, when he found Elena, they would be together from then on forever. Not so, it seemed.

"*Why*," she said, "is the question that tormented me for years. But let's forget why! We're together, you and me! That's all that matters. We must savour every moment while it lasts."

"While it *lasts*?" echoed Jonathan.

Looking serious now, she gazed into his eyes. "You've already explained to me once that if the past of a person contains the future of another person, there must be a certain indefinability, or a definite uncertainty, so as not to destabilise the continuum and let things carry on."

"I told you that?" He felt he was in a trance.

Elena nodded.

"Excuse me," said a supersize mother who was trying to approach the toilet.

When Jonathan had got to know Elena for the first time for Physics lessons, so far as he knew no older version of himself was her partner – so for some reason he wouldn't spend the rest of his life with her right till the end. Maybe the older version died before his eighteen year old self met her. That would happen in her future, so Elena couldn't know this yet. Not unless he already told her in her past, but he didn't know this because that would only happen in his own future... always assuming that an older and younger version of himself from separate timelines could both occupy the same timeline, all be it at different times.

"Excuse me! I have a right to use the toilet."

As Elena stepped further back, the vast woman moved between her and Jonathan like a total eclipse, filling all the available space. With difficulty the woman passed through the doorway to the toilet. As she did so, slowly she uneclipsed... a *blank wall.* Had the supersize woman dragged Elena with her, attached like an inadvertent parasite on a whale? No – Jonathan had stopped observing Elena and now she was gone!

Jonathan staggered, bewildered, panicked, and desolate. To have found Elena and lost her because a mountainous woman wanted to use the MacToilet! Elena had been solid and real, but the continuum had destabilised due to local obesity. Too much mass occupying one location, too much definability. Maybe!

Jonathan returned to his table where *Death Kisses Me* lay open, and slumped. For a while he stared at the street door, willing Elena to walk in to MacDonald's again, as if reality could simply reset itself by a few minutes. Instead, an even larger woman overlapping a power wheelchair entered. Jonathan felt unreal by comparison, as though he lacked enough substance. MacDonald's was a risky place to try to meet Elena! Yet it also remained the most logical place. Oh why had Elena lingered with him beside the MacToilet? They should have run hand in hand out into the street where there was more free space.

If Elena had vanished, that meant she had only *probably* been present in MacDonald's that day. The probability had been very high, maybe 99.9 per cent, but that left 0.01 per cent of improbability, which the sheer bulk of the supersize woman displaced into reality, rather like a black hole in reverse. Right now very likely Elena was somewhere else in the city where she might most likely be, unaware of having met Jonathan yet perhaps thinking about him and wondering *why*, at this particular time.

A whole new vision of the world came to Jonathan, one which explained how he had been able to travel by willpower to an alternative timeline, and which also explained socks lost in washing machines…

There must be an infinite number of timelines with a greater or lesser degree of probability – but never with *absolute* certainty. In the least probable timelines, the whole human race might become sapient dinosaurs and the sky might turn green. In less (but not least) probable timelines a man might become a woman, or your pet cat an iguana – flux, though not so chaotic. The most probable timelines would be very stable but not totally so. You might put twenty socks into a washing machine and only retrieve nineteen. Sometimes crazy coincidences would occur. A child called Ruby Gumdrop of 52 Weasel Road would release a balloon with her address attached – the balloon would land 200 miles away at 52 Weasel Road in a different city, to be found by a different girl of the same age who was also called Ruby Gumdrop.

So Jonathan had become very improbable in one timeline, and very probable in this one.

Now that he knew Elena was here, and that she knew who Jonathan was, why not put an advertisement in the local newspaper to arrange a meeting place? Ah but no, he must travel further into her past to tell her about uncertainties because that had already happened. If he didn't do so, *everything* might become uncertain.

As he had done in that other MacDonald's, he closed his eyes and concentrated.

And presently he opened his eyes, to behold what was apparently the same eternal MacDonald's. However, the staff were other, different people – and *prices were cheaper.*

About 20 per cent cheaper!

When he went to the MacToilet and glanced in the mirror, he had a shock. He looked about ten years older. Initially he was gobsmacked, but then he recalled his previous indefinable sensation of greater maturity and decided that travelling backwards along any timeline must come at a cost, of proportionate ageing. This time devotion had cost Jonathan dear – ten years of youth.

But there was one advantage! Here in the past, fewer customers were supersize. Maybe a quarter instead of a third. Presently he went to the same rubbish bin where he'd found *Death Kisses Me.* Of course that same book couldn't be there for another ten years, but instead Jonathan found *A Treasury of Turkish Proverbs: The Mother of All Proverb Dictionaries* in Turkish and in English. The back had been torn off and the last hundred pages were missing – maybe those pages had been torn out for nose-blowing or grease-wiping.

Thus commenced two weeks of MacWater, and "Love is a burning chickpea," "An ugly woman tidies her house, a beautiful woman roams the streets..." But on the fifteen day an Elena in her early twenties came into MacDonald's for a pee. Quickly Jonathan stationed himself outside the door to the toilets, wary of the approach of any supersize persons. As soon as Elena emerged, he blocked her way.

Calmly she said, "Will you let me past?" Ah, she hadn't recognized him! Thank God he wouldn't need to go further back in time.

"Pardon me," he said, "but I'm an inspector of the quality of the MacToilets, as customers perceive them. Could you spare me a moment for a few questions? First of all," he improvised hastily, "did you do a pee or a poo?" God, he had been overhearing too many mothers with their toddlers. It had been ages since he talked normally to anybody.

"You're a *pervert*," she exclaimed. And then her face turned pale. "Jonathan...?"

"You know who I am?" In fact, thank God she knew him – that was better than being thought a pervert.

"This isn't possible! It's a hallucination! Let me out of here!"

"Elena, my Beloved, everything's all right, don't panic." He was detaining her by force, but Elena suddenly stopped opposing him.

"Your smell, I'd know it anywhere. Oh, my God, I'm dreaming... dreaming..."

"You aren't dreaming, my love. Relax. Pretend this is an enchantment and let yourself be cherished by the impossible. The impossible loves you."

Elena closed her eyes for a moment, then she began to cry.

"I must be dead! Something like this can't happen in reality."

"I need you alive! I mean: you're alive, and I need you. I've been sitting here for weeks waiting and drinking MacWater. Don't cry."

"Because my tears aren't MacWater?" She laughed crazily. "You're *young*!" And she began to dance. And he'd thought he looked ten years older!

To establish continuity and make things more probable, quickly he gabbled at her about definite uncertainty and a certain indefinability, the same phrases she had used to him – as if reciting a prayer or a magical formula. Soon they would be in bed, either at his hotel or wherever she lived.

Big mistake.

Jonathan had stopped paying attention to his surroundings. At that very moment a voice wheezed, "Move aside."

Maybe the supersize man only had enough breath for two words, however he also sounded militant. Either because of Fat

238

Power or momentum he acted militantly: vast arms followed by a great body intruded between Jonathan and Elena, forcing them apart. When the eclipse passed, Elena had vanished.

Anguished, Jonathan returned to his table.

During their brief encounter Elena had seemed amazed by his young looks compared with when she'd last seen him, in her past. Was he condemned to sit in MacDonald's for years reading peculiar Turkish proverbs until he aged naturally sufficient to travel further back in time, to arrive – plus travel time – looking very mature? True, his most recent jump had added a decade to his apparent age, but a further decade of ageing due to a further jump seemed frankly insufficient.

He mused on the indelible image of her corpse after the night of love she had spent with him in his past, which was her future. He so wanted to be completely transparent in her eyes, for such is the nature of a true and absolute love – there should be no secrets between them. Yet in no event should she ever learn of her own death in his arms, during her last and his first embrace! This exception to transparency hurt him, yet paradoxically further fueled his immense love, and his pain at their separation.

His yearning grew uncontrollably till it was a blazing forest fire from which he must flee – to dive into the life-saving lake of her presence, as it were. As the Turks say in the section on *Yokluk*, or Absence: *Hasret ateşten gömlektir*, Longing is a shirt of fire. Consequently he forgot all about time and age, shutting his eyes and concentrating. He scarcely even heard, "Hey, I can't get my power wheelchair past..."

MacPrices were even cheaper. *The Mother of All Proverb Dictionaries* had disappeared, praise be to Allah. Only one supersize customer was in the establishment.

Like a swimmer after surfacing, Jonathan ran his hand over his hair, and found not much hair, so he went to the MacToilet to check in the mirror.

A sixty-year-old Jonathan, approximately, looked back at him! Maybe 58, maybe 62, no way to be certain. Evidently going back in time was like trying to reach the speed of light! In the case of space travel the more you accelerated, the more your mass increased until masswise you were supersize, although the same in appearance. In the case of time travel, the further you went the more rapidly *your age* increased. If he had to go back another couple of years, probably he'd become 100 years old. Where had his intervening life gone to? It had been used as time-fuel.

How could he possibly appeal erotically to an even younger Elena?

As a sixty-year-old man approximately, Jonathan was out of place among the many youngsters who visited the MacDonald's. They might regard him as a sort of MacTeenophile. So now he needed to remain vigilant while giving even less appearance of staring round repeatedly. Fortunately the same waste bin came to his rescue once more (or for the first time), suggesting that destiny was perhaps collaborating with him.

This time the discarded book was entitled *Golf Rules Explained.* "Golf is a lonely game," advised the book. Likewise, trying to find Elena! "Golf is difficult because we make it so. All manner of inhibitions and fears rise up in the mind of a man about to hit a golf ball, some of them demons of his own creation and some impressed on to his imagination by the daunting sight of the way ahead..." Yes, this was wise. Jonathan must relax.

"Know your own ball": that was good advice too, but Jonathan was sure he would recognise his Beloved at any age. Above the age of 13, anyway! Below that age, for the sake of decency he would have to let her grow up a bit, even if he himself continued ageing.

In golf sometimes you needed to drop a ball vertically over your shoulder to put it back into play. Beware, if you had a big bottom and the ball bounced off your bum! Sitting in MacSeats for weeks, or years, might well be enlarging Jonathan's bottom, yet what could he do about this? Perform callisthenics or yoga in the MacToilet?

Fortunately, only ten days passed before unmistakably a young Elena came into MacDonald's with a girlfriend – not to pee, but to eat! All youngsters go through a phase in which they think that fast food is good. Having learned patience, Jonathan observed her dirtying her lips with ketchup and slowly sucking a milk shake through a straw, offering an involuntarily wonderful show of spontaneous sensuality. She wasn't more than seventeen, he estimated. Her look was pure and completely innocent, yet in her eyes he already caught glimpses of the light that in the years to come would irradiate that look of hers. Uniquely in the history of the world, Jonathan was looking at the girl who later would have been the love of his life before any of this happened. In fact new verbal tenses were required to express his experience.

By now he was wary of MacToilets, which had proved dangerous and were in any case unpoetical even though they got cleaned every hour. Igniting Elena's love for him couldn't be a simple and immediate affair. If he failed this time, the entire bubble of reality where he had seemingly lived for the greatest part of his life might dissolve into nothing, leaving less trace in the universe than a bubble of soap that pops!

Besides, that girlfriend was with Elena. An old man making an approach in such company would cause embarrassment or giggles or even screams. When Elena left the MacBuilding, he followed at a discreet distance, pretending to study the book about golf.

And after he had discovered where Elena lived, he went to an Indian restaurant. Finally, some interesting dishes!

Elena knew that she was a special girl, yet this was a source of worry. Most of her girlfriends already had a boyfriend, or at least they'd had one. Why couldn't she find a boy who interested her?

She hadn't the slightest idea what she was looking for, but she knew exactly what didn't interest her, and the world seemed full of uninteresting boys. Maybe this was because psychologically males mature later than females. She could only wait and wait, and try to understand herself better. By doing so, perhaps she would discover what exactly she wanted from life, and from men. Meanwhile the intact energy of her youth gave her the strength to tolerate the big mystery.

Every Sunday lunchtime Elena would visit her beloved grandparents. She adored the *Borscht* soup such as only her grandmother knew how to make – alternatively the *Kapustnyak* soup – followed by a dish of *Vareniki z Tvorogom* or *Ghalushki Poltavskie*. But what she was really crazy about was *Nalystniki*, also known as *Deruny*, small potato pancakes made in a unique way, and of course drowned in *Uzvar*, a refreshing beverage made from berries.

One fine Sunday, Elena found a new guest at the home of the grandparents. Her grandparents were very gregarious, although in common with most old people they had a stable circle of friends. Rarely indeed would new acquaintances pop up in their life. This was one of those exceptions.

The newcomer had become friendly with Grandfather at the city golf club, which was where Grandfather and his friends played chess now they were incapable of playing golf due to arthritis or lack of breath. People who formerly played golf, and who liked the club house, graduated to chess. The newcomer seemed to know a lot about golf, even though he didn't possess any golf clubs, consequently chess was ideal for him too.

When you have lunch at your grandparents you don't expect originality, but the comfort of a familiar experience. However, conversation that lunchtime was more original than usual, with strange speculations about time, and even some Turkish proverbs, such as *Vakit gelmeden horoz ötmez*, The cock does not crow until the time comes. So when it came time for the new guest to leave, Elena felt a bit guilty at not having paid more attention to his name earlier on when he was introduced.

As she shook his hand, she frowned and said: "Mister..."

"Call me Jonathan," the guest answered, gazing into her eyes in a strangely significant way. However, she forgot about him later that afternoon.

In the months which followed, Elena became accustomed to Jonathan's presence in her grandparents' home on Sundays. Grandfather had really taken a shine to him. Within the 60-year-old body there seemed to be quite a youthful soul, yet a wise one with an interesting vision of the world – which Elena realized was helping her discover a lot regarding *her own* vision of the world. It wasn't that Jonathan taught her anything but rather that she discovered inside herself concepts for which until then there had been no words. She felt she was evolving. All week long she was looking forward to Sundays.

Yet her evolution had no urgent timetable – to understand yourself too quickly might imply you were banal.

Finally a chance came to see Jonathan outside of the bosom of the family. He mentioned that he had a couple of invitations to a private viewing at a gallery specialising in modern art, and Elena grasped this opportunity to hear his opinions in a different setting.

The exhibition consisted of broken, reassembled clocks on which dead chickens lay, some still in their plumes with boiled eggs forced into their mouths, some plucked, some roasted, though all were varnished to delay putrefaction

Jonathan commented, "*Ay gör, oruç tut; ay gör, bayram eyle.*"

"Don't count your chickens till they're hatched?" She understood him perfectly.

"And soon," he said, "*tempus fungus.*" Yes, mould would grow on the dead birds.

A young woman was carrying around a tray of drumsticks

and quail eggs.

"Cluck," he said.

"Yuck," she said.

"Would you prefer to go to a café for a latte?"

Thus the pretext of the art show evaporated, allowing them to leave rapidly for a lovely conversation about entirely different matters in a coffee house.

From that day onward, they frequently met in town. By seeing Jonathan thus, Elena began to perceive much more of herself too. His understanding of her helped her greatly to explore herself, although, as often happens, knowledge generated more enigmas than it resolved. One day, while they were lunching in a Pakistani restaurant, she said impulsively:

"There's a question I'd like to ask, but I don't want you to feel I'm intruding."

"Don't worry," replied Jonathan. "You can't possibly offend me."

"Well then, in a purely hypothetical way, would you ever consider the idea of making love to someone much younger than you?"

"Woman or man?" he asked.

"I don't know your tastes for sure, but I would more or less have thought a woman."

"Are you are asking if I could feel *interest* in a woman much younger than me – or whether some moral imperative would prevent me from making love with her?"

"I don't exactly know. Maybe both."

"Mature men never stop liking young women, Elena, unless the men are brain-dead. And I can't think of a meaningful rule that would rule out such a possibility."

"Have you ever followed any rules when it comes to love?"

"My only rule, probably of genetic origin, is that I can only love one woman totally during my life, and once she's been found all other women are uninteresting to me any more."

"Oh...," said Elena. "Your woman must be a very lucky person."

"My opinion too. But suppose she doesn't know?"

Elena laughed. "You're joking!"

"In that case, I'd still be a virgin. What year is it now? Hmm, I'm positive I'll lose my virginity within the next 40 years. Probably, when you're my present age. It's the universe which jokes. You too are made to love only one person, Elena."

"How do you know that?"

"I remember the future very well."

She laughed again. "You're funny."

"Not just me. It's life which is funny."

"I imagine one can see it like that."

"Likewise with many tragedies. Only the fact that they're fundamentally funny stops them from being ridiculous."

"So now life's a tragedy?"

"Elena, it's the mother... or rather, the *matrioshka* of all tragedies. Open the big doll up, and it contains a more miniature tragedy – and so on. That's what ultimately makes it funny."

"Life can be a beautiful tragedy."

He nodded. "If you interpret it in the right way."

"You've lived a lot more than me. How have you interpreted it?"

"I've done my best."

"And are you satisfied?"

"I've no complaints. It would make no sense to."

"I hope I'll be able to interpret life in the right way too."

"Oh, you will."

"How do you know?"

Jonathan winked. "I've been in the future and I've taken a peek."

Of course she laughed again. "When *I'm* in the future, I'll come back and tell you if you were right."

It was Jonathan's turn to smile. "No need! I'll be around to listen to you when you're old."

"You do like to dream."

"Don't dreams shape reality?"

"That sounds such a cliché."

"Dreams are ancient enough to be allowed to be clichés. After all this time they can hardly be original."

"You always have an answer ready! There's really no way to have the last word with you."

Did a shadow of pain cloud his eyes?

"The last word," he said, "is when the mother of tragedies happens."

"So that can only happen once?"

"Once is more than enough – once contains all other tragedies."

"I think I understand."

"Not yet you don't. But there's no hurry."

She said archly, "Presumably you're right about that too."

"Being right isn't necessarily a pleasure."

Elena felt provocative. "Would making love with me necessarily be a pleasure?"

"*Inevitably* is a more appropriate word."

Of course Elena did not know that their love might be a powerful necessity, but not something inevitable.

Time typically passes, and the things that must happen, usually happen. Or not. This time they did.

Elena and Jonathan had been dining together often at many exotic restaurants in the city, but on that particular evening for the first time they were in Jonathan's flat – he'd offered to outdo those restaurants, or at least to try.

Soft light came from two tall candles on the dining table. The dinner was as extravagant as he'd promised. To describe it couldn't possibly honour him enough since describing tastes is senseless. Yet we might mention the starters of sea urchin in lettuce parcels, since the insides of sea urchins resemble little brown labia which taste the way rockpools smell at low tide.

Sitting opposite her, Jonathan watched her with a piercing gaze, in which something was making itself manifest. Was it happiness, was it melancholy? Was the light too dim to distinguish between sadness and joy? Had she drunk too much Red Paradox Cabernet? All Elena could tell was that a strong feeling had arisen inside her.

What Jonathan represented to her had undergone a sea-change into something rich and strange. No longer did she see the somewhat elderly person whom anyone else would have seen, but someone so rich in significations that he almost eluded objective scrutiny. Who knows how many times female eyes must have seen that profound unexpected beauty in Jonathan during his long life! Yet perhaps right now she was the only person able to perceive that beauty in its wonderful totality. She would like to think she was unique, and that to all other women, blinded by banality, Jonathan would seem merely a man of sixty-something. And she believed that he perceived her completely.

When he spoke to her he was talking to her in her entirety, not to any petty secondary part of her the way other people commonly did. When he listened to her, he heard what she was actually saying, not what ordinary listeners would hear, namely their own preconceived notions.

Communion between herself and Jonathan had become a spiritual phenomenon of absolute intensity. People are like soap bubbles which float in the air of the world. The bubbles wander at random. Every now and then they bounce against another bubble. Sometimes two bubbles fuse into a single one, bigger and more brilliant. Sooner or later all bubbles pop, shrinking to the insignificance of a droplet, but, while the bright bubble endures, that's of no importance. Right now she and Jonathan were within the wonderful bubble of communion.

When does the first kiss become inevitable? What of time

247

itself, during the kiss which inaugurates a timeless love? What of space when the first kiss abolishes all distance? And why do questions regarding love have to sound so kitschy and commonplace?

Then their kisses diffused and diversified, and seemingly without transition the dining room became a room with a large soft bed. Clothes were a useless relic. Nothing could intrude upon the bubble of Elena and Jonathan, impenetrable for now by the ordinary world, a bubble in which warm and beautiful things were happening.

Jonathan paid attention to every inch of Elena before finally paying tribute at the ultimate shrine. The heat within the bubble crescendoed.

"I've been waiting so long for this moment," Elena murmured, her words surprising even herself. Objectively it wasn't so much time, yet of a sudden it seemed an eternity.

"I've been waiting all my life," he whispered. Indeed this was true, even though decades of life had disappeared as time-fuel.

"I already felt you were inside me for a long time. Shall we erase the gap between imagination and reality?"

"Yes, yes."

The embrace was long and very sweet and filled Elena with enchanting emotions.

She cried out, clutching Jonathan to her with all her force. In the soft aftermath she and he exchanged long effusions and sweet words.

"I love you Jonathan."

"I love you too."

"So now you've finally lost your virginity," she said with such a sweet smile.

"I've *regained* my virginity," he answered. "It isn't time yet to lose it."

"You always say such funny things."

"Why should I choose tragic things?"

"Jonathan, I've no way to compare, but I'm sure you're the perfect lover."

"It was you who taught me."

Elena gazed passionately into his eyes. Her cheeks were enflamed.

"I want you," she said from the depths of her.

And they began making love again.

Elena recalled things she'd heard about the diminished potency of elderly men. Those must be groundless legends! At least, they didn't apply to Jonathan. Very soon thought was replaced by atavistic sensations and she cried out again as her whole universe became a synonym for ultimate pleasure. How could life be so wonderful? For the rest of the night they embraced, scorning wasteful sleep, kissing, chatting, joking, loving.

As dawn brightened, the force was with Jonathan once more. Elena thought herself the luckiest girl in the world. She felt as if Jonathan were channeling power from the entire cosmos to dispense to her during this first night of love of her young life. He was the pole around which all the love of the universe gravitated and concentrated itself so as to be rhythmically pumped into her till she exploded with ultimate joy. The universe itself was loving her, and Jonathan was he whom the universe had created to show its love for her. She knew she would love Jonathan forever.

His orgasm erupted within her at the very moment when she screamed the climax of her pleasure. Their cries mingled in primordial melody which should last forever in that bubble of time.

But then came a discord – a strangled sound from Jonathan's throat as he sank heavily upon her and moved no more.

"Jonathan...?"

No answer came.

"Jonathan!"

And she understood and screamed again more loudly than ever before. Though not, this time, from pleasure.

Years later, after she met the younger Jonathan in MacDonald's, and he gabbled to her about uncertainty and indefinability, and she found his abandoned book of Turkish proverbs, she vowed that she must study Physics until she understood the nature of time.

After she met him again and a supersize customer intruded, she found his copy of *Death Kisses Me*.

He had kissed her and initiated her in the past and had died. In a way this made Jonathan's life, and their love, immortal, since unlike everybody else in the history of the world Jonathan certainly wouldn't die any year *after* he was born,. When he departed from her on his time-crusade, how would she cope with his absence? Probably that would become more obvious as the intervening years went by, likewise spent coping with his absence – a special love demands special sacrifices, as in the case of Héloise and Abelard, or Tristan and Isolde. Meanwhile, she had something to look forward to in later life, which was more than most people did.

On no account must she go looking for Jonathan prematurely!

She redoubled her studies of Physics. Occasionally she reread *Death Kisses Me* and *The Mother of All Proverb Dictionaries*. Despite transparency and communion, she must never let the even younger Jonathan scrutinize those two books – otherwise what fresh experience could he occupy himself with in MacDonald's? Certainly not the MacMenu.

My Beloved Cascamorras

Well now, my Beloved, Guadix and Baza are two rival towns to the east of Granada – which was the capital of the last kingdom of the Moors in Spain. In 1490 Baza had only just been reconquered by Christian soldiers, and in September of that year a labourer from Guadix was in Baza helping to clear the site of a wrecked Moorish shrine. Juan's pickaxe hit what he assumed was a big buried stone, so he really walloped the obstacle. Whereupon he heard a sweet sad voice call out, "Have Mercy!"

Soon crowds and dignitaries arrived, including the brave knight Don Luis (who had helped to liberate Baza) accompanied by his jester dressed in motley – and within a rough shell of disinterred plaster proved to be a statuette of the Virgin Mary!

Consequently a church must be built to house Our Lady of Mercy – and Our Lady would need a festival every 8th of September. Juan the labourer returned to his native Guadix together with the jester. For some reason they'd become bosom chums, perhaps even Beloveds, eh? A year later Juan and the jester returned to Baza accompanied by many Guadixians. Why the devil should Baza retain a virgin found by a man of Guadix, eh?

This dispute resulted in a remarkable festival. Every September from that year onward, a champion from Guadix – representing either Juan, or the jester, or both men simultaneously – would try to escape through the streets of Baza without being hit by anyone local. His only defense was a ball on a pole, which he would swing around him. If the champion could get away untouched, the virgin would go to Guadix.

Obviously the champion never succeeded, because hundreds

251

of Bazans gave chase. Some champions from Guadix may have been badly injured, or even killed. The name of the champion, and of the ceremony too, is *Cascamorras* – which means something like *bash his head*.

Around the 1940s, so as not to seem uncivilised, the spectacle was changed. Instead of bashing the Cascamorras, hundreds of Bazans would dress in old clothes, cover themselves with dirty black motor oil drained from cars – yes, that's what I said! – and if anybody could touch and stain the Cascamorras, the Guadixian would lose. Naturally he continued to lose, although now without risk of broken bones.

By the way, in Spanish – due to lisping – Baza is pronounced *Batha*, and on festival days it certainly looked as if the inhabitants had taken a *bath* in sump oil! But Baza's festival of filth is the reason why, by the second half of the 21st century, that provincial Andalusian town became one of the most important places of pilgrimage on Earth, for those who could get there.

All because of oil, my Beloved!

How many times do I have to listen to this shit?

I'll ignore that. Now obviously the Cascamorras must be a tough chap, to endure several hours of oily slaps in the hot sun. A well-muscled, strong-thighed man, like Achilles showing off his masculine beauty in marble. Such was my Beloved Miguel, who had come with me to Baza from Antibes – where we were then living – to compete in the selection for Cascamorras, as had seventeen other men of assorted nationalities.

Thank God I was very wealthy. Or rather, thank my parents! The shrinkage of oil supplies and escalating cost caused a veritable holocaust of the Middle Classes. The objects of their desires had become unattainable, only a dream – package holidays and sex in Thailand, neon lights and lycra tights, private cars. You do love me, don't you, Antoine? You wouldn't try to fool a seasoned old fellow such as me?

Love you? Fool you?

Do have another banana. Bananas are such an erotic shape, and so expensive, they're a scandal!

I was talking about cars. Loss of cars was a castration, inability to use cars was impotence. When billions of cars stand empty, deprived of gasoline and engine oil, little wonder that the annual anointing by dirty engine oil in Baza assumes such magical, iconic significance. Maybe some year the ceremony will conjure the renewed ejaculation of oil wells.

I suppose you want me to ask, how come if cars stand empty there's a lot of used car oil in Baza?

Presently, presently. Let's not get ahead of ourselves. First I want to mention alcohol. Candidates for Cascamorras are tested for their resistance to alcohol – because once in the distant past a Cascamorras turned up too drunk to run.

Well now, the Spanish have a custom of drinking wine from a vessel called a *porrón*. It's a bit like a glass bagpipe. You hold the *porrón* above your face, tilt it, and out of a long thin spout pours a thin stream of wine... ideally, into your mouth. Quite often, especially after repeated use, you *pour* the wine *on* to your face, and your hair, and your shirt.

Several days before the race (to allow time for the resulting hangover to go away) a drinking contest decides who will be Cascamorras; and this contest is vigilantly invigilated. Soaking your hair and your shirt instead of swallowing the wine is cheating. Yet just as the ceremony of the Cascamorras changed from fists to oil-stains, so did the nature of the *porrón* employed in the selection test. No longer a glass bagpipe, but an upside-down skull with a long spout fitted to one eye socket. And the other eye socket blocked up, yes yes, obviously – very acute of you, I know you aren't just a pretty face. Otherwise the wine would simply pour out on to the floor. Likewise from the nasal orifice, et cetera. Wax is used.

What had happened was the discovery that some wine matures wonderfully not in barrels of oak but in human skulls. A serial killer oenophile of great cunning and patience, Pedro de la Mano, pioneered this method. When the police finally caught Pedro after ten years, they searched his cellar – or shall we say catacomb? – and found a hundred cranial vintages all labelled with the name of the victim and the date of bottling (or rather, skulling), and with a big cork in the right eye of each. The police Captain who led the search, and who pulled out a cork to investigate, thought at first that the red liquid might be the blood of the murder victims, diluted by some method to preserve and prevent coagulation. As soon as congeners evaporated, the bouquet (rather than a stench) told his nose otherwise.

Report has it that the Captain poured a glass, just to confirm his realisation, and he promptly cried out, "It's the whore's mother!" which is an Andalusian way of saying, "It's excellent," rather than being the identification of a victim. A British Inspector from Scotland Yard Sud, who was liaising with the Spanish police, also sampled some of the wine and exclaimed, "It's the dog's bollocks!" which is an English way of expressing appreciation.

Scotland Yard Sud? My Beloved, millions of British people had moved to the South of Spain before the oil ran short with all sorts of unfortunate social consequences. Many desperate geriatric English, impoverished and deprived of their pensions, took to crime and in the hilly inland coastal parts of Andalusia it was like the old days again – bandit territory. Have you heard of Marauding Maggie?

No doubt you'll tell me all about Marauding Maggie another time.

If you're a good boy. Well, in view of the name of the serial killer, de la Mano, which means 'of the hand,' might he conceivably have masturbated into his trophies through the eye socket before corking the skulls? Serial killers sometimes get their rocks off in some such way. Forensic tests proved otherwise: the skulls had been specially varnished on the inside to exclude air, and the wine was simply wine.

Did I say *simply?* This wasn't merely Cosecha or Crianza category, or even Gran Reserva. It merited a new appelation, Grandísima Reserva. Storage in skulls worked wonders. The deplorable origin of this discovery shouldn't cause the new-found technique to be spurned.

Yes, Antoine, wine matured in skulls is much rarer and consequently far more expensive than wine matured in big barrels of oak. And candidates to become Cascamorras must be rich to participate. Or at least their Beloved must, in the case of my Miguel. Before I discovered Miguel, he was merely a waiter in a café in Asturias.

Asturias is a bizarre region of Spain. Its people believe they are Celts and play the bagpipes. It rains constantly in Asturias – and something else which rains down, in many cafés, is cider. The locals insist on drinking cider by holding the bottle high overhead in one hand, a big glass down by their knees in the other hand. Without looking at either the bottle or the glass, but gazing piercingly straight ahead like a kind of Zen matador, they then pour, listening attentively for the tinkle of liquid against the glass. Often much cider soaks the sawdust on the floor. The idea is to oxygenate the drink immediately before serving, about two centimetres of it being all you get. If you, the customer, take half a minute to complete your sentence to a companion, in disgust the cider pourer will toss your cider into a bucket, promptly snap to attention again, and pour a fresh couple of centimetres into your empty glass.

How I admired Miguel's tight-trousered buttocks as he stretched tall in the Asturian *sidraría* and as a distant look came into his dark brown eyes. Miguel knew a lot about accurate pouring, which could help him to become Cascamorras.

The wine to be drunk in the selection contest was Grandísima Reserva from skulls, their righthand eye sockets fitted with long thin spouts. Those vessels are called *anthroporróns*, being made of human bone rather than glass. A couple of hundred *anthroporróns* were waiting on shelves beside the judges in a railed patio. Spectators crowded beyond the rails to watch.

The competitors would take turns to drink by groups of six, each of the six judges carefully eyeing a single drinker, and taking notes. Miguel was in the first group. Each contender took a full *anthroporrón* – and suddenly Miguel froze, staring fixedly at the vessel.

"My God!" he exclaimed. "I knew him well!"

Was Miguel parodying Shakespeare's *Hamlet*? That scene where the Prince of Denmark addresses the skull of Yorrick? Ah, but Miguel was no intellectual. He was gaping at the label on the *anthroporrón*.

"What's wrong, my Beloved?" I called.

"This… it's my paternal uncle. I'm sure of it… The name, the date…"

To obtain enough skulls for their Grandísima Reserva, wine makers couldn't simply dig up old graves. The public health authorities worried about ancient bacteria and viruses. Nor could the vintners import the skulls of North Africans since those would probably be Moslem skulls, and the Koran prohibits any contact with alcohol. What the vintners did was rent skulls all over Spain from impoverished relatives of the deceased for a period of twenty years, at the end of which the skull would rejoin the rest of the bones. For poor people, there was prestige in such use of a skull. That a superb Grandísima Reserva should fill the cranium after a life far from superb was really something. Quite a few members of the aristocracy even insisted in their wills that their skulls should be rented for what, to their families, was a mere pittance. You could say that the *anthroporrón* system established a new kind of aristocracy among connoisseurs of quality.

"Was he a proud man, your paternal uncle?" I called out to Miguel.

"Most men are proud," Miguel replied.

"Think how proud he would be to help you become Cascamorras!"

Whereupon Miguel tipped up the *anthroporrón* and began to drink.

Eventually, after numerous rounds of drinking, Miguel was down dizzily on his knees. However, his rivals were all stretched out flat. Some had vomited and thus been disqualified. Great was my joy and pride as I helped haul my Beloved to the shaded area deep in straw where he could pass out.

What's that, Antoine? Ah yes, where do they get all the dirty car oil from? Quite right, my treasure.

In Baza, almost uniquely in the world, old cars are still much used *specifically* to dirty the oil which the town council purchases – expensively, as expensively as they purchase all those *anthroporróns* every year. In fact the spectacle of the Cascamorras generates a lot of income, in particular from worldwide television rights, and Baza charge a big fee to outsiders who wish to coat themselves in used oil and participate in the chase. (As you know, most TV sets are powered by alternative technologies, such as stationary cycling while you watch, a much healthier option than lounging on a sofa.) So only rich visitors can afford to become dirty. Since being covered in oil is so prestigious, those rich people stay dirty for as long as possible, weeks or even months. What's more, the oil-dirty man is the ultimate sex attractant for many women because of the association with lots of money. Personally I was sure I would find dirty Miguel extremely exciting after the chase through the streets.

The main problem for oily men, who let eager women into bed with them casually, is that the men get *cleaned* in contact with the women, since the eager women gain status by being dirtied by an oily man. Wearing a thick layer of black oil on the skin makes a woman prouder than wearing a diamond necklace. Consequently some rich newly-weds deliberately visit Baza in September for their honeymoon, which will be their oilymoon, and in bed they exchange bodily oil-stains. In a sincere relationship both parties ought to be dirty, since if only one lover is oily, you can't be sure that the other lover isn't merely attracted by the dirt, not by the person. How weird the implications of love become! But you know something about that, don't you, Antoine?

A couple of mornings later I accompanied Miguel, my chosen Cascamorras, to the MacDonald's on Calle Alhamillos which was gearing up for the finals of the American Eata-thon. The whole world was looking to Baza at that time of year, so whatever else you did there would grab media attention parasitically – and profit Baza, of course.

You know about the Eata-thon, Antoine?

Of course I fucking know about it!

Patience! There's a skill to story-telling, a proper pace.

Well now, traditionally during the three-hour Super Bowl 130 million Americans viewing at home consume 8 million pounds of tortilla chips, 3.8 million pounds of pretzels, and much more besides, usually amounting to 156 billion calories in total, quite an achievement. Since for most of the time nothing much happens in American football, a TV channel began filming in several hundred selected homes the munching spectators, accompanied by a scaled-up score of calories consumed across the nation. *Beat 156 Bill!* was the message, beloved by sponsors who manufactured tortilla chips, pretzels, nachos, nuts, pizzas etc.

Thus was born the Eata-thon, like a marathon but less mobile. Soon it involved millions of Americans – every American has a patriotic surveillance microchip implanted for reasons of homeland security, so the exact quantity of food ingested by each can be known constantly. The victors from each state participate in regional Eata-thons, and that particular year the grand final was in Baza. The previous year, the final had been in Yokohama, hosted by the All-Nippon Sumo Federation. Part of the reward for finalists was exorbitant travel to somewhere exotic.

Libertarian Americans had objected to having microchips implanted in them, until it became clear that without microchips you couldn't participate in the Eata-thon, whereupon objections faded away. The certified amount of calories consumed during a particular Eata-thon was proudly worn on XXL t-shirts and often featured on business cards.

The competition hadn't started yet, or we wouldn't have been allowed into MacDonald's, but the American Champions were already training their jaws and keeping their giant stomachs pressurised. Occasionally one of them would stare at us in superiority or pity, or maybe disgust. For my Miguel was slim, with the perfectly shaped muscles of a sculpted God; and I was also quite lean.

"Will you ever let me grow fat?" Miguel asked me, with big sad eyes. As a Cascamorras he was a hero of mobility – his mission, to run fast enough to escape a herd of people covered with oil – yet paradoxically he was dreaming of becoming an *anti*-hero of inertia.

"Only at the cost of my love," I said. And my money, I might have added. "You can get fat when I'm not around any more."

About half of the Americans present, including TV journalists, were dressed as Arabs. The war for oil was long finished, not least since a lot of oil was burned to win the war. Also, Al Qaeda had allegedly been defeated, in the sense that Moslem men no longer existed.

Do you want me to ask why *that was?*

Not yet. I wish to emphasize that a victor needs trophies to remind him against whom he triumphed.

Thanks to vanquished Native Americans, the world enjoyed the Cherokee Jeep, the Indianapolis car racing circuit and the Apache HTTP server. These days we have The Al Qaeda American Dream, which began life as a nightmare. Theme parks such as Disney's Jihadworld, featuring Osama bin Laden as the Santa Claus of Evil, Snow White Prom-Queen and the Seven Dwarf Suicide Bombers and so on, and the Al Qaeda fashion label. As the world runs out of Muslims, Americans ape their disappeared traditions. But we shouldn't analyse these things in public – not that you'll ever have much chance to, my dear Antoine.

Don't remind me!

Anyway, I ordered a MacFelafel for Miguel and a MacBaklavaMuffin for me, spurning the MegaMacs which the Eato-thon people were practising on. Naturally, I paid with my Oil-for-Food card. Few of us can afford a Swiss bank account in oil. What a shame for democracy that credit cards disappeared during the Greatest Depression, and were never restored! But can a delusion be restored once it's revealed as an illusion and disappears?

Miguel eyed my choice. "I could die for a MacBaklava stuffed with cream."

"And you'd never," I reprimanded him, "be stuffed again."

Obesity is the ultimate result of any individualistic society, my dear Antoine. You're still too innocent to understand sociology properly, but you know how I like to fill gaps in you. Am I or am I not your Pygmalion, honing your beautiful body and polishing your mind? You see, my dearest, once upon a time before the era of individualism, boundaries between people were very blurred. People would even sacrifice themselves for one another, or for the sake of the community! Now, contrariwise, it's society that must sacrifice itself for the sake of the individual. Yet since society consists of human beings, paradoxically everyone will blithely renounce his rights as a human being to protect his rights as an individual.

Why did things change so much? My Antoine, many bad things happened during human history, usually due to collective madness. A wrong idea is harmful only if shared among masses of people, which gives it power. So maybe extreme individualism is evolution's answer to the catastrophes caused by collective madness – who knows? That's why democracy is so unpopular nowadays, because it involves collective opinions. A political opinion is only legitimate if it expresses an individual point of view shared by nobody else, for who can share it yet still remain truly individualistic? Shared opinions would violate the rights of single individuals not to have a collective opinion. In your eyes I can see that you don't understand me, Antoine. But never mind! If people began to understand my opinions, necessarily I'd become an outlaw.

Anyway, I understood Miguel's dream of becoming fat. Becoming as fat as possible is the ultimate individual right, because then you occupy more space, and the more space you occupy, the more you affirm your individual rights versus the the community.

Miguel glanced around the Eata-thon champions chomping in MacDonald's.

"Normal people," he said rebelliously, "start supersizing themselves from an early age. If I wait too long, I'll never reach a profitable size."

Ah, well now, my innocent Antoine! How long have you been here?

I've told you – since I was twelve.

˙ Very well. I'll explain.

You're always fucking explaining! Even when you're fucking.

Consider. Fossil oil, almost finished. Forests cut down and turned into deserts. The only surviving mammals being ones we eat, but several times bigger due to genetic engineering, and unable to move much. Plant biodiversity a memory of the past, due to MacAgriculture. And for Joe Average to get enough to eat, first of all he needs to supersize.

This is the bit I never understand.

Listen carefully this time. Supersize people sell their own fat on the human fat market, which has flourished since the end of oil. Once a month they undergo liposuction, and in return for their extracted fat they get vouchers to convert into more food. In modern times the economy has always been strange and bizarre, so by selling your own fat you earn a lot more food than you need to produce the fat. This keeps people busy, since eating a lot demands a lot of time. Also, this produces political stability, for fat creates physical inertia. How can you make a revolution if you can barely move? On top of this, no revolution can possibly happen in a world of egoistic, egocentric individuals. So here is the state of the art of the status quo triumphant.

Talking of the economy being crazy, look at bottled water.

I'd rather not.

No, look! Billions of litres of ordinary water came out of springs in Evian or San Pellegrino or somewhere, only to be put into plastic bottles made of ancient oil, then transported thousands of kilometers by burning gasoline, a much rarer fluid extracted from the bowels of the Earth to be shipped thousands of other kilometers to be refined and re-transported to fuel trucks to move the water, just to pee down a drain.

Miguel said bleakly, "You love only my body."

"That's what I can see and touch," I replied. "And penetrate, also. You can touch a soul with your mind, and that's perfectly beautiful. But penetrating a body is so charmingly absurd! It makes no intellectual sense at all, yet it's dense with mystery and a source of bizarre sensations such as orgasm."

A thin man was sitting at the table near to us. What a rarity in a MacDonalds! I'd hardly noticed him since he occupied so little space, but he must have listening to our words, since he intruded:

"You talk about love, but you know nothing!"

"Does somebody truly know anything about love?" I responded sarcastically.

"I was in love with a woman dentist." The thin man's eyes became sad. "She paid no attention to me till I became her patient – whereupon I discovered that she adored extracting teeth because this gave her a sexual thrill. After my first extraction we had beautiful sex while my mouth was still bleeding. But she refused to meet me anywhere afterwards for a candlelit meal. So I had to make another appointment to have another tooth pulled out – and after that she made love like Delilah – "

"Who liked men's hair to be cut off – "

" – or like Salome – "

"Who liked men's heads cut off. That's displaced penis-envy."

"Each intercourse cost me a tooth. We could only have sex 32 times." The thin man smiled, and I saw he had no teeth to

263

smile with.

"So why not have artificial teeth implanted?"

"I did – by another dentist. But my beloved erotic dentist wasn't turned on by implants. Thus we never had sex again, and I lost all my new teeth for nothing."

"Why did you insist on having all your new teeth pulled out, seeing that it produced no result?"

"Love is blind," said the thin man. "Hope never dies."

"What a beautiful love story. No wonder you're thin."

"You see! What do you know?" The man sucked his MacMilkshake, probably one of the few things he could still consume.

A young woman journalist was videoing us, as an alternative to filming the jumbos in training for the Eata-thon. I suppose she was glamorous, but I have no interest in describing women.

"Who are you?" I demanded.

"My name's Angina. It was supposed to be Angelina."

"Do I know you?"

"Not in this world," she said enigmatically.

"Keep out of my world," I advised her.

The thin man said, "My name's Felipe." Probably he was tired of always being categorised as 'the thin man.'

"What's your job, Felipe, if I may ask?" Obviously he didn't survive by selling the fat he grew.

"I'm a human rights designer. Now and then I sell some new human right to Amnesty International, and this keeps me alive."

Indeed, Antoine my sweetheart, this was a much better business than growing your own fat, though of course you needed imagination to be successful. An individualistic society needed more and more human rights, since it was a fundamental human right to have access to new and better rights. After a while it became difficult to find new rights, so Amnesty International had started a revenue-sharing program with a 1% royalty to anyone who could design a new right. 1% mightn't sound much, but Amnesty International had a virtual monopoly. Once a new human right had been defined, Amnesty could sue multinationals for lots of money, which it could use to buy shares in those same multinationals. It could also sue governments, which have less money but still quite a lot.

"I hate these fucking milkshakes," Felipe said. "I think it's my human right to be able to eat cheeseburgers even if I don't have teeth. MacDonalds must find a way or be sued. This is the project I'm working on at the moment."

"Ah, so you're here for research. But are there enough people on Earth without teeth to justify a lucrative lawsuit?"

"Of course! In Absurdistan a biological attack blamed on MacQaeda caused the population to lose all their teeth, so that multinationals can sell more milkshakes there."

I understood immediately what he meant by MacQaeda. Here was a man after my own heart – metaphorically, at least.

"And," said Felipe, "the presence of all these supersize people here gives me emotional trauma."

"Exactly. So that's why you came to the Eata-thon. For special trauma."

"You're queer, aren't you?"

"Why do you ask?"

"Homosexuality is rising at astonishing speed. Some say this is due to American military viruses escaping. You know, the Americans were researching weapons to trigger outbreaks of homosexuality among enemy soldiers." He frowned. "But *I* say that *heterosexuality* is a violation of individual rights, perpetrated by our species so as to perpetuate itself. Homosexuality means freeing oneself from the enslavement to the species. Look what the human species has done to me!" His empty-mouth smile was grotesque, like a wet cave.

"Hmm," I said, "queerness might be a natural homeostatic adjustment to limit population growth."

But Felipe wasn't paying attention.

"There has to be a way to sue the species for forcing me into heterosexuality and depriving me of my teeth!" he ranted. "I'd solve all my financial problems forever. The human species would pay the bill!"

"Hang on," I warned him. "Human nature reflects the will of the *genes*, not of the species."

"Then we'll have to sue the genome!" Felipe brightened and rubbed his hands. "No, I'll sue the people who sequenced it. Next they'll try to patent it, and I'll be waiting – because a patent is ownership, which means legal responsibility."

Miguel kicked me beneath the table. Obviously he was getting jealous, as if a skinny toothless man could trigger my fantasies. This annoyed me, so I told Felipe, "We're planning to share a *porrón* of good wine somewhere. Would you care to join us?"

"That's kind of you, but I'll stay here. I'll treat myself to a MacHappyProstate session."

You never had any problems with your prostate, did you, Antoine? No, you're too young. So you probably don't know about the big step forward in the treatment of prostatitis made by a brilliant Russian doctor, A.R. Guskov?"

Antoine groans.

Well, Guskov developed a unique technique of prostatic drainage by electronically controlled rectal pneumovibromassage – but as well as medical benefits the procedure turned out to have the side effect of significantly increasing male potency! Greater sexual power is of course a fundamental human right for males. So MacDonalds, because of its leadership in globally franchised happiness, was obliged to provide this service in special little booths, where you can eat your HappyMeal at the same time.

"That was my idea," boasted Felipe.

Miguel and I quickly left MacDonald's before Felipe could

intrude any further, and we went for our *porrón* to *La Boca Abierta*, a pub whose name means 'the open mouth.'

In *La Boca Abierta*, where a TV blared, I noticed a short hairy man, who wore much golden jewellery, having a private conversation with another short hairy man who was bare of jewellery.

"¡Estoy hasta los cojones de que no me pagas ni un puto duro!" the second man shouted, untranslatably.

"¡Vete a la mierda, gilipollas, cabrón!" shouted the first, also untranslatably.

"Why are they shouting?" I shouted at Miguel.

"Ah," shouted Miguel proudly, "that is because in Spanish we use *double* exclamation marks."

We went through the pub to a rear courtyard, but there the Andalusian mood was polluted by too many foreigners, rich pilgrims of dirty oil. That reporter woman, Angina, was busy doing an interview, which was a fast transition from her being in MacDonald's. She must be highly professional.

A cheerful long-haired lottery ticket vendor was making his way around the courtyard handing out fliers, which proved to be bilingual.

MÚSICA PARA PAJEARSE / MUSIC FOR MASTURBATION, Miguel and I both read. That same evening in the Baza concert hall.

"Wow," said Miguel, "a whole auditorium masturbating. Will you take me?"

"No, it's the pianist who wanks while he's playing. Look at the programme: Ravel's *Piano Concerto in D major for one hand*, Scriabin's *Prelude and Nocture* for the left hand, and Godowsky's left-handed *Capriccio*."

"He must be a virtuoso penist."

"Pianist," I corrected.

Miguel looked smug. "I mean both."

"You're running tomorrow, so we need an early night."

267

This is difficult in Spain because night only starts when the evening ends, round about midnight anywhere else, just as morning lasts till late in the afternoon.

Angina headed for our table and addressed Miguel:

"I just realized, you're the Cascamorras! But not yet in costume."

Miguel beamed proudly and rippled some muscles, making me wonder how queer he really was.

Have you ever felt you're being chased by a character from a different story?

Now don't you start getting intertextual – that's perverted.

"She's a lesbian," I told Miguel, "so she's irrelevant. Let's go."

So we went to have some coffee and cake, only to come across Felipe once again, in apparently reluctant company with three tall young men, muscular and blond, dressed in tight white shorts and t-shirts. The trio had surrounded Felipe, up against the plate glass window of a café. While two of the men restrained Felipe's arms firmly though gently, the third was sliding his fingers in and out of that toothless mouth.

"Goo-wa, goway, gloog," Felipe was protesting.

I admired the young men's thighs and biceps, then I interrupted:

"Excuse me, but I think you may be violating his rights."

"He sucks well," declared Henrik – I was to learn his name later – in a Danish accent.

Ah, these were Danes, in disguise as Danes!

I should explain, Antoine…

Do you think I don't know!

These days Danes usually wore Arab clothing, although not

268

quite for the same trophy reason as Americans. It was several years since the last of the Al Qaeda suicide bombers sentimentally set off dirty little nukes in Denmark to avenge some old cartoons depicting the Prophet Peace-Be-Upon-Him. This killed a few hundred thousand Danes, and forced the surviving few million quickly to abandon their contaminated homeland. This was the same time as all Islamic men were turning into women, so obviously the world's Islamic population would diminish considerably as time went by. Consequently the UN assigned Morocco to the refugee Danes. This has led to the creation of many Danish harems, which UNESCO declared a treasure of mankind, to preserve the culture of a people being extinguished. Local traditions must be treasured. It's very noble to respect the heritage of a people you've exterminated.

And of course among the Danish harems were many gay ones, such as I judged Henrik to come from, which is why he was testing Felipe's mouth.

"Excuse me again," I said, "but unlike myself this man's a heterosexual. He had his teeth removed not to suck cocks but to seduce a woman dentist."

"Goo-waa," said Felipe, maybe agreeing with me or in protest.

"So you already tried him?" said Henrik. "He is no good?"

"As an expert connoisseur," I replied, "I've no interest at all, not while I have my beloved Miguel here to suck me."

Henrik appraised my handsome Cascamorras.

"I warn you," I added, "that Miguel is mine." Being rich, I could be stern. "I also warn you that you're violating the rights of a designer of rights, and that isn't wise."

"Hmm," said Henrik, eyeing me. He exchanged glances with – as I learned later – Hans and Sven, and they released Felipe then sauntered away, whispering in Danish which is like Swedish with a throat disease.

Felipe expressed his gratitude by offering to design a human right for me, but I simply patted Felipe on the cheek and ushered Miguel into the café. Various other things happened that evening; however, I don't wish to be tedious – the art in narrative is brevity.

The next morning we lay in bed late, which was the only way to fit in enough night. Finally we rose and Miguel washed himself carefully, to become as clean as possible. I smelled abounding *eau de cologne*. Thousands of people in town would be doing the exact opposite, dirtying their bodies with expensive black oil. The acrid reek of oil seemed to be insinuating into our room, borne on the whiffs of breeze coming through our shutters, an appetizer of what would happen later. Miguel slowly dressed in white Y-fronts with protective codpiece, an immaculate frilled white shirt, and the striped red and yellow trousers of a buffoon, a delightful reverse strip tease. Then we watched a few bullfights on TV, hoping to gain tips from toreros about how to manoeuvre and not be touched.

Eventually the two official Escorts of the Cascamorras arrived, wearing white suits, white shirts, white ties, white roses in their buttonholes, and carrying white capes draped over swords. Anyone who tried to touch the Cascamorras prematurely would have to touch them first! Accompanying them was a waiter bearing a tray of milky coffees and plates of split toasted half-baguettes spread with pieces of ham and tomato and olive oil. However, this oil wasn't a trick by the clever Bazans, for the waiter produced a huge barber's cape to tie around Miguel to keep oily crumbs at bay. On the tray were also glasses of some strong-looking liquor, yet only a can of MacCola for the Cascamorras – again, no tricks. The final arrival was an elegant señora wearing a polka-dot flamenco dress and a bright red hat, and equipped with a guitar.

One of the Escorts read from a scroll in the Spanish of Don Quixote. Then we toasted Miguel – the drink proved to be a

heady mixture of anis and amontillado – and to guitar chords the
señora sang:

Echada está ya la suerte;
yo he de seguir mi camino,
aunque me lleve a la muerte.

"What's that mean?" I asked Miguel.
"My luck, no my fate, the dice, they've been thrown. I have
to follow my path, even if it takes me to death."
"Let's hope not, dear boy!"
I gave him a last kiss, then he took the ball on a pole which
he would use to defend himself. I opened the shutters upon
blinding sunlight and dark shadows and watched the little
procession process up the street, the Escorts flourishing their
white capes, the señora playing and singing and even adding in
some flamenco steps, while white-shirted Miguel swung the ball
overhead. When I next saw him he would be very dirty in a
completely new and sexy way.

Presently I went out to mingle. Black human magma flowed
through the streets, getting ready for the dirty run, many
participants darkly bare to the waist. Numerous carried flails of
oil-soaked cloth. Skirts and shirts, cut into ribbons, exposed oily
legs and chests of men and women alike (the women wore
saturated dirty bras). Black tentacles swung from the bums of
girls. I noticed how awkward it was for one youth to use a
cigarette he'd been passed, without setting fire to himself.
Whitish bands were around many heads as if those people
were kamikazes – and in fact I spotted quite a few undoubtedly
rich Japanese, and Chinese and Indians too, thus the magma
wasn't as homogeneous as it once would have been. People from
different countries look different from one another, often
stridently so, which is why different countries exist. Yet, all the

same, the oil homogenised Orientals and Europeans, making them look more similar than they usually would – which seemed to me a kind of poetry; the rhyming of Europe and the Orient.

Trying to avoid being jostled and oiled, I walked the traditional course from Fuente de los Caños Dorados, the Spring of the Golden Spouts, to Plaza de las Erras where a fine statue of the Cascamorras stands upon a plinth, onward to the Plaza de la Merced, the Square of Grace, thence to the Plaza Mayor, where the final catharsis of the event would took place – the ritual miracle of the transmutation of a fountain's water into oil.

Millions of people worldwide would religiously participate live on TV in this sacred transmutation. The shock of the end of oil had badly hit the collective unconscious. Oil had signified power and freedom, especially the power to burn in 100 years all the oil that millions of years of life on earth had produced to give mankind its aura of omnipotence.

Didn't you say this before?

Ahem, I wish to introduce a metaphor and a simile. When the illusion of an endless free lunch of oil collapsed, that was like a second expulsion from Eden, from the garden of plenty. Oil was the forbidden fruit that mankind had greedily devoured, condemning itself for the second time. Since oil did not look like an apple, experience gained from the previous sin was useless.

Messianic expectations were flourishing around the globe: a messiah would appear to announce a new world of oil to burn! This was common to every cult, though UFO cults had an edge in plausibility since alien worlds might realistically be full of oil, although the pipeline to Earth would be a very long one with many possibilities of leaking or being punctured. Truly, only a miracle could eventually give back to mankind the oil it had wasted. Thus the ritual transmutation of water to oil in the Plaza Mayor was a moment of high mysticism for all the world, and this year my beloved Miguel, by then covered in dirty engine oil, would be the agent of that miracle, the knight of hope and faith for millions of suffering believers. In a few more hours how proud I would be! A memory to treasure forever.

Of course technically I knew that the annual miracle was a fake, performed by imported Italian specialists of the San Gennaro cult in Naples – where, ever since 1389, dry blood liquefies thrice a year. Yet every miracle is what you believe it to be. Miracles would be impossible without the impossible.

It was a Chinese who first spied the Cascamorras emerge from hiding and shouted out. Only other Chinese understood his cry, so the first group to give chase was entirely composed of Chinamen, an unusual sight in a town lacking Chinese take-aways. Very soon I was treated to the spectacle of a whole cosmopolitan black herd stampeding towards me in hot pursuit – the temperature was about thirty Centigrade. Seeing this blackened crowd gave me the impression that the Moors had newly reinvaded the Kingdom of Granada, not to pick tomatoes in plastic tunnels but to conquer once again. This was unlikely now that all Moorish warriors were women, but archetypes die hard. Spectators crowded the railed balconies of yellow- and white-painted apartment buildings.

Once the Cascamorras was spotted (I mean visually, not by oil) his route was traditional, as I've said, which made escape even more unlikely. I don't know whether Miguel panicked because of the howling mob running after him, maybe remembering how he'd once experienced a gay gangbang by some members of the Basque separatist movement, but he must have deviated, for I next saw him on Calle Alhamillos. I'm spry and agile and in very good shape, and I took some random short cuts.

Just ahead of the mob dashed Miguel with that ball on a pole. Oily palms were reaching out eagerly to besmirch him. They were going to catch him very soon.

As I've said, MacDonald's is on Calle Alhamillos, and the Eata-thon finals were now in progress. Since supersize Eata-thon contestants can only waddle very slowly, it made no sense for them to participate in the Cascamorras run even as spectators. Enough tele-journalists were in Baza to cover both events, and split-screen allowed a fascinating intersection of a stationary and a mobile marathon.

MacDonald's was already crowded. Six supersize finalists, male and female seemingly, were munching their way through Big Macs while supporters cheered and organisers watched carefully and kept the score and telejournalists filmed.

Just as the vanguard of the oil mob was about to overtake Miguel, instead of swinging the ball around him to keep people away he dashed through the open doorway of MacDonald's – to be followed by a dozen oily pursuers, then fifty, then a hundred more. Soon the complete filthy mob was trying to get inside, and as more and more people poured towards the blocked doorway, they became completely crazy. Some of the most cheerful and richest individuals of the globe were now a hysterical orgasmic mass. The walls of MacDonald's and the now smeared, blackened windows bulged outwards. The building was about to burst, unless it could supersize itself!

And this, Antoine, is the last I ever saw of my Miguel.

For in the mad confusion, this is when those three gay Danes – behaving like Viking raiders – grabbed hold of me. "We have an expert connoisseur!" I heard Henrik cry in triumph. They hauled me to a side street, and bundled me into a solar-powered van, to immobilise and gag me with bondage gear even as the van started driving away to take me to the final destination of the rest of my life – this gay Danish harem in Morocco where you'd soon join me, Antoine, kidnapped from the beach at Torremolinos.

I fucking know where I was kidnapped from.

After so much time, you may have forgotten.

Well, you've fucking forgotten to mention why *Moslem men all turned into women!*

Oh, that. It was all the doing of those Christian fundamentalist scientists researching how fish can change sex spontaneously. You see, the Christian symbol is the fish, *ikthus* in Greek, an acronym for 'Jesus Christ Son of God Saviour' – a Greek called Basil Panglotis, a Professor of Erotics, told me this. Other scientists had already found a gene for faith. When the fundamentalists found some Lamarkian DNA which encoded belief in Islam, the result was a Christian fundamentalist bio-weapon. All Islamic men and boys became women and girls.

Couldn't they have become Christians instead?

No! There cannot be Lamarkian DNA for being a Christian, or else Christianity wouldn't be fundamental! It was either a sex-change, or turn into fish.

Anyway, hidden cameras broadcast worldwide whatever happens in all these harems, as a cultural and historical reality show. All of this violates our personal human rights, but it was traditional for Arabs to violate human rights, so UNESCO declared our own violation of our human rights a treasure of mankind, occurring inside another treasure of mankind. So we'll never leave here, my dear Antoine. The Danish sheikh who uses our bodies for his pleasure may eventually die, but another sheikh will take his place.

At least the place where we are is beautiful! Even though it's a gay harem, the walls are adorned with beautiful posters depicting female nudes, by grand masters such as Helmut Newton and Konstantin Krasnobaev. Gays often appreciate female beauty more than straight men, since our perceptions aren't polluted by the deceiving force of lust. We inhabit a luxury cruise ship hauled inland and bedded in the sands of the Sahara, surrounded by about 50,000 land mines to deter us detainees from diving overboard. Swimming pools, saunas, jacuzzis, gyms, a casino, massage parlours, masturbatoriums!

Thanks to the arrays of big solar panels on masts to provide power for the air-conditioning et cetera, from a distance our home must look like a huge motionless sailing ship, a galleon with many glittering sails. Nor is ours the only 'ship of the desert' – a name once reserved for camels. The UN dragged many redundant ocean liners inland for displaced Danes to use as harems. Herds of pigs and cows, wearing sunblock, graze upon the decks of many of these harem-arks to provide continuity of the famous Danish butter and bacon. I believe the animals eat food-pellets rather than grass, but the flavour of the meat is still superb.

Everything is perfect here, except for you, Antoine, which is why I love you so much. Exceptions are the jewels of life, and you're the only mistake the raiders ever made, since you aren't gay at all. Your angelic appearance fooled them. Antoine, my Antoine, do you realize how lucky you are in having being unlucky?

My name is Carmelo, you old goat.

So you tell me, not for the first time. But I can call you what I please.

I hate being called Antoine.

That's perfect, since I know how much you love to hate.

I especially hate having to love you.

I'm your only option, Antoine, and you know it. Our banal sheik doesn't care about your existence. He has hundreds of men in his harem whom he can fuck as he pleases, and they're all gay and enjoy their position, except for a bit of jealousy. I'm your only interface with sociality, since I alone am intelligent enough to embrace the abnormal. Most of the other guys are stupid, so we only have each other to talk to, you and I, eh? You've no hope with the guardians of the harem, them not being eunuchs but doctrinaire Danish lesbians. They'll never satisfy you, only torment you by their inaccessible presence. Your only chance of happiness is a paradigm shift, so you can start enjoying what happens to you. You've no choice but to love me, Antoine.

You know I hate you. **FOR THE SALVATION OF TREES, OR TO SAVE BREATH (WHICH IS SIMILAR), EXCESSIVE SPACING IS BANNED FROM NOW ON.**
"But that's your way of saying you love me!"
"I know. Why do you think I let you do everything to me? How to explain to oneself that you love the person you hate? Can something like that be explained?"
"If love can be explained, Antoine, it isn't true love."
"Tell me, do you still love Miguel?"
"Did he even survive the super-pressurisation and flesh-explosion of MacDonald's? For your sake, Antoine, I wish I could regain the virginity of my feelings! I know that you're jealous. My love for Miguel seems forever – yet if you could feel physical desire for me…"
"I'm definitely disgusted by your body and what it does. So it must be that I love your soul – sufficiently to let you use my body as you wish, even though this gives me no pleasure, quite the contrary."
"Women may often feel that way about men."
"Which forces me to hate you at the same time," says Antoine.

"The truth is," I philosophise, "you love me so much only because you hate me immeasurably. You *have to* love me so as to perceive clearly and vividly, by contrast, the reality of your loathing. So therefore I fuck you every day to stoke the hatred that fuels your paradoxical love."

"What else can I do? Is love a choice?"

"Beloved Antoine, are you quite sure you hate me for what I really am?"

"Oh yes, beloved goat, I'm sure I hate you for what you really are."

The Illustrated Tumour of My Beloved – part two

Sooner or later there always comes a time when the ideal world of poetry collides with the implacable gears of society. That's probably due to a basic law of the universe, to which every layer of reality must bow. The universe is intrinsically fractal, which means that it *loves* self-similarity, or at least it needs this. If you analyse the jagged geometry of a coastline, you'll discover that this doesn't change if you alter the scale of your observation. Take a photo of a coastline from 100 miles high, 10 miles high, or 100 yards, and you'll find that the geometric equations defining what you see are always the same. This is an example of self-similarity, at the root of fractal geometry. The universe works like that. Nobody knows why.

Because of the self-similarity of the universe, the ideal world of poetry likewise exists both in the maximal and in the minimal systems. Probably it was a poetic intuition to hypothesize the splendor of a universe even at a time of no-time when not even nothing existed. To generate a universe was in essence poetical, but then poetry collided with that nameless antithetical Force which in every time and place operates as an elixir of Normality to freeze the world into one shape rather than a multitude of possibilities. This Force of Normality raped the purity of the original poetic intuition, giving it the aspect of a noisy and vulgar big-bang; and from that moment onward Normality continued to rape the world, forcing everything that was evolving on an ideal plane to become normal.

And so, it was fated that my pure, innocent and immortal

love for my Beloved – in the form of my material, spiritual and sexual devotion to her illustrated tumour, that tumour grown inside the mould of her and perfectly identical to her – would be fatally assaulted by the squalid influences of Normality.

On the fractal plane of Mankind, the Knight of Normality – sworn enemy of the poetry of the universe – is society. My love story with the illustrated tumour of my Beloved didn't remain a secret. People found out, and after a while *too many* people knew. Some journalist thought to amuse the sheep who were his readers with a morbid and sensational story, and from that moment *everyone* knew. That's a lot of people!

At the time, much public dispute was going on between the World Wildlife Fund for the protection of animals and Amnesty International, regarding the natural rights of tumour cells.

An American court had decreed that because tumours possess a genetic aberration compared with the organism in which they grow, and because they pursue aims at variance to those of the host body, they must be regarded as sovereign entities independent of the bodies in which they grow; and since tumours too are undoubtedly creatures of God, they possess rights that must be safeguarded. The World Wildlife Fund pushed the argument that tumours are not really human beings, so they need to be regarded as animals of a different and endangered species, and as such must be protected.

Amnesty International, on the other hand, considered tumours to be absolutely human, but they were *dissident* persons in opposition to the organic homeland in which by chance they were born. Essentially tumours were a political minority persecuted by the owner of the body and by doctors collaborating with the regime of the owner – so they must be protected by Amnesty International. Admittedly tumourous cells might be classed as enemy aliens by the majority shareholder of the body, but if so they should be accorded protection under the Geneva Convention. This point was held in great esteem by the

American public. Americans are usually obsessed by the thought that everybody, except their own government, should respect the Geneva Convention, maybe as unconscious compensation for the fact that their government usually indulges in disregarding it.

This dispute over the legal rights of tumour cells was no joke. On the table was business worth billions of Euros in lawsuits – which the organization that won the dispute would commence against everybody affected by tumours who tried to cure themselves in violation of the legal rights of their tumours.

Was the fight against cancer a political crime, or a crime against an endangered species? Human Justice had yet to decide.

One fine day the illustrated tumour of my Beloved was invited to participate in a well-known TV talkshow. People usually hate tumours, and television needs to invite guests whom the public may hate because TV already has far too many guests whom people are supposed to love. The tumour of my Beloved was elegantly dressed, made up and posed on its own chair so as to resemble a normal seated human being. For marketing purposes popular talkshows always have a very low intellectual level, and this let the A.I. program inside the tumour come over rather well in verbal confrontation with the other guests.

The program in the tumour wasn't the sort you read about in science fiction stories. It would never pass the Turing Test, that famous test to decide if an artificial intelligence can be mistaken for a genuine human being. Although actually, from what I understand about all this, it's senseless to think of a Turing test as being unique, unambiguous and universal. Really we ought to be thinking about a whole series of scalar Turing tests depending on the intelligence or stupidity of whoever has to be fooled or otherwise by the A.I. program. In a typical TV talkshow the right setting for the Turing test would be *idiot mode*. It takes very little for an A.I. program to seem like a true human being to such an audience.

"What does it feel like to be an authentic tumour?" asked the anchorman at one point.

"You feel like you're an authentic tumour," was the simple answer, although it seemed acute and sarcastic.

"Is it true that you have frequent sexual intercourse with the husband of the woman that you killed?"

"That's true."

"How can a man possibly couple carnally with the cancer that killed his wife?"

"By undressing, then taking me from all positions, repeatedly."

"Is there only physical attraction, or love as well?"

"There is much, there is infinite love between my Beloved and me."

"How can a tumour *love?*"

You could have heard a pin drop.

"There are no limits that love can't surpass. Love is the magic of the universe."

"But you don't think. You have no brain! You can't know what love is!"

"Thinking is not necessary for love. A brain is not necessary. Why can't a tumour know what love is?"

And so on.

It was a huge success. The illustrated tumour of my Beloved had an extremely high rating. Paradoxically, people were identifying with that tumour, humble and dignified, an involuntary killer in the past but a generous lover in the present. My wife had been good-looking and so was the tumour grown in her mould. Its beautiful crystal eyes – glassy, of course, and unfocused since they were seeing nothing – hypnotized and seduced millions of spectators. That way of talking without moving the lips, nor even a single muscle (which the tumour lacked), gave to my beloved tumour a completely special charm, never before seen on TV until that day.

Love e-mails for the tumour of my Beloved began to flow into my mailbox. Death threats came from feminists scandalized that I'd grown a tumour into the form of a woman. The die was cast; the chain reaction of banal human lunacy had started. And nothing would stop it.

As I said, the tumour of my Beloved was growing eternally, and at regular intervals tumourous excess was ejected from an orifice that for aesthetic reasons was where people have their anus. I'd been disposing of this excess in the dustbin along with the regular trash. Somebody with a bit of imagination searched my garbage and took away the residues of tumour. Soon, items of the tumour of my Beloved started to appear as collectables at auction on eBay. The illustrated tumour of my Beloved was already famous, and it became even more so after the inevitable pseudo-ethical discussions in the media caused by its abusive auctioning. The pieces offered on eBay grew in number. Probably the pirates had set up their own little tumour-of-my-Beloved factory.

Thousands of people all over the world got hold of a piece of the tumour of my Beloved to display in their sitting rooms. Some people kept it in a little see-through freezer shaped like a coffin. Others people put it in the aquarium where it wouldn't stink and would make a interesting feature for a few weeks before the fishes ate it all. A few people had it embalmed. The lazy majority kept it in the refrigerator till it began to rot.

Several lawyers were inciting me to fire off lawsuits in all directions, but I wasn't bothered. I'm not daft. Why on Earth should I be jealous of the tumourous substance itself? The illustrated tumour of my Beloved with the digitalized voice of my Beloved – that and that alone was the unique entity! Moreover, it was unique only inside my own mind. I knew my mind well, and had great respect for it (otherwise I couldn't have respected anything else), so where was the problem? Why were people so fascinated by a tumour that represented nothing personal for

283

them?

But then the first Sexy Tumour Dolls started to pop up, mercenary versions of the illustrated tumour of my Beloved which people could buy for sexual entertainment purposes. Probably by this time the tumour of my Beloved was being hyper-cloned on an industrial scale, and its total biomass could be many thousands of tons. Tumour was grown inside the mould of famous pornstars, and anyone could install the result in their own bed for the pleasures of night. On demand, the skin of those tumour-pornstars could display pornographic images, a twisted and vulgar adaptation of my original poetic concept. Many males need to watch pornography while they fuck, and what better place to watch it than on the surface of the object they're fucking?

The originators of the moulds received royalties, but not my Beloved, originator of the tumour that filled those moulds making live, warm tumour-dolls with no legal rights. The World Wildlife Fund and Amnesty International both pressed me to behave in a normal manner by filing lawsuits against the cowboy cloners of the tumour. But my world is one of poetry. So far as I was concerned, the sirens of banal normal lunacy could sing for centuries but I wouldn't heed them. And because of the sex-dolls there never was any need for me to sodomize or whip the tumour of my Beloved – many of those exploiters of the tumour-dolls were humiliating the tumour sufficiently on a grand scale; so I felt that my promise to Amanda was being fulfilled vicariously.

In human society, sexual novelties are often the source of new levels of Normality. Some legislators tried to have laws approved against the the flood of oncophily, akin to the international laws against cloning actual humans, but this was a lost cause; the rising tide of triumphant fashion had already altered the human *Zeitgeist* irreversibly for the umpteenth time. People loved the slogan *Fuck Your Death*. Having a tumoural lover became a nihilist status symbol among intellectuals, and then a banal mass marketing phenomenon. Tumour Bodies Franchising won the prize for best and most innovative company of the year. Talkshows filled with more and more tumoural stars, displacing old-style human guests. Verbal duels between the stolid artificial intelligences of tumour-puppets with petrified expression fascinated audiences.

The new Zeitgeist! Sexual oncophily extended to other spheres of human endeavour. An expanding population of tumour clones became a legal inevitability because people sick with cancer were only allowed to cure themselves if *first of all* they guaranteed to provide an adequate alternative body for their tumour, where it could live and develop according to its own nature and right. The immortality of a tumour was a clear sign of the will of God; no human being could be allowed to deny its vital spark. Church and White House were both adamant on this point, even though both disapproved of the use of anthropomorphic tumour clones for sexual purposes. But also, the typical total passivity of the clones was seen as the achievement of a state of nirvana, of Zen internal enlightenment; people should copy their example. Monasteries filled with men and women nourished by liquid nutrient, imitating cloned tumours.

More and more people adopted the so-called tumour lifestyle, of complete idiotic inactivity. Tumour stars were all the rage. Youngsters assumed the typical petrified countenance of their TV favourites. Facial expressions became *out* amongst teenagers. Having a less than glassy look was a cause for social ostracism.

The demographic problem of the proliferation of anthropomorphic tumours was worsened by the fact that they were immortal, and that it was forbidden to kill them or let them starve. In some communities the percentage of tumours with a human aspect surpassed that of human people.

Then somebody started to eat them, by cutting off pieces which in due course would replace themselves.

No law forbade oncophagy, probably because no legislator ever thought that someone would like to feed himself or herself with cancer. But a tumour is only abhorrent from the point of view of a body in which it has ceased following the body's rules – when all's said and done it's just meat, which therefore can be eaten.

As usual, sex had opened the way to a whole new trend.

An innovator fitted two little nozzles to the sheath of an onco-lover in the nipple positions, and put a cork in the anal vent, causing the ever-growing excess of tumour to exit from the breasts like exotic spaghetti growing down in nice spirals. In the fire of sexual passion that innovator discovered that by sucking the tits prolongedly he was nourishing himself from his own lover. He sold photos of his unique perversion to a sensational magazine, and the rest all followed. The law prohibited killing a tumour entity, but not eating part of it so long as enough remained to be considered alive. Just as the sexual taboo was transcended, so was the alimentary taboo.

Bored mankind didn't pass up this opportunity, and so was born Nouvelle Cuisine de l'Oncophagie. American oncophagists started to nourish themselves with MacTumour sandwiches drowned in ketchup, while French connoisseurs – who love *crudités* – preferred to eat their tumours raw with just some lemon, salt, pepper and Worcestershire sauce, or in very elaborate gourmet dishes such as *Pâté de tumeur grasse*. Italian oncophagists elaborated delicious recipes such as *Risotto ai frutti di Onco*, a summer dish with rice where the seafruits were replaced by delicate tumourous nodules, and the proverbial *Pappardelle al Forno con salsa di Cancro*. German oncophagists were known for their excellent *Tumorbraten mit Kartoffel und Preiselbeeren*, and the very popular *Krebswürstel mit Senf*. Just order a *Paella* in Spain, and you can be sure the meat in the rice isn't chicken. The British serve *Roast tumour with Yorkshire pudding and two veg* as well as *Full English tumour breakfast*, but these dishes are laughed at by most people of taste, likewise the *Tumour tikka massala* favoured in Birmingham.

We were at the zenith of the oncocentric age of mankind. But I was keeping myself out of this crazy decadence, even though I was best placed to benefit. In vain did the World Wildlife Fund and Amnesty International pressure me to exploit commercially the illustrated tumour of my Beloved in partnership with them. My whole life was the illustrated tumour of my Beloved exactly in so far as my love for my deceased Amanda could thereby carry on expressing itself effectively, enabling me to communicate directly with the soul of my Beloved in paradise. The only thing that made sense to me had become the *Leitmotiv* of the collective nonsense of mankind, but what did I care? When, in the silent nights of intimacy and poetry, the illustrated tumour would look at me without actually looking at me, between one sigh and another in a whisper it would ask:

"Do you really love me for what I really am?"

And I would answer:

"I really love you for what you really are."

THE END

287

Acknowledgements

"The Grave of My Beloved" first appeared in *Weird Tales*, 2006.

"The Penis of My Beloved" first appeared in *Lust for Life*, edited by Claude Lalumière & Elise Moser, 2006.

"The Mass Extinction of My Beloved" first appeared in *Helix*, Spring 2007.

"Beloved Vampire of the Blood Comet" first appeared in *Flurb* #3 edited by Rudy Rucker, April 2007.

"The Colonoscopy of My Beloved" first appeared in *New Writings in the Fantastic*, edited by John Grant, Fall 2007.